THE HAWTHORNE SCHOOL

THE HAWTHORNE SCHOOL

A NOVEL

SYLVIE PERRY

CROOKED
LANE

NEW YORK

Published in the United States by Crooked Lane Books, an imprint of The Quick Brown Fox & Company LLC.

Crooked Lane Books and its logo are trademarks of The Quick Brown Fox & Company LLC.

Library of Congress Catalog-in-Publication data available upon request.

ISBN (hardcover): 978-1-64385-792-3
ISBN (ebook): 978-1-64385-793-0

Cover design by Patrick Sullivan

Printed in the United States.

www.crookedlanebooks.com

Crooked Lane Books
34 West 27th St., 10th Floor
New York, NY 10001

First Edition: December 2021

10 9 8 7 6 5 4 3 2 1

For Tom: Thanks for the vanilla soy lattés and kind support.

1

THE HAWTHORNE SCHOOL stands rooted on its hill, surrounded by woods and fields. A breeze rustles its coat of wet and trembling vines so that it seems to breathe in and out like a living being. Its black window panes glint at the tiny boy, and he pulls on the arm of his young mother. She pulls back, not letting him go, although he twists his little hand in hers, trying to get free, trying to run from her and toward the enchantment.

"It's a magical castle!" cries Henry. "*I* want to go to the magical castle!"

Once a convent, The Hawthorne School reaches its gothic peaks toward heaven while small pale faces carved into the moldings gape in mute astonishment at the two people below.

The air is heavy with the scent of wood fires and damp earth. Green maple leaves shake with each breeze. The sun sends spears through the clouds, and the vines and trees sparkle.

Claudia's car is parked down the hill, beyond the open wrought-iron gate, at the side of the road. She considers picking Henry up and going back, but she doesn't know why. She intended to come here for help. She needs to find a school that will understand her boy. She walks forward with Henry, hand in hand, toward the main entrance of the school.

This is the moment when The Hawthorne School inhales new life.

CHAPTER

2

CLAUDIA LET HENRY guide her toward The Hawthorne School, her eyes not on him, but on the second-story cloister walk and the arches over the heavy wooden doors. This school had the look of an old European convent plunked here, incongruously, in the American Midwest.

Claudia, an artistic soul, was deeply affected by beauty of all kinds, and she fell under the spell of the school at first sight. She was well and truly charmed, like a character in a fairy tale entering the grounds of an enchanted palace.

The medieval-style door to the main entrance was made of planks of oak studded with large black nails. She stopped there, looking for a posted sign of some kind instructing her to ring or push an intercom button, but there was nothing.

With a sensation of passing through a portal into another dimension, Claudia pushed open the heavy door and stepped through with her child.

Inside, it was cool and slightly humid. As Claudia's eyes adjusted to the dimness, she saw that she and Henry were in a long, wide, darkly paneled hallway with rooms on either side all the way down. She could see a steep stone staircase leading up on her left, and another one to the right, far down at the end of the hall. An enormous wrought-iron chandelier hung over their heads, lit with electric bulbs in the shape of candle flames.

Immediately, a figure came toward them as if she'd been expecting them. She was dressed in sandals and a flowing maxi dress, with a soft shawl draped over her narrow shoulders. She moved with the easy grace of a twenty-year-old, but her face was much older. Her hair was in a loose, gray chignon, and her pale eyes sparkled blue behind round spectacles.

"Welcome!" she said, extending her hand to Claudia and reaching her other hand to gently grasp Claudia's arm above the elbow. A warm, almost possessive touch. Claudia's shoulders relaxed. She'd been half fearing "getting in trouble" for trespassing, feeling that she had no right to come onto this property with her son, but now this woman who looked like a grandmother in a children's book was smiling at her and Henry, greeting them as if they already belonged.

"I am the director of The Hawthorne School. My name is Zelma Huxley. And you are . . .?"

"Claudia Vera."

Claudia thought Zelma must be what she would consider well beyond retirement age. Eighty, at least?

"And this is my son, Henry. He's four. Say hello, Henry."

Claudia saw Zelma's fleeting reaction, the same reaction all strangers had when they first looked at Henry. His black hair and blue eyes caught people's attention, and just as they were about to say something positive about his appearance, Henry would ruin it by doing or saying something obnoxious.

Henry, of course, did not say hello. He never did when she asked him to. He never did anything she asked him to do. That was the problem. One of the problems. Instead, he asked the director, "Does a giant live here? Are you a witch? Or are you the giant's wife?"

Zelma fixed Henry with her pale gaze and a faint smile. She searched his face, as if trying to place him, as if she had met him before. After the briefest pause, she said, "Hello, Henry. I am Mrs. Huxley."

Henry, clearly awed—probably still under the impression that he was speaking to a giant's wife—replied, "Hello." He continued looking at Zelma, who reached out her hand to him. Claudia winced, knowing that he would refuse to take it.

But Henry solemnly shook Zelma's hand and continued to stare at her, fascinated.

Signaling the first room on the right, Zelma said, "Come into my office, please."

She led them into a high-ceilinged room that was bright, despite its rich dark paneling, because of the sunlight streaming in through a row of casement windows with diamond panes. Facing the windows was the director's mahogany desk. In the center of the room was a large mahogany table.

Zelma said, "Let me offer you both a glass of juice. I was just going to have one myself." Claudia thought this woman was eccentric, but adorably so, offering not water, but juice. Zelma poured a liquid of a rich green color into two small glasses. It looked like a beverage in a health food store. Claudia thought Henry would never accept it, but he did touch it to his lips, and then drank it all straight down. Claudia tasted it and found that it was sweet and delicious.

"It *is* good, isn't it, dear heart?" said Zelma, the skin around her mouth and eyes crinkling with pleasure.

Claudia thought she was too old to be called "dear heart," but she liked it. She liked this twinkly little lady. There was somehow something captivating about her.

Zelma took a stack of paper and square crayons from built-in shelves and set them out for Henry. To Claudia's surprise, Henry set to work right away, glancing up from time to time at the director.

Claudia noticed a framed poster enumerating the "The Hawthorne School Ideals":

1. Be cooperative.
2. Be loyal.
3. Be just.
4. Be self-controlled.
5. Be humble.
6. Be steady.

"So," said Zelma to Claudia, "you are interested in our school for your son?"

Claudia blushed. Of course, she'd love to be able to send Henry to a school like this. What parent wouldn't? But she didn't dream she could afford it, a school as beautiful, as grand as this one. What would the tuition be? She couldn't even guess. She was barely able to pay the rate at Happy Start Preschool, and it was known to be the cheapest. She felt guilty about wasting this nice woman's time, but she also wanted to know: What was Henry not getting? What privileges did other children have, what enrichment and opportunities, only because their parents were wealthy?

"Yes," said Claudia. "I am interested. First, may I ask what the tuition is?"

Zelma, relaxed and friendly, smiled. "We'll come to that. But first, would you tell me a little about yourselves? How did you find us, to begin with? A referral perhaps?"

Claudia thought, *You couldn't actually call it a referral.*

Miss Patty at Happy Start Preschool had only mentioned The Hawthorne School sarcastically. The parent–teacher conference had not gone well. In fact, it had been a disaster. *"Your son,"* accused Miss Patty, "is not like any child I've ever taught before, and I've been teaching preschool for thirty years."

Claudia knew Henry could be frustrating to deal with. But could he really be so different from other children? This seasoned teacher should know. Claudia had never had much experience with children before she'd had Henry, and he'd been challenging for her from the beginning.

"He spends more time in time-out than he does participating with us. He refuses to cooperate in any way at any time." As if naming the worst offense of all, she added, *"He does not know how to cut with scissors!"*

Miss Patty had looked with false pity at Claudia, who was biting her lower lip and tucking her hair behind her ears. "I'm sure it's hard, being a single mother. You don't have time to work with him at home, do you?"

Claudia had had no idea she was *supposed* to be teaching Henry how to use scissors at home. Were other parents doing crafts with their kids after school? She'd felt humiliated.

"He can't even identify the letters in his own first name! Academically, he's very far behind his age group. But the biggest concern is his behavior," Miss Patty had continued.

Claudia had tried to advocate for Henry. "Do you think he could have a different learning style?"

Miss Patty—whom Henry insisted on calling Miss Potty—curled her lips in disdain. "A different *learning* style? Henry Vera has *no* learning style. He refuses to learn anything. He's too busy knocking down other children's blocks, drowning out instruction time by singing at the top of his lungs, and trying to climb out the window during circle time."

Unfortunately, Claudia was not surprised. Henry had already boasted to her that he had taken Miss Patty's "special teacher markers" and thrown them over the fence at recess. When Claudia had asked him why, he'd only laughed. "And then she chased me. But she couldn't catch me!" Henry jumped up and down with pleasure at the memory. "She huffed and she puffed, and her eyes got real big."

"If it's a different *learning* style you're after, you could always try *The Hawthorne School*!" Miss Patty snorted, as if the very idea was beyond ridiculous.

"Where *is* The Hawthorne School?" Claudia had asked. It seemed to her she'd heard of it before, but she couldn't remember where.

"Way out beyond the edge of town, on Route 171. They say it's based on the Scandinavian nature schools. Unconventional. It's an old convent, I think, that was built in the 1920s on several acres of land, lots of trees. People say the kids are outside all day in all kinds of weather, and the teaching methods are . . . unorthodox. Not that I know anything about it. Just what people say." Miss Patty had suddenly looked alarmed. "I'm *not* seriously suggesting you take Henry there! It was just a little joke. We *can* work with your son. But we will need your help to make him understand that we expect him to behave. He seems to think he can do whatever he wants whenever he wants to, and that has to stop."

Miss Patty looked kindly then at Claudia, who was beginning to feel hopeless. "I can see that you would do anything to help your son. Of course you want to do what's best for him. And you're a fighter; he's lucky to have you in his corner."

Claudia knew what Miss Patty meant by the word "fighter." She'd been "fighting" with this woman about Henry for three months, ever since she'd enrolled him here. Not aggressively, but nonetheless insistently. She'd countered all the negatives with positives. The whole time, Miss Patty had only pointed out his faults and complained about how difficult he was. Claudia admitted he was a handful, but she also knew he had his strengths. He was bright and funny and loving too. Didn't that count for anything? Miss Patty dismissed these qualities, leaving Claudia feeling childish.

Miss Patty had paused. "Let's try this. We'll make a reward system with stickers and a chart to help Henry with his behavior, and I'll give you your own copy so you can use it at home with him. Consistency between home and school is key. Have a serious talk with him. Let him know your expectations for his school behavior. I also suggest you work with Henry on letter recognition and on cutting with scissors."

Claudia, who had tried everything to rein in Henry's behavior, including stickers and charts, felt discouraged. At home, he screamed like a toddler when he didn't get his way; he seemed to take joy in frustrating her: pulling food out of the pantry and throwing it all over the floor and, most recently, stripping off all his clothes, charging out the door, and streaking down the street as she ran after him, praying he wouldn't run across the road. She'd tried being more strict; she'd tried "choosing her battles"; she'd tried crying in frustration and begging him to be good. She was at a loss when it came to raising this boy, and she was very afraid that she was failing him.

Claudia had never planned to be a mother; she'd never seriously thought about what type of mother she'd be until she saw the positive pregnancy test.

She had only been twenty at the time, and she'd feared that she wouldn't be equal to the task. This wasn't the way she'd thought her life would go. She had seen herself finishing fine arts school and then becoming a graphic artist. She'd expected that someday, after establishing herself in her career, she'd get married. She hadn't made up her mind about whether having children would be part of the picture. And then, suddenly, life had taken her by the shoulders and turned her from one path and set her on another. There hadn't been a question in her mind about keeping the baby. From the minute she knew he was there, he became her focus. She would just have to figure everything out, that was all. Devin, the baby's father, had his faults, and she had never thought of him as marriage material, but now they would both have to see things differently.

Devin, however, had had the freedom to take off, and he did.

But at the time, she'd had her mother to help her. Her mom had done a good job herself as a single mother, and Claudia told herself that she could do it too. She and her mom grew closer through their shared responsibility of raising Henry. As she struggled through those early years, her admiration of her own mother grew. She'd never known before how hard it was to be a mom. And when her mother became ill, and Claudia took on her mother's care as well as Henry's, instead of pursuing her own ambitious goals, she'd just congratulated herself on each day of survival. She thought—she hoped—she was doing okay.

But here was Miss Patty letting her know she was doing a very bad job indeed.

That evening, after the conference, she'd searched the internet to find out about the school Miss Patty had so sneeringly mentioned.

Strangely, she had not been able to find any website for it— not even a listing for its address. Then she'd texted Maggie, her new friend in an apartment down the hall.

Claudia: *Got a minute?*
Maggie: *Come on down!*

CLAUDIA HAD MET Maggie soon after she'd moved into their apartment building.

As she and Henry had walked from the residents' parking lot one day, a voice called out, "Oh hey! Are you new?"

Claudia turned to see long, golden, glowing sunlit hair above wide, bright eyes, a woman about ten years older than her who looked like a glamorous celebrity from another world. With car keys in her left hand and extending her right, she was hurrying over to Claudia.

"Hi. I'm Maggie Timmerberg. I live here with my daughter. I just saw you with your little boy and thought I'd say hi."

"Hi. I'm Claudia Vera." Claudia moved her hand reflexively to her hair, which was probably a mess. She always took more care with Henry's grooming than her own now. Whenever she saw another woman who had "salon hair," she felt self-conscious. "And this is Henry." Henry ran behind her and clutched at her jeans.

Maggie leaned sideways and peered around Claudia, and Henry peeked up at the stranger and screamed. Maggie's first glance at Henry lasted a little too long for his comfort—and for Claudia's. She felt judged. But Maggie put her at ease.

"Aw. Someone's a little shy," she said indulgently. Henry screamed again. Claudia didn't know what to do. Any attempt to pull him away from her calves would only make him worse, so she ignored him, hoping that not feeding into the behavior might help.

"I have a little girl just about your size," said Maggie.

Henry went silent as he poked his head out of hiding to see a miniature Maggie who came forward and said maturely, "Hi, Henry. My name is Violet."

She was a bright-eyed, friendly, and contented child. The kind of child that always made Claudia question her own skill as a mother. Were kids like this temperamentally different from her own son? Maybe, as people said, girls were just easier than boys. Or did Maggie's mother just do a better job than Claudia?

Maggie said, "I've been waiting for a chance to introduce ourselves."

Claudia said, "You're the first neighbor we've met. We just moved here from New Jersey."

"Well, welcome to the neighborhood! I'm in apartment eight. Actually, I've noticed you. Don't think I'm a nosy neighbor or anything. It's just that I work from home—at my computer— and it's right by the window that overlooks the parking lot, that's all."

Claudia wasn't especially good at small talk, but she tried to keep the conversation going. She needed to make some friends.

"Right. How nice, to work from home. Oh, and I'm in apartment thirteen."

"I know," said Maggie with a wink. "Nosy neighbor! Where do you work?"

"At the chiropractic clinic. I'm a licensed massage therapist."

"Well, that's interesting."

Was it? Or was Maggie just being polite, also trying to keep the conversation going?

"How did you decide to become a massage therapist?"

"I kind of fell into it, actually. I'd been going to a fine arts school, and I had to change gears when I got pregnant. All of a sudden I had to get practical. I love working with my hands, and I liked the idea of making people feel better, so . . . I don't know—it just sort of came to me, you know? And I really enjoy the work."

"So you have a *calling*!" said Maggie. "I wish *I* did. I still don't know what I want to be when I grow up! Did you have to go to school a long time to get your license? Was it hard?"

Maggie listened intently, her luminous eyes fixed on Claudia.

"It was a yearlong program. And yeah, it was intense. There was a lot of anatomy involved. But I liked it."

Maggie asked a lot of questions, simple ones, and she was equally willing to share her own personal details with Claudia.

"Oh, so *you* were a good student. *I* never was. I remember hearing my mom tell someone I wasn't 'the smartest crayon in the box.' I was just a kid, and I was so confused, trying to figure out which crayon *is* the smartest one in the box. Which I guess just proved her point."

Here Maggie laughed good-naturedly at herself. "Well, great! Hey, I should have you and Henry and your partner over some time for dinner or something."

"That's so nice of you. Henry and I are alone."

"Well, hey. We have so much in common already! Violet and I are alone too. It's really hard to be doing everything all by yourself and have no one to count on, isn't it? I'm really glad you're here, Claudia."

* * *

Maggie proved to be an interested and reliable friend from the start. When Claudia told her about the miserable parent–teacher conference and Miss Patty's offhand remark about The Hawthorne School, Maggie laughed.

"You *know* that's where Violet goes, right?"

"*That's* where I've heard the name before. The wonderful private school *Violet* goes to."

Maggie was always singing the praises of Violet's progressive school where she was getting "the most amazing education." Claudia was sure it would be out of her price range. Maggie and Violet seemed to be taken care of financially somehow. Claudia perceived there were no money troubles for them. That was not the case for Claudia and Henry.

"Ugh. I hope I don't sound like I'm bragging about Violet's school. I hate bragging. But it's been a real game changer for us. I can just *see* Henry at The Hawthorne School. If you ask me, it's just what Henry needs. He would be so enriched there." Seeing Claudia's hesitation, Maggie pushed. "You at least have to go for a tour."

"I don't really have the money for a private school," Claudia admitted, feeling her disadvantage, Henry's disadvantage. She looked at Violet, who was playing sweetly with Henry. Violet was a lucky girl who went to a school where children flourished.

"It can't hurt to go and look. Ask about financial aid. I know they work with some parents. I bet they'll work with you, Claudia. Let me tell you a little secret." Maggie leaned in. "I probably shouldn't tell you this, but they're giving me a really good deal on Violet's tuition. I've even heard that they waive some students' tuition completely in exchange for volunteer hours from parents. Not for everyone, of course. But it's been known to happen. They have alumni and community support, so they can help a lot of kids out. Just go talk to them. What have you got to lose?"

4

CLAUDIA HAD DRIVEN out of town on Route 171 until she came to the wrought-iron gates and the words engraved in the tall stone wall: "The Hawthorne School." The grandeur of the place had intimidated her, but it hadn't intimidated Henry. She'd allowed him to pull her along and had brought him into the Main Hall.

Now she said to Zelma, "I have Henry enrolled at Happy Start right now, but I'm not sure it's the best fit." Claudia felt like a hypocrite saying this, as if she had a choice in the matter. It wasn't as if The Hawthorne School was a real possibility, but she wanted to keep pretending. She liked sitting here with the director and acting as if she were in a position to school-shop, to find the "best fit" for her son. She enjoyed being in this room, in this building. She felt calm. She didn't usually feel calm.

"And my neighbor, Maggie Timmerberg, has her daughter Violet enrolled here too." Maybe that would help.

Meanwhile, Henry was neither singing loudly nor trying to climb out the window. Claudia could tell he liked being in this place, too, and was continuing to fill sheets of paper with color.

Zelma was looking at Henry thoughtfully.

"A very good child," she murmured, as if for Claudia's ears only, though of course Henry heard her and sat a little straighter in his chair. "He puts me in mind of another little boy, one I knew long ago."

Claudia confessed, "Henry doesn't know his letters. Not even the letters in his first name. He can't cut with scissors, and he won't try. And his teachers put him in time-out every day."

There, she'd said it. The director might as well know the worst before they went any farther. And Claudia also had the secret hope that this kind-looking woman would give her a different perspective, perhaps would tell her that he didn't need to know the letters in his own name yet, that there was still plenty of time, that Henry was fine, and that she was fine too.

Henry glanced up at her and returned to his coloring with a frown.

Zelma said, "You're a very wise mother, to be so aware, so *in tune* with your son. Your little boy is so lucky! Do you know, most parents have no idea what their children need in a school environment? *I* see what the problem is."

"You do?" Claudia opened like a flower in the sunlight of Zelma's wisdom. She hadn't felt so open since her mother had passed away.

"Yes! And I get the feeling that you ignore your own awareness sometimes. *You* don't see what is right in front of you." Zelma smiled, as if to say she meant no offense. "You need to get him out of that one-size-fits-all factory. He shouldn't be there. He is a very special child." That was exactly what Claudia's mother used to say: that Henry was special—remarkable, in fact. "I think you know that Henry needs something more too, or you wouldn't be here today." She stopped to observe Henry, who was pretending not to listen to her as he colored carefully and with raised eyebrows. "Schools like that do so much harm to a child's natural development. Your son is only four years old. Time-out? If they were doing their jobs and working properly with him, they wouldn't have any reason to even think of time-out. Time-out does not exist here. We do not push academics on four-year-olds. At this age, he should be playing."

"Well, that's what *I* always thought!" said Claudia.

"And you thought right!"

Claudia flushed with pleasure.

"*Our* children don't learn letters or cut with scissors until they are developmentally ready. That way, it's organic, and there's no frustration. Why *should* there be frustration? Why push? What's the rush? Now, at this age, your son should be spending time in nature, running, breathing in fresh air, using his muscles and his imagination. Our children spend the majority of their day outside, in the fields, on the playground or in the woods. They come inside calm and ready to do art." Zelma's bespectacled eyes peered into Claudia's as she spoke, and she nodded with each assertion. Claudia nodded along with her.

"Oh!" said Claudia, her heart lifting even higher. "Do you have art? I mean, like, real *art*?" She would love to have Henry immersed in art.

"Do we have *art*? It's an art-centered school, didn't you know? Art is the way to awaken the spirit of every child, of every person."

"It *is*! I've always felt that way too!" Claudia could not hold her enthusiasm in. Art, for Henry! If only he could be a student here!

Zelma said, "It's easy to see you're an exceptional mother. It's always the exceptional parents who find their way to us."

Tears of relief flooded Claudia's eyes at Zelma's words, and to her embarrassment, Zelma saw.

Claudia couldn't take in the compliment. She couldn't believe she was an exceptional mother, as much as she wanted to. She hoped that Zelma saw something in her that she didn't see in herself. She only knew how hard she was trying, how much she worried and felt unequal to the task of raising her boy, and how much she loved him.

Zelma smiled, as if she could read Claudia's thoughts. "I will hazard a guess and say that in addition to being a very loving mother, you are also curious and open to different ideas. Am I right? Or . . .?"

Claudia laughed. "Sure, I guess so." Now, Claudia felt she might be in love with this little old lady.

"In that case," said Zelma, "I'll take you on a tour of the school. Do you have time?"

Zelma rose and went to Henry. She looked thoughtfully at each picture he had made, and commented, "These are very interesting, Henry. I will keep them. Thank you."

Claudia noticed that Zelma did not say, "I will keep them, *okay?*" the way most adults would. She had made a clear affirmative statement, and Henry was nodding, pleased. There was no condescension, no false delight or forced cheerfulness. She spoke to him minimally and seriously with the expectation that he would respond with dignity, with the unspoken message that their interaction would be peaceful and collaborative. Claudia could see: Zelma knew how to bring out the best in Henry. And Henry liked Zelma.

"Yes," said Claudia, "we have time. I have the afternoon off. I'm a massage therapist at Dr. Wesley's Chiropractic Clinic downtown."

"Ah," said Zelma. "You are a healer."

"Sort of," said Claudia, humble. Then, gaining confidence, "I do really love my job."

"I can just tell. I myself have a little gift for reading people. I know you make people feel better. It's in your very nature, isn't it?"

It was true. Making other people feel better was what Claudia did best.

"I'm sure you are gifted at what you do."

Claudia had not heard this assessment from Dr. Wesley, although she had been wishing for some positive feedback. Dr. Wesley was a man of few words, and Claudia didn't know what he thought of her work. She was already building a steady client list, though. She hoped that meant that she was good at her job.

"Henry is an only child?" asked Zelma as they walked down the hall.

"Yes."

"Ah. And you yourself, do you come from a big family?"

"No, I'm an only child too."

"Do you know, some of the greatest artists and most brilliant minds have been only children? In mainstream society, the only child gets a bad rap, I'm afraid, but it's not deserved. There are inevitable benefits that come from getting a lot of individual attention from adults. A more mature point of view. Independence of spirit. Are Henry's grandparents in the area?"

"No. I never actually met my father, and my mother died this past winter."

"Oh, my dear. I am so sorry."

"Thank you." At this expression of sympathy, Claudia felt a wave of grief rising up from her heart to her throat, and she fought to keep her composure. Fortunately, the director continued.

"So you have no family at all?"

"No. No one."

Zelma nodded, as if these details of her life were of any interest to her. Claudia was sure she was only being polite. "Have you lived here a long time?"

"No. I'm from New Jersey. We just moved here three months ago."

"Ah. You, Henry, and Henry's—"

"Just Henry and I."

"I see," said Zelma. "And Henry's father? If it's not too personal?"

"We're—estranged, I guess, is the best word."

Zelma's face clouded. "Estranged," she repeated. "In my experience estranged parents have a tendency to pop up in time. We've had problems in the past when both parents were not on the same page concerning their child's education."

"There's no chance of Devin 'popping up.' He walked out on us very decidedly four years ago, and he's never turned up so far."

Zelma, sympathetic, asked, "And his family? Does Henry have grandparents on his father's side?"

"I'm afraid not. Devin's family was broken and scattered."

She turned to Claudia and beamed at her as they walked down the cool, echoing hallway. "I see! Then you need *support!*"

Claudia felt the relief of recognition: that was exactly what she needed. Zelma was so perceptive, seemed to see inside her and to really care. It hadn't occurred to her before.

Yes, that was exactly what she needed.

"And that's what we give our parents at The Hawthorne School. Lots and lots of support."

5

"THIS IS MISS Applegate's room. She has one section of the four-year-olds—the fours, as we say. It looks like they're just sitting down to lunch."

Claudia didn't see Miss Applegate, but she heard someone in the kitchen area, just out of her line of vision, and she smelled corn cooking. Henry stood by Claudia, one arm around her leg for security. She sensed he was curious but still a little shy. Claudia took in the room: against a wall, there was a child-sized throne made of branches with bright ribbons wound all around it, and a wooden doll house with tiny cloth dolls. An array of corn husk dolls stood in the deep windowsills, some looking in and others looking out. A large photograph of a dark-haired man hung prominently, bearing a golden plaque reading "Gabriel Hawthorne." Bright artwork covered all the walls and the chalkboard. There was a series of swirls in chalk on black construction paper—one by each child in the class, Claudia assumed. There were also paintings of colorful, hooded, elf-like creatures marching gaily through a garden, as well as some mythical animals. Claudia felt strangely moved by these chalk paintings.

The children were so quiet that she noticed them last of all. At a low table were seated a racially diverse group of six children about Henry's age. None of the children wore T-shirts with logos or words; they were all dressed differently, yet in a similar, plain fabric. None of them looked up at Claudia, Henry, and Zelma. Perhaps they were used to tours coming through.

"They're so well behaved," Claudia murmured, so as not to disturb the class. She wondered how her son would fit in with a group like this.

"Yes! They've been outside the entire morning, of course. Climbing, running, making nature crafts—like that vine wreath you see on the table? That's the kind of thing they make when they're outside. They feel relaxed and free of tension after two and a half hours out there. Every child does. When children are immersed in nature, there are no behavior problems because they don't feel restricted, you see. And then when they come in, they go straight to music."

Claudia was thrilled. "You have *music* here?"

"Of course we have music here! Music is everyone's birthright, you know. Each child learns to play the recorder. When they get older, they go on to learn the flute. And of course, a little Spanish. The preschoolers learn little songs and rhymes. It develops their ear for language."

Claudia was sold. This was what Henry should have. Nature, art, music, and Spanish. If only she could find some way to pay for it.

"Now, the lunch and snacks," said Zelma, "are all provided. Our parents don't have to pack anything. All of the food is organic, plant-based, and gluten-free. We obtain some produce from outside: pineapples, bananas, and avocados. But most of our food comes from our own garden, which the children plant and tend."

As if on cue, a woman came from the kitchen area with a steaming pot and spoon. She glanced unsmiling at Claudia, and served the children. This must be Miss Applegate. She did not introduce herself, and Zelma did not introduce her either. Miss Applegate had a way of turning and tilting her head that put Claudia in mind of a delicate bird. She looked to be about forty-five, and her figure was strikingly thin and flat. Her hair was black, straight, and feathery, and her bangs were long, curling in toward her eyelashes. She wore no makeup and was dressed in a maxi dress with low-heeled boots. It was a sort of boho look: very aesthetic.

Claudia observed that there was no chattering, no bicker-
ing, no surreptitious poking, and no elbowing. The children sat
calmly, waiting for everyone to be served. The ambiance was
tranquil and muted. Claudia looked up at the ceiling for a light
source and saw there were no panels of fluorescent tubes. There
was an emerald cast to the sunlight that filtered through green
vines and broke through the diamond-paned windows, which
faced west, beyond which were the green leaves of a woods.

Zelma, following Claudia's glance, said, "Sunlight, natural light, is best for children's learning. On a very dark day, of
course, we turn on the floor lamps. But the fluorescent lights
you find in most classrooms are *proven* to cause anxiety and
stress, and even hormonal changes. It's no wonder schools have
so many behavior problems to deal with: confining children
indoors under fluorescent lights is activating in the most harmful way. And of course, you won't see any computers here either.
Even the teachers don't have cell phones, iPads, or computers of
any kind. We know too much about electromagnetic radiation
and the damage it does—even on a cellular level—to people,
and especially to children, who are so vulnerable." Zelma gestured toward Henry, who was avidly searching the room with
his eyes. He looked longingly at a wooden playhouse—two stories, with an arch-topped door and covered with painted green
vines. Claudia expected him to tear away from her and run to
that little house, but mercifully he stayed by her side and came
along as she and Zelma exited the classroom. She thought to say
goodbye to Miss Applegate, but in that quiet, she felt it would
be a disruption.

As they walked back down the corridor the way they had
come, Claudia was lost in thought. She was trying to imagine
a school day without the internet. At twenty-four, she was of
the first generation said to be "native speakers" of technology.
However, she didn't own a TV, and she regularly challenged
herself to go half a day without turning on her smartphone. She
had a vague feeling that there was something unhealthy in the
way most people connected with their devices. She wanted real
experiences, human connection, and time in nature for her and
for Henry.

They were passed by a file of older children—Claudia guessed they were ten-year-olds—who marched with purpose, trailing odors of sweat and the outdoors, before disappearing through a door ahead and on the right.

Claudia and the director stopped before an oil painting that Claudia had noticed before. It was the full portrait of a seated, earnest-looking, silver-haired woman. She wore a calf-length black dress, and her hand rested on a white book on her lap. The background was in the shades of blue and rose that were popular in the 1980s. At each lower corner of the frame were decorative wires that held small vases in which stood water and fresh flowers—white hydrangeas. At the bottom of the frame was a golden plaque that read "Julia Hawthorne."

"This is our founder. She passed away six years ago. Now her son, Gabriel, or "G" as we call him, is the president of the Hawthorne Foundation. You're standing in the first Hawthorne School Julia Hawthorne started, but of course there are now Hawthorne Schools in three states and even two in Europe and one in Asia. We're growing steadily. We sometimes joke: the Hawthorne Schools are taking over the world!" She chuckled softly, and Claudia smiled.

"Let's take a look at a section of sevens," Zelma said, leading Claudia and Henry away from the portrait and to another door. "This is Miss Kincaid's classroom."

In this room, the teacher sat with eight children in a circle—five girls and three boys—knitting. Each child sat on a wooden chair with a pair of knitting needles and a furrowed brow. Miss Kincaid was in her thirties, serene and slender. She wore a long linen skirt and knitted sweater. She looked up briefly on the entrance of her visitors and then seemed to tune them out. Claudia allowed that they had interrupted Miss Kincaid while she was working. It couldn't be easy to keep children of this age focused on knitting. While seven of the eight children were concentrating deeply and had swatches of varying lengths of accomplished work already, Claudia was relieved to see one little boy twisting around in his chair and sliding off it, first left and then right, in a slow and controlled way—clearly resisting the knitting lesson. He never hit the floor, but pulled himself back in time and slid the other way. She'd known there *had* to be some children here who didn't cooperate all the time. That little boy's knitting swatch was less impressive, only about two inches long, and falling off its needles as he fell off his chair. He did not seem concerned that the little work he had already done was slipping into destruction.

Neither Miss Kincaid nor Zelma made any remark about the falling boy. Claudia broke the silence with a question for the class: "That's some beautiful knitting you're doing there. Is it hard?" Only one child, a little girl, looked at her. The rest continued to work just as if she had not spoken, as if she were not there at all. Claudia sensed surprise in Miss Kincaid and discomfort in Zelma, but she didn't know why. She repeated, "Is it tricky—to learn to knit?"

The little girl said brightly, "It's not very tricky if you practice. When you first learn, it's very slow. But if you practice a lot, it starts going fast, and it gets easier and easier! And then you love it, and you want to do it all the time. See?" Obviously pleased with herself, she held up her knitting—the longest swatch of all—for Claudia to appreciate. Neither Zelma nor Miss Kincaid made any comment, but Zelma opened the classroom door to lead Claudia and Henry out.

They walked past closed doors, hallways, and staircases. She could hear children's uproarious and contagious laughter coming from somewhere, and she turned to smile at Zelma, who smiled back. "It's time we got Henry outside to the fields and the playground," said Zelma.

Once again, Claudia noticed that Zelma did not ask for Henry's buy-in; she did not say in a falsely cheery voice, "Wouldn't you like to see our playground?" She simply stated what he would see next. She was not trying to make him like her or think she was fun. As connected to him as Claudia was, she could feel not only his curiosity about what they would see outdoors but also that Zelma's matter-of-fact, take-charge manner was somehow calming to him. Perhaps, Claudia wondered, she should take that approach with him at home. Maybe she tried too hard to win his cooperation.

Claudia and Henry still wore their jackets. They had never thought to take them off since they'd entered the building.

Claudia noticed now, for the first time, that it was very chilly inside. She thought of the children in the classrooms and wondered if they were cold.

As Zelma brought her own cloth jacket from her office and put it on, Claudia said, "It seems a little cool in the building."

"Cold temperatures are healthy for children. A cold environment is best for promoting brain growth and stimulating the immune system. You'll find that all our classrooms are quite cool."

Outside, the sky shimmered mother-of-pearl. They walked along curving, tree-lined paths around and behind the school, until they came to the immense expanse of land that Zelma called "the grounds." From an upper window somewhere drifted the notes of a flute accompanied by piano. The tune was Celtic and touching, the notes twining around the grandeur of the nearby woods, the soaring birds, and the passing clouds above them as they darkened and brightened the scene. When the playground came into sight, Henry took off running.

Claudia understood his enthusiasm. The playground was not like any Claudia had ever seen before. Here, there was no plastic in primary colors. Everything was made of natural materials. There was an immense wooden structure with ladders, platforms, and bridges made of rope and enclosed with netting. This was surrounded by patches of flowers and mature trees. Zelma encouraged Claudia to walk on with her, although she wanted to hover close to her son.

"He can see us. Let him use his muscles and run and climb. Let him be free." They walked on, slowly, with Claudia looking back over her shoulder from time to time. Led on by Zelma, she walked farther away from him than she ever would have thought safe.

"When the children go in after a morning of immersion in nature, they have a snack, of course, and then they have a teaching. After the teaching, comes the silence."

"A teaching? Is that a lesson?"

"Yes. We educators do love our special lingo, you know. We at The Hawthorne School call it a teaching."

"And then, did you say, 'a silence'?"

"Yes. In this chaotic world, people seldom have enough silence. We need the silence, to remain sane and present. In schools—out *there*—children are being talked at constantly. Even adults these days are being talked at constantly. Conditioned to the constant yack-yack-yack in schools, they feel the need to keep the noise going with TVs, car radios, internet videos, and on and on. There's so much anxiety and depression in today's world because, for one thing, people are not letting in sufficient quiet, you see. The silence, coming after the teaching, allows each child to absorb and integrate what they have learned."

She walked Claudia past a fountain with metal frogs that spewed water from their mouths into the pond. On the grounds, there were tiny wooden houses for children to play in. For as far as she could see, there were woods on one side and fields on the other.

"How much land *is* this?" she asked.

"Thirteen acres of field and forest. That big barn there is our carpentry shed. The older children build furniture and do crafts there. Beyond that is our vegetable garden. As I mentioned, the children work there too."

Zelma was silent, lifting her gaze to the sky and closing her eyes, breathing in the cool air. Claudia stood with her, soaking in the loveliness of nature all around them. She turned to watch Henry in the distance, swinging from the bars and running along the bridges.

After a few minutes, Zelma asked, "Do you have any questions?"

Claudia was overwhelmed with emotions. The aesthetics of The Hawthorne School, its architectural grandeur, its attention to beauty in every interior and exterior detail, the progressive and commonsense approach, the enlightened focus on what was truly good for children, filled her with hope that Henry could fit in here, that the only problem had been small-minded, inferior, mass-market "education," that he really was fine, that she was not a failure as a mother, and that this school could prove it.

And besides the wonder and the hope, she felt despair. Despair because now, having seen this place, she would have to live with the knowledge that there was a school where her son could be all right, but she couldn't afford to get him into it.

She was used to doing without. She had learned to manage and accept her limitations. But now she had Henry. It hurt her heart to think of him being deprived of advantages like this.

"Zelma, it's a beautiful school. I'd love to have this for Henry. But I'm afraid I won't be able to afford—"

"We do work with our parents who can't afford the tuition," Zelma said, waving away Claudia's angst. "In fact, most of our families are on scholarship to one extent or another. It *is* very expensive to run a school like this, but keep in mind, we have many donors. Grateful alumni are very generous to us. We are fortunate to have the funding that does allow us to offer financial aid to deserving families. And you and Henry *are* a deserving family. I can see that."

Claudia said, "Could you just clarify—what do you mean by 'financial aid' and 'scholarship'?"

"We can get into all the details later. But generally, what I mean is this: we do take all you can give. But if that does not pay tuition in full, and if you commit to the Hawthorne Way, you can certainly 'have this for Henry,' as you say. Of course, you'll need to provide us with records of all of your financial assets so that we can assess how much aid to offer."

"Naturally," agreed Claudia.

"Be assured, we will make it work, no matter how little you have. You can pay off some of the tuition through parent volunteer projects."

"But—that's all? I just give you my bank records—there's nothing much to see there—a record of my apartment rent, things like that? And then I do volunteer work here—and we're in?"

Claudia looked around herself again, thinking she wouldn't mind coming here often to do volunteer work. She liked the way she felt here. She wouldn't just be dropping Henry off, the way she did at Happy Start. She would come in with him and become a part of this beautiful place.

"Well, I want you to be prepared: the volunteer work is a real commitment. You should be prepared to give us several hours a week. This is not a free ride, of course. This is an exchange. We do expect a lot. We will keep you busy! Very busy!"

"That's fair enough. I'm happy to help. But of course I have a job too."

"I know that, dear. We'll work with your schedule."

"Perfect! And that's all there is to it? There's no wait list? It seems too good to be true!"

Zelma laughed, her eyes sparkling periwinkle. She pressed Claudia's arm affectionately and said, "When you join us, you become a part of our family. And you and Henry *need* family. I can see that."

Claudia had given up all hope of having any kind of a family beyond Henry. Since her mother died, it had been just Claudia and Henry against the world. This gentle woman's words warmed her heart.

Henry ran to join them, and Zelma, to Henry's delight, pulled a red apple from a tree and, receiving a nod of permission from Claudia, presented it to him like a gift. He bit right into it. "It's *sweet!*"

Zelma invited Claudia to pick one for herself, and she did. The apple was pure juicy sweetness, not like the supermarket apples she was used to, but full of flavor.

Claudia promised to bring back her financial paperwork as Zelma accompanied her toward the gate. Henry spun in circles and hopped on both feet, behind them as they walked.

As Claudia and Henry rode home, she asked him, "Do you like The Hawthorne School?"

Henry said, "I don't like it."

Claudia, surprised and disappointed, asked, "You don't?"

Henry said, "No, I don't like it . . . I *love* it!" And then he laughed at his own joke.

Claudia, reassured, said to herself, "I think I've found an answer for us."

CHAPTER

6

AT HOME, AFTER bath and before bedtime, Henry was his best self: placid and affectionate. They sat on the couch with an open picture book. Although he hated cutting with scissors and having letters of the alphabet pointed out to him, he did love stories. He could sit still and listen to fairy tales for as long as Claudia could keep reading them. He could draw and paint and play with clay for hours. He could run around at the park for as long as Claudia could stay. What he could not stand, though, was being taught or told what to do. Told to put on his shoes, he would take off his socks. Told to connect the dots in a workbook, he would roll around the room. Gandhi could have learned a lot about passive resistance from Henry.

But now, he was cuddling close. Claudia loved these fleeting moments when he was a little sleepy and she could put her arms around him. She was thinking about the decision she had before her: to keep Henry at Happy Start, which after all was a normal, regular school and would probably prepare him for all the other schools he would have to go to in his life—or to move him to The Hawthorne School, which was unconventional. She'd always preferred unconventional things herself, but this was her son's education, and she didn't want to make a mistake.

Maggie seemed very happy with The Hawthorne School; she'd talked of support for parents and said it was a "game changer" for her child. Violet was thriving. But Violet was the sort of child who would blossom anywhere, who could adapt to any environment. Henry was different. How would Henry fare at The Hawthorne School?

While Claudia had been with Zelma Huxley, she'd felt as if she were under some sort of enchantment, and she loved everything she saw and heard. But now, in the ordinary world of their apartment, she slipped back into the despondency and uncertainty that had taken over her life ever since her mother had died.

She thought now of Zelma and was aware that the allure of The Hawthorne School was twined with the allure of Zelma. Zelma stood, vivid and dominant in her mind. A kind and supportive older woman, she made Claudia feel safe.

Zelma had seemed to see right into her, to know all about her. But how could she put faith into the compliments that Zelma had given her, the ones that had touched her bruised heart and brought tears to her eyes? How would this stranger know if she was a "wise" mother or if Henry was "special?" Was the director being overly kind? And the offer—it appeared that Zelma was ready on this short acquaintance to simply waive tuition in exchange for some volunteer work. Things like that didn't happen. They had never happened in Claudia's world. But couldn't it be that Zelma was especially perceptive and saw how deserving Claudia and Henry were? Maybe things like this did happen for some people, and this was her lucky break.

Luck of this kind had never been a part of Claudia's reality before. She was used to working hard for modest rewards. And yet she'd inherited from her mother a sort of stubborn hope, despite whatever current circumstances might be. A belief that Magdalena Vera had always held, that better times were just around the corner. Whenever Claudia thought of her mother— which was every day—she saw her laughing. Claudia's mother often broke into contagious fits of laughter, even when things looked dire: when there wasn't enough money to pay the bills and even when Claudia went to sit by her side at the hospital. She'd lain in the narrow bed, exhausted, thin, and sickly, waiting for her next chemotherapy treatment, and when Claudia had appeared around the door frame with Henry by the hand, true to form, her mother had laughed quietly, her head shaking from side to side. Claudia, with grief in her heart, couldn't help but laugh too.

"Mamá. What's so funny?"

"Nothing. It's just so good to see you."

The two of them had laughed for no apparent reason until tears streamed down their faces.

Her mother's strength was in her ability to laugh at whatever life threw at her.

She thought back to when Henry was a baby and wouldn't stop crying, no matter what Claudia tried. Her mother was the baby whisperer, her confident embrace sending him off to sleep. And as Henry grew, his grandmother became, as she was for Claudia, an important source of comfort and security. If she were alive now, she would love to see Henry getting a wonderful opportunity. Maybe, in some way, her spirit was behind this lucky break.

There was no doubt in her mind that Henry *was* deserving of an education based in nature and the arts. He needed educators that liked and understood him.

She held Henry close to her and felt the gravity of her decision. The Hawthorne School was a beautiful gothic building on a lot of land, but it was "unorthodox," as Miss Patty had said. Henry was already different enough from the mainstream. Wouldn't this school just encourage that differentness? And wouldn't most people say that was a bad thing? Or was it exactly what he needed, so that he could grow up self-confident and free to be himself? She wished her mother were alive to advise her, but there was only Henry, and he was only four.

"Henry, let's talk about the school we went to today."

"It isn't a school."

"It isn't?"

"No. It just looks like a school. It's pretending."

"Pretending? To be a school?"

"Yes. Because it's really a giant's castle."

"Oh!"

"Yes, and I live there."

"You mean, you want to live there?"

"No. I live there already. It's my home. And it's magical."

"Oh, okay . . . And what about the director, Mrs. Huxley?"

"She's the giant's wife. You have to be good with her, Mom. Always be good with her."

"Me? *I* should be good with Mrs. Huxley?"

"You have to. Or else she'll tell the giant. And that would be bad."

"Oh, okay. Gotcha."

"I will always love you best, Mom. Will you always love me best?"

"Yes, Henry. I will always love you best."

*　*　*

After Henry was asleep, his little chest rising and falling, his arms flung above his head and his legs splayed out, Claudia tiptoed to the living room and called the phone number for Happy Start Preschool. She didn't know when she'd made the decision. She only knew that this was the path that she and Henry had to take. They'd been given an opportunity, and she was going to be grateful and accept it. After all, what was the worst that could happen? If, at some point, she decided it wasn't the right choice, well, then at that time she would simply make a different choice. Nothing was forever.

And once she decided, she felt flooded with relief. She and Henry would be a part of that beautiful place. It was meant to be. She remembered how everything felt right while she was there.

Claudia left a message for Miss Patty that she was withdrawing Henry from Happy Start, that she had decided that a "private school" would "better meet Henry's educational needs." She felt satisfied with herself as she spoke those words. She felt like a mother who knew what she was doing.

7

CLAUDIA HAD GIVEN Henry a haircut in preparation for his first day at The Hawthorne School. He looked bright and shiny, with his hair slightly wet and brushed neatly to the side, and over his white undershirt she put him in a blue-checked, button-down shirt that brought out the blue in his eyes.

As she looked at his baby face in the bathroom mirror, she saw herself, her mother, and Henry's own strong individual self, all combined. She felt a surge of pure love for the sweetness of him, balancing out her more frequent feeling of frustration with him. He was just a little boy, learning about the world. She had never loved anyone, not even her mother, as much as she loved Henry.

She resisted a temptation to tell him to be good at school, because she knew from experience that such instructions never worked.

He had not misbehaved during the tour, but then everything was new. As she buckled him into his car seat, she had the feeling she was forgetting something. But no, the list of first-day instructions Zelma had given her at the end of the tour had specifically said that parents were asked not to send snacks, lunch, or food of any kind with their children. One less thing to worry about.

Zelma met her at the door and invited Claudia to wait in her office while she personally delivered Henry to his classroom. The invitation was more of an order, and Claudia understood the reason for it. Henry was less likely to balk with Zelma than with her. She gave him a kiss and watched him walk down the long hall, holding the hand of the director. He did not turn to look back at her.

Within minutes, Zelma returned. Her smile told her that Henry had gone into his classroom without incident.

"He's nicely settled. This would be the best time to get the finances out of the way once and for all. Have a seat, please. You've brought all your financial records?"

Claudia gave her most recent pay stub from the chiropractic clinic and her latest checking account statement to Zelma, who took them with a nod and glanced over them. "And your savings? Investments? IRAs, stocks? Any mortgages, anything of that nature?"

"I don't have anything like that at all," said Claudia, "but here's my apartment rental contract, if you want to see that."

Zelma browsed through it.

"Any car payments?"

"No," said Claudia. "I paid cash for my car."

Zelma glanced up from the document she was reading.

"I bought it used. Four thousand dollars cash."

Instead of looking disappointed, Zelma became more cheerful with each piece of financial strain that Claudia revealed.

"Now, your own expected contribution will be . . ." Zelma penciled calculations as she looked from one document to the other.

Claudia waited, unconsciously biting the inside of her cheek.

The director looked up brightly and as if delivering good news. "Well! I think we can bring your payment down to five hundred a month?"

Claudia felt stricken. She was just scraping by as it was. But what had she expected? To pay nothing at all?

Zelma searched Claudia's face.

"Have I overshot the number?" Zelma set the paperwork to the side. "Don't worry, dear. Let's do this: we'll leave it flexible. Honor system. Each month, you pay whatever you can. I know you will be as generous as possible within your own limits. What you can't give us in dollars, you can give us in hours.

We'll set you up with enough volunteer hours to compensate for the financial shortfall. I did tell you—didn't I?—that we'll keep you busy!"

"Yes," said Claudia, gratefully, "I'd love to help the school in every way I can."

"*That's* what we love to hear! Now, the next item of business is this little stack of registration forms for you to go through and sign."

Claudia took the forms and sat down at the table.

Zelma went on. "Please bring Henry's birth certificate tomorrow so that we can verify his identification. It's a requirement," she explained apologetically. "Today, we just need your signature on these papers. I'm afraid they make rather dry reading!" quipped Zelma, her face jovial.

The forms looked standard. She flipped through the pile and signed on each line that was highlighted in yellow. As she handed the papers back to Zelma, Claudia was gratified to feel that she was performing as Zelma would wish. She wanted so much for this little woman to like her, to approve of her, even. She wanted to stay on her good side and not feel like the failure she'd been with Miss Patty. So far, Zelma had seen her as an excellent mother and Henry as a special little boy. Claudia wanted to keep it that way.

Claudia still thought of herself as a girl, not as a woman. She was sure she wasn't "adulting" correctly, and expected that true adults could see that. She felt exposed all the time. It was discouraging to her that even motherhood had not conferred on her a sense of maturity.

But Zelma looked happy with her.

"And now," said Zelma, "I'll let you get out of here and go to work. In the meantime, I'll think of some volunteer projects for you. I know you are artistic?"

Claudia felt a thrill of excitement. "Yes, I am. Well I *used* to be. Since Henry was born, I haven't actually done any art."

"Naturally. You've been dedicating your time to Henry."

"Yes. But put me to work painting a mural or teaching an art class! And massage, of course—I could offer massage sessions to the teachers, maybe?"

"Do you know how to sew?"

Claudia wanted Zelma to keep seeing her as a parent who fit in at The Hawthorne School, one who knew some traditional skills. "Actually, I do—a little." Claudia hadn't thought of it in years, but her mom had taught her when she was twelve how to sew a pair of shorts. They had turned out a bit wonky, but she'd worn them with pride anyway. She thought she could still remember.

"I may have you mend some of our costumes. Every class has a dress-up cupboard, of course, and the costumes require some upkeep. We've been amassing a pile of silk capes that need to be repaired. There are lots of different things for you to do.

"But for now," said Zelma, standing and moving toward the door with flexibility that belied her age, "Toodle-oo!"

Claudia followed her and wiggled her fingers like Zelma. She felt silly, but she laughed and repeated the childish farewell.

"Toodle-oo."

CHAPTER

8

STEPHANIE, THE RECEPTIONIST, called out gaily, "Good morning, Claudia! You have a packed schedule today. I'm making sure you still get your breaks, but some clients are insisting on seeing only you now. They won't let me schedule them with another massage therapist. They'd rather wait for you."

"Aw, well, good," said Claudia. She suspected Stephanie was being kind to her, trying to make her feel comfortable, because it must be so obvious that she still felt ill at ease in her new job. The only time she ever really relaxed was in the small, dark massage room with meditation music playing, her hands pressing into and subduing the tightly knotted back and neck muscles of a client.

Stephanie tapped with blue fingernails on the calendar as Claudia looked over the day's schedule, and observed, "You don't know how good you are, do you? I don't think you really give yourself credit."

"Well, thanks." Claudia smiled to acknowledge the compliment and headed toward the massage room to set up for her first appointment.

As her hands worked through the day, her mind was free to float. She thought of Henry, the wonder of his being a student at such a school, and the hope that this forward-thinking method of education would allow him to behave within expectations. She thought of her mother and imagined sharing the good news with her. "I've found the perfect school for him, Mom. Things are really working out for Henry." She imagined her mother smiling with her eyes, sharing in Claudia's hope.

Claudia felt the pull of grief and tried to work it out with her hands.

* * *

Henry's first day at school—according to him—had gone well. According to Henry his school days always went well. His teachers, though, tended to have a different view.

"I'm the most special boy now," he assured her. "Another boy was the most special before, but now I am."

Claudia arched an eyebrow at him as she took a bag of rice from the pantry.

"And what did you *learn* in school today?"

"Mm. Mostly about spiders. We saw one eating her lunch. She uses her little fangs—they are so sharp! She sticks them in the fly." Henry showed his upper teeth to illustrate. "Then she squeezes out the poison in her. Then the fly can't move. Then it's safe for her to eat the fly."

"Oh! Poor fly, huh?"

Henry shrugged, unconcerned. "The spider has to eat."

Claudia's cell phone buzzed with a text.

Maggie Timmerberg: *Hey Claudia! I'm just making dinner. Come on over with Henry if you want to. There's plenty.*

* * *

There was a sweet charm to Maggie's apartment, reflecting Maggie's own simplicity and beauty.

In contrast, Claudia's apartment looked like a teenage boy's bedroom: nothing aesthetic or tasteful or planned. Nothing inspiring on the walls. Strictly utilitarian, and not especially orderly. As if the inhabitant were only passing through and would be leaving soon anyway. Claudia's artistic flair never translated to interior decorating skills.

Violet took Henry's hand with maternal care and led him to an assembly of her stuffed animals, which she had set up in hasty preparation of his visit. Henry allowed himself to be led and obviously relished the older child's attention. So far, so good.

Dinner was a frozen deep dish pizza and a tossed salad.

"Sorry, I don't actually cook," apologized Maggie. "You probably do. I hope this is okay."

"This is great! We were just going to have rice and beans."

"Oh, see? You *do* cook! I never learned how. I'm hopeless at it. I admire people who can."

"I wouldn't call rice and beans real *cooking*," said Claudia, amused.

"*I* would. It's more than I could do. We just do microwave dinners and takeout."

"Your place is awesome," said Claudia. She wanted Maggie to stop deprecating herself. Why did women feel the need to compare themselves to one another and to always find themselves lacking? Claudia hated her own insecurity and how weak it made her feel, and she hated to see that same insecurity in other women.

"Thanks for suggesting The Hawthorne School. I still can't believe our good fortune, that they took us."

Maggie looked up with surprise as she removed the plastic covering from the deep dish pizza.

"Of *course* they took you. I knew, the minute I first saw you, that you would be just right for The Hawthorne School. Henry will really like it there."

Claudia thought that Maggie's child had probably never had a bad school experience. Violet was so compliant, not the type to throw fits or call teachers names. The kids were playing together peacefully, and that was a nice surprise. Henry didn't usually "play well with others."

"Oh gosh, it's great!" continued Maggie, licking sauce off her fingers. "It's such a helpful school for single moms like us. You'll meet people who will help you with everything. Whatever you want or need, there will be someone to help you. It's like a family."

"That's what Zelma told me." Claudia studied Maggie's face. Maggie had a movie-star glow, but beneath that Claudia saw sweetness, a desire to be helpful and kind.

Maggie cast a glance at the children, and then said in a low tone to Claudia, "Tell me about Henry's father. Were you two in love?" She sounded like a starry-eyed adolescent. She put the pizza in the oven, set the timer, and settled in to hear Claudia's story with wide and interested eyes.

Claudia recounted her brief and tempestuous relationship with Devin. "Did I love him? In the beginning we were obsessed with each other. I was head over heels. Just the sound of his voice would start my heart beating faster. Corny, huh?"

"Oh no! It's *romantic*!" Maggie urged her on. "So, what was he *like*?"

"As I see him now? Smart, but not as smart as he thought he was. He liked to 'speechify,' you know?"

"A 'mansplainer'?" supplied Maggie.

"A know-it-all. Loved the sound of his own voice."

"Yeah, but then, you were both younger then."

"It was only four years ago."

"Still. There's a big difference between twenty and twenty-four."

"Maybe for some people. Anyway, *he* was twenty-one at the time."

"Right. So by now, he could have matured a lot. *You* probably have."

"I've *had* to. I have Henry. I'm sure his life has changed too. By now, Devin could be married—who knows?"

"Ohh," said Maggie, crestfallen. "I didn't think of that. Funny, I never thought of that with Violet's father either. She was two months old by the time I figured it out."

Claudia was hit by a sympathetic wave of hurt. "That must have been awful." She thought of the betrayal of trust and hoped Maggie would tell her more.

"Yeah. You know that feeling—when you think you know someone, and then you find out you don't? Maybe not. It happens to me a lot."

Claudia looked at Maggie's open face and her wide eyes and believed it must be so.

"But you and Devin—it sounds so classic: art students falling in love and all. Did he work?"

"Yeah. We both worked retail. The funny thing was he worked at Health for You—a natural foods store."

"What's so funny about that?"

"He was the biggest junk-food junkie I ever saw."

"Well, there are worse things. You know what *I* think? *I* think you should look him up."

Claudia shook her head vigorously.

"No, really," Maggie insisted. "I just have a feeling. I'm very intuitive. Did I ever tell you that? I get hunches all the time, and they turn out to be true. I just have a feeling: you two should totally be together. Don't ask me how I know—"

"Okay," Claudia laughed. "I won't ask. There's no way I would take Devin back after he walked out on us like he did. No way."

"I'm just saying people change. Especially in their twenties."

Maggie called the children to the table: Violet, leading Henry by the hand, and Henry tolerating it. Once seated, he didn't grab his piece of pizza and run back to the toys. He was keeping an eye on Violet and doing as she did.

"Enough talk about men," said Claudia.

Maggie acquiesced.

"Honestly," said Maggie, her mouth full and her fork gesturing in the air, "I don't know what I'd do without The Hawthorne School. I get a lot of guidance from them. They're the best."

Claudia smiled. "You sound like a true believer."

"Well, I am that! I mean, between you and me, I don't always have a lot of confidence that I'm doing okay as a single parent, you know?"

Claudia glanced up from her plate at Maggie. There was another mom who felt the way she did?

Maggie continued, vulnerable. "In some ways, I don't feel my age, you know? Thirty-five, in case you're too polite to ask. I look around myself . . . I mean, some moms, even single moms, seem to know what they're doing."

Claudia couldn't agree more, but said nothing.

"Take you, for example, Claudia."

"Me?"

"You're so sure of yourself. You were so *brave* to uproot Henry and move out here. I wouldn't have done it, not in a million years. I would've been too afraid. Your doing that shows you have confidence. You're not worried that you could make a big mistake that would have a terrible impact on him for the rest of his life. I'm always worrying about things like that."

Claudia felt these words as a punch to her solar plexus and searched her new friend's face for signs of malice. But she saw only sweetness.

"I didn't uproot him." She glanced at Henry as if checking for signs of damage. He was chewing and swinging his legs. He looked fine.

"Oh gosh. Oh, sorry. I didn't mean it that way. *Why* do I talk so much?" Maggie bit her lower lip. Claudia thought she was right: Maggie really was a little young for her age.

"That's okay," said Claudia. "But just for the record, it wasn't like that. He's only four years old. You can't uproot a kid his age. A four-year-old doesn't *have* roots." Claudia doubted these words even as she said them. She hadn't even considered the possibility that Henry might have had a connection of some sort to their life in New Jersey. But, no. The only thing tying them to the old place was Henry's grandmother, and she had passed on. There was no one else and nothing else that either she or Henry was attached to there.

Claudia told Maggie about her mother's death and the feeling of drifting out to sea that had followed. She told her about how she and her mother had moved every year or two, and that moving felt natural, especially after something bad had happened: a bad breakup, a falling out with a landlord.

By now, the children had gone back to play, Violet announcing rules and assigning roles, and Henry alternating compliance with playing in his own meditative way.

"It's a strange coincidence, Claudia, but we're both orphans, you could say. My parents died years ago. I miss them. But not like you miss your mom. I can see that. You two were really close and depended on each other. And she helped you with Henry, I bet, didn't she? Yeah. My parents died before I had Violet.

"They left me a little trust—nothing extravagant, but enough to cover basic expenses. And I do work too. I work remotely, just part-time, with a flexible schedule. If I had to depend on my work to support us, well, it wouldn't. I know we're lucky my parents made sure they set up the trust for me. They were always worried I wouldn't be able to take care of myself. I don't know why. I guess because I was never good at school. I was no scholar. But *you* were, weren't you?"

Claudia thought it was a good thing Maggie's parents had left her provided for. There was something stunted about Maggie, in spite of her beautiful sheen. She was in some way unfinished, and yet touching in her eagerness to share, to be friends, to be liked.

"I wasn't the best student," answered Claudia. "We moved so much, it was hard to adapt to every new school. But I always did like to read."

"I thought so. You seem like a reader. And you were popular in school. I can tell. Not me. I was sort of bullied. It was awful."

Claudia took in Maggie: her glowing skin, her bright eyes, her general charisma, and found it hard to believe that Maggie had not been the center of admiration all her life.

Claudia said, "I was *not* popular. I was always the new kid, with no friends! But you? I don't believe you. You don't *look* like a scapegoat, that's for sure."

"Thanks. I've changed a lot over the past couple of years. I give all the credit to The Hawthorne School. They don't just educate the children. They do just as much for the parents, I swear."

Claudia watched Violet brushing Henry's hair with a doll's brush as he sat cross-legged, leafing through a picture book.

"How do they help parents?"

"Well, they only help you if you need it. Like I did. But you, Claudia, you're different. You're strong already."

"Strong? Is that how you see me?"

"Mm-hm. Strong. And solid."

Claudia wondered how Maggie couldn't see how unsolid she really was. Maybe it wasn't as obvious as she thought? "Oh well, you should see me on my darker days."

"*Do* you have dark days? Really?"

"Yeah. My days off are the worst ones. Well. You don't want to hear about it."

"I *do*."

"Oh, it's no big thing. I just have days when I can hardly get out of bed. Or I'll get up to feed Henry breakfast, and then go back to bed again."

Maggie looked sorry. Her voice was soft. "Oh. Because of your mom, right?"

Claudia shook off the pity. "I have more good days than bad," she corrected.

But was that true?

All her life, her mother had been the one and only constant. The apartments changed; so did the neighborhoods and the acquaintances. The classmates and the boyfriends cycled through. Her mother's presence had always been the one reliable element in her life.

"Well, the next time you have a dark day, you just text me, and I'll come right over." Maggie smiled, like a child who was pleased with her own idea.

Claudia laughed, knowing she would never send such a text.

"Honestly, Claudia, you are so stable—and so smart. You're ten times smarter than me."

Claudia laughed again. "Maggie! Stop flattering me."

"Flattering you?" Maggie looked perplexed. "I wouldn't do that. I really mean it. I wish I could be more like you. Getting along on your own with a child in tow. I know how hard it is. And there you are, figuring it all out for yourself. You're incredible. Like a warrior or something. I don't have half your courage."

Claudia searched Maggie's eyes but found only sincerity there. She laughed off the compliment. "Oh, Maggie. Go ahead! Tell me sweet lies!"

9

CLAUDIA FELT SHE should be encouraged by Henry's success at The Hawthorne School. All through his first week, Zelma had assured her at pickup that Henry was excelling. She would hardly have believed the director's reports, but they were confirmed by Henry's obvious happiness as he climbed into his car seat and chattered all the way home about his day.

"I still haven't seen the giant. But I will."

"Tell me about Miss Applegate." Claudia wanted to ask if he'd gotten in trouble with his teacher yet, and this was her indirect way of finding out. If Henry said he hated her, that would mean he'd already been disciplined.

"She's nice. She's nicer than you, Mom."

"Nicer than *me*?" Claudia was caught off-guard, surprised that she wasn't pleased, that she could actually feel a pang of jealousy toward her son's teacher.

Henry insisted, "Way nicer. She lets me do whatever I want."

Claudia smiled, imagining how a classroom could be run if a teacher let the children do whatever they wanted.

"I can climb trees. And stick my hands in mud. And yell in the forest. She never tells me to stop anything. She's bee-yoo-tee-full."

Ah, yes. He was spending a lot of his schooldays in the great outdoors. So it was possible that he had more freedom to do as he pleased. It was no wonder that he came home tired but happy each afternoon.

Still, once at home, the happiness began to wear off. Going back out then to do an errand usually didn't end well.

A quick run to the grocery store turned out to be disastrous, as she knew it would, but they were out of all of Henry's favorite foods, and that would lead to stormy moods in any case. The cashier, Laurie, always kept up a bright banter with her customers, and remembered something about each of them. Today, she tried to engage Henry, but he only stared straight ahead, plugged his ears, and puffed out his cheeks in a dramatic expression of disagreeableness.

The cashier was a talker; she loved to give advice on what to buy and not buy, and to disapprove of products in Claudia's cart that Laurie considered too expensive.

Unfazed by Henry's histrionics, Laurie said cheerily to Claudia, "You know what *you* ought to buy? Fruit leather. All the young moms buy fruit leather for their kids' school snacks. Kids just love fruit leather."

Claudia said, "Oh, in our school, all the snacks are provided. They give the kids organic fruits and vegetables."

Laurie said, "Well, that's handy, isn't it? One less thing for you to think about. I didn't know Happy Start was so health conscious."

"Henry doesn't go there anymore. I moved him to The Hawthorne School." Claudia felt privileged as she said it.

"The Hawthorne School? Isn't that the one way out there in the country? On route 171? The one you always hear about?" Laurie froze with a bag of green pears in her hands and searched Claudia's face.

"Yes, it's a wonderful school," said Claudia, then added, "What have you heard about it?"

"Well, I'm just impressed that you were able to get him in there. You must know someone! Connections in high places?"

Claudia laughed. "You're joking. I don't know anyone."

"Huh. Then how'd you do it? I don't know anyone who's been able to get their child in that school. You're the first I've heard of. Of course, I don't know anything about it, really. Just what they say, you know. They say the wait list is *years* long. You have to get your kid on the list before they're even born!"

Claudia smiled politely. Laurie was always happy to be informative, but most of her information was unreliable.

Claudia thought of Zelma's kind words and realized they must have been sincere. She didn't know about any wait list. But The Hawthorne School was special, and yet Zelma had taken Henry right away and made the path easy. She felt humbled and affirmed. And very grateful.

Henry cut Laurie off with a piercing scream. "I want to *go* now! I want to *go* now!"

Laurie continued to talk, but Claudia couldn't hear her over Henry's tantrum. She held out her hands for the bag of pears, smiled apologetically at Laurie, and rushed her cart out of the store, ashamed once again of Henry's behavior.

* * *

On days off from the clinic, grief rolled in like a black wave and dragged her down to the depths of something far below the undertow of misery. Her mother's absence tore at her soul and left her in a place of emptiness that was primal. There were no words for it, this thing that left her feeling that she could scarcely breathe.

On these days, Henry, of course, had no pity. He might squeeze all the toothpaste out of the tube, creating lines across the floors of every room in the apartment; he might stand on a chair and turn on the knobs of the stove; he might run to Claudia's bedroom and deliberately pee on the carpet. When she dragged herself out of bed, trying to pull up anger from the place in her where anger used to be, he would hop from foot to foot in excitement, watching her face.

Sometimes she felt Henry hated her. Why else would he behave this way?

She wanted to cry but couldn't summon the tears.

Guilt crushed her. His awful behavior was no doubt a reaction to her grief. She was ruining their lives with her negativity. Henry was at last in a school that understood him, where he would be able to flourish, and she was dragging him back down into gloom and failure. *She* was the problem. She was damaging him. All because she couldn't or wouldn't summon the strength to rise up out of this suffocating darkness.

On Sunday morning there was a knock on the door. Claudia was on the floor, sweeping up the oats Henry had dumped there.

Henry, against the rules, ran to open the door.

It was Maggie.

"What's the matter? You don't answer texts?" She walked in, Violet following.

Claudia sat back on her heels and then stood, her shoulders heavy. She wished these visitors gone. "Oh, hi, Maggie. Hi, Violet."

"You look awful."

"Thank you."

"No, I mean it. Like a truck hit you. But hey, you told me, days off are the worst. That's why I'm checking on you."

Maggie looked around Claudia's apartment, so different from her own, and then at Henry, who stood slack-jawed, and then at Claudia.

"Okay. Grief. I get it. My parents died too. I remember. But then one day someone told me, life is for the living. You can't sink into this bereavement. Not for too long, you can't. Come on, now. You have to pull yourself together."

Claudia looked at Maggie and saw the concern on her face, but she had no answer.

"I know, I know. If it was that easy, you would have done it already. Okay. That's why I'm here."

Maggie snapped into control, giving orders.

"Here, give me that broom. You, fill a glass with water and drink it. I bet you're dehydrated. Go!"

Claudia found herself obeying. How long had it been since she had drunk or eaten anything?

"Put your shoes on. We're going outside. You need fresh air, sunshine. Then we're getting food. Move." Maggie put her hand on her hip, and Violet put her hand on her hip too.

Claudia shrugged, looking at the floor. "I don't really feel like—"

"Did I ask what you feel like? I don't recall asking you any-thing. Go!"

"Maggie, I appreciate your concern. But I can't go anywhere. Not today. I just can't. Go home."

Maggie said, "Henry, where are your mom's shoes? Go get them."

Henry stood gaping at this woman who had come into their home, commanding his mother. Then he ran to Claudia's bedroom and came back with her sneakers.

* * *

Claudia felt better the next day, driving Henry to school. Maggie had dragged her out of her isolation into the light of day. She had made her eat and drink and move her body, and it had worked. The grief was still inside of her, of course. But she was back in functioning-mode, and it was due to someone caring enough to throw a rope down to her where she had been stuck in the bottom of a well.

Maggie was a good friend.

At The Hawthorne School, Zelma was all smiles, and Claudia was able to smile back.

"So! Your first volunteer day!" Zelma took Henry's hand, and he craned his neck to look up at her. "I'll just take Henry up to Miss Applegate. Henry, you are doing well with us here. Your mother can be proud of you. And I believe your teacher has some very special things planned for your class today. Claudia, I've made you a cup of tea. Make yourself at home."

Claudia kissed Henry goodbye, and he struggled away from her, eager to get to his classroom.

Zelma's office was quiet and calm. Claudia sat at the dark wood table, sipped the tea, and looked out the window at the expansive lawn, the beautiful grounds. As she heard Zelma's quick steps coming down the hallway, she drained the cup and set it in its saucer, wiping her lipstick from the rim of the cup with the cloth napkin.

"Come with me. We'll be going down to The Pit."

"The *Pit*?" asked Claudia, sure that Zelma must be kidding her.

Zelma laughed, gently teasing. "That's just what we call it—someone's idea of a little joke. It's just a storage room downstairs. Quite colorful and pleasant, as you'll see. You can leave your purse in my office."

The stone staircase leading down to the tunnels was steep, and Claudia put one hand to the cold wall, but Zelma hurried on ahead of her with the balance and grace of a teenager.

If Claudia had thought the school was cold, the underground passageways were glacial. The tunnels were lined with dim electric lamps that resembled candles. Their flickering made her feel a little dizzy and disoriented. Claudia imagined the nuns of the past who had walked through this labyrinth. She envisioned them in their habits, rosaries at their waists, speaking in low tones. On each side there were large, numbered, metal doors. Zelma chatted as they went, indicating one room that housed school supplies; another, garden tools; another, furniture not currently needed.

Zelma took out a key ring as they came to one of these doors, and opened it, saying with theatrical flair, "Open, Sesame!" and stepping in to snap on several lamps that illuminated a large table piled high with glistening silks of brilliant colors and a wooden sewing basket.

Claudia was reminded of the miller's daughter in the fairy tale, who is brought to a room filled with straw and required to spin it into gold if she wants to save her life. This did not look like a fun parent volunteer project to her. There were so many capes! This looked like drudgery. However, she would make the best of it. Henry was upstairs at an extraordinary school, and she would pay his tuition by stitching up rips in costumes. It was a fair deal. She was sure there would be other volunteer jobs that would be more to her liking in the future.

As Zelma had promised, the room itself was charming and contrasted sharply with the dim tunnels. On all four walls were a mural, hand-painted in brilliant colors, depicting children— or were they elves?—wearing caped hoods of various hues, and walking down a path into a cave. Flowers taller than the little people towered over their heads. The brightness of the art made up for the lack of windows.

Zelma left the heavy metal door propped against the tunnel wall when she left. After Zelma's steps had receded, Claudia realized how alone she was.

Left on her own then, Claudia set to work, sifting through the pile of hooded capes that tied at the neck. She assessed the repairs to be done and inspected the tools she had to work with: a box containing an array of colored spools of thread and a new-looking sewing machine in full working order. She pricked her finger on a pin, and she smiled as she remembered another fairy tale, the one about the princess who pricked her finger on a spinning wheel and fell into a deep sleep, a sleep that lasted one hundred years. Why was she recalling fairy tales here? It was something about this place. Henry had called it a "magical castle."

After stitching ripped seams in several costumes, her eyes felt strained. Her stomach growled, and now she wished she *had* rebelled against the rules and brought a candy bar in her purse—until she remembered that she didn't have her purse anyway. Zelma had told her to leave it in her office. She had a brief image of Zelma pulling out the contents of her purse and examining them on the mahogany table, and then smiled at her own paranoia. As if Zelma or anyone else would be interested in her thin wallet, package of tissues, keys, and makeup bag.

Her fingers were stiff with the cold, even though she had dressed herself, like Henry, in layers. Her nose was cold too. She wondered what the temperature could be down here. It was silent. *Silent as the tomb,* she thought. It was even a little creepy. She wondered if anyone else was in the tunnels, perhaps sneaking around on tiptoes, perhaps even watching her from somewhere. She realized her imagination was running away with her. There was no clock. What time could it be? It had to be midmorning by now. She began to wonder, should she call it a day and find her own way back upstairs? Is that what Zelma was expecting her to do? Or was Zelma going to come downstairs to get her at a certain point in the day? She hadn't said.

She stood and stretched her neck from side to side, and heard footsteps coming down through the tunnel. They were heavier than Zelma's.

CHAPTER

10

GIVEN HER SURROUNDINGS and fanciful thoughts, Claudia was prepared to see someone like the stocking-capped Rumpelstiltskin or perhaps even a vampire in a black silk cape appear in the doorway, but instead she saw a blond, blue-eyed man of about thirty. She could not help noticing that he was seriously handsome. "Seriously handsome" was the phrase she and her high school girlfriends had used back in New Jersey, and she smiled as she remembered it. It had been a long time since the phrase had come to her mind; a long time since anyone had made her think of it. Frequent moves, changes in life direction, and then becoming a mother—all of these things had combined to make her lose track of every friend she'd ever had.

The handsome apparition flashed perfect, white teeth at her, pausing only a second as they locked eyes. His were bright; the illumination of the bare bulb in this dim little room made them look like blue glass.

He said, "Zelma sent me to rescue you from the Pit. My daughter Taylor is in your son's class. I'm Zelma's assistant. My name is Niles Holloway."

Of course it is, thought Claudia with amusement. What other name could he possibly have? It struck her as a name that would fit a hero in a legend.

"I'm glad you've come to 'rescue me.' I was wondering how I was going to get myself out of here." She laughed and added,

"I'm Claudia Vera, but I guess you already know my name." She reached up to tuck loose strands of hair behind her ears, and closing the sewing box, she joined Niles in the tunnel. He shut the door with a clang.

"Do you need to lock it?"

"No, it locks automatically when you close it." Claudia felt the cold grip of alarm around her heart. Why had she agreed to sit alone in that subterranean, windowless room, with no one in the world but Zelma knowing where she was, for hours? But then again, what was there to be afraid of? No one had thought of shutting her in. This was the downside of an artistic mind, she thought: her imagination had always been both a blessing and a curse to her.

"Zelma wants me to take you to the kitchen and show you the ropes up there."

Claudia walked along with Niles and stole a glance at his left hand. No wedding ring.

"So your child's a student here too," said Claudia, making conversation.

"Yes. This is a great school for Taylor. It's more than a school for us, really. It's become our way of life—and our family."

He hadn't mentioned a wife.

"What brought you and Henry here? How did you find The Hawthorne School?" he asked, turning his attractive face to hers.

"The teacher at Happy Start mentioned this place. So we came to check it out. I'd only ever seen the sign from the road. You can't see the building from there. Do you know, you can't even find the school online?"

"Yeah, The Hawthorne School doesn't advertise to the outside world. *You* have to seek *us* out."

Claudia saw how closely he identified himself with the school, using the word "us." He felt a part of the school. She wanted to feel that too.

Eager to keep talking about herself and Henry, Claudia went on. "We came out for a tour. From there, I guess things moved pretty fast. I mean, I didn't need to take much time to think. I've never seen such a beautiful school before, and I was impressed right away with the focus on nature and art, you know?"

"Right," agreed Niles. He exuded a fragrance of outdoors. He was about a head taller than she was, and he had a manner that made her feel comfortable. He was so easy to talk to. "Forest schools are common in the Nordic countries, I guess, but we're lucky to have one right here."

"I don't know much about forest schools, to tell you the truth."

"Well, the basic idea, I guess, is that children learn best in nature—not in stuffy classrooms. Outside for hours, they learn science by exploring plants, insects, animals, and weather. They breathe it, live it, it's all hands-on. They hike, run and climb. They get their hands dirty. They get to be kids, discovering all the life forms in the woods."

"That's interesting. It seems so obvious, now that you say it, that this is what kids need." Claudia was eager to keep the conversation going. "The Hawthorne School is everything I could ever want for Henry. I'd never even heard the term 'forest school' before, but Zelma showed me some of the grounds and talked about the children spending two and a half hours outside every day."

"It's very healthy and natural for children—for everyone, really—to be outdoors. At least *I* think so."

"So do I! But what about rainy days or cold days?"

"They bundle up."

"Don't they catch colds?"

Niles shook his head, laughing. "You don't catch a cold from being cold. You catch a cold from being confined in a closed space with people who *have* colds. Look: kids need to know that they can be cold and still survive. It should be normal to get cold—and wet. Our kids are much healthier than indoor kids.

"There are acres of forest on this campus. Woodland full of all kinds of creatures: owls, deer, raccoons, possums—you name it. There's a pond with frogs and salamanders. That forest is our children's classroom. It's fantastic. Right now, your son and my daughter are out in those woods."

Claudia felt a shock of discomfort. No one had asked her if they could take Henry into the woods. Would they keep a careful eye on him?

"The problem with most parents of our generation," Niles went on, "is not trusting that kids can explore and be safe."

She was pleased that he said "our generation." He seemed to assume she was his age. She was sure he was older. Although he was very interesting, and getting more interesting by the minute, she needed to know that Henry was safe in the woods right now.

Niles had warmed to his subject and continued with increasing passion. "Children need to discover wild animal tracks out in the natural world, and follow those tracks, follow their own curiosity and learn for themselves, you know? In the modern, artificial world, children are surveilled all the time, overprotected. They don't get enough chances to take risks. All that helicopter parenting—it stifles them. *That's* why you have kids acting out. That's why you have attention deficit disorder and stuff like that, if you ask me. Kids need to run free. Well, I guess I'm preaching to the choir, talking to you."

"Right, I think you're right," agreed Claudia, her mind working. She did not want to be in the kitchen while Henry was "taking risks" and "running free" near a pond. "As a matter of fact, I'd love to go out there and watch the kids learning for a few minutes. I mean, after being in that underground room all morning, I'm kind of craving the sunshine and fresh air, if you know what I mean."

"Well"—Niles hesitated—"there's a lot to do in the kitchen. I have to show you how to prepare the smoothies, and then we have to chop the vegetables for the salads, and after that, cook and freeze veggies for lunches. But—"

Claudia was already heading toward the first exit she saw, a door at the top of the stairs.

"Sure, why not, just for a few minutes."

11

OUTSIDE, IT WAS blessedly warmer than it had been in the Pit, and the sun was streaming down, diffused through swift-moving clouds and the lacework of leaves. Niles led her around the building, out toward the woods.

There were bands of children everywhere, some climbing and hanging from the wooden bridges and ladders on the playground, some running through a distant field and calling to each other, some with heads bowed over rows of green in a large, fenced vegetable garden. Each group had its accompanying teacher, dressed in flowing clothing and standing a little apart, solemnly observing the children.

As Claudia and Niles walked, he peppered her with questions, and she felt with a thrill of emotion that he was curious about her.

"Is Henry's father volunteering too?"

"No. He's not in the picture."

"Really? Why not?"

Claudia smiled to herself at the tactlessness of the question. "Devin left us when Henry was three weeks old. He said he wasn't 'a family man.' Whatever that means."

"That's too bad. Does he visit Henry?"

"No. He never has. We met in fine arts school. I dropped out when Henry was born, but he kept studying. He was in theater. I guess maybe he's an actor somewhere. Or he could have dropped out later. I really don't know; I lost track of him, but it's okay. We get along fine without him." Claudia wanted to present herself as independent and sure of herself. A woman who didn't need a man. Solid, like Maggie said.

"What kind of guy leaves his own kid? I'll never understand men who do that. He just abandoned you?"

"Yes. Or, no. He did, but actually, I was the one who gave him the ultimatum. He just picked the wrong option."

"Oh" Niles stole a glance at her. "Do you want to say any more about that? Or . . .?"

Yes. Yes, she did want to say some more about that. She wanted to tell this sensitive and interested listener about her life. She took a breath of fresh, clean air.

"We had a fight when Henry was two weeks old. I was exhausted and trying to figure out being the mother of a newborn who never seemed to sleep, and Devin came home, his eyes all wide and weird, tripping. He'd been experimenting with hallucinogenic drugs—all for the best reasons, of course. He was trying to understand the purpose of life, and expand his mind, or *some* BS.

"So I was sitting there with our baby crying in my arms, and Devin was sitting there gripping the arms of his chair, his eyes bugging out at shadows on the wall. I was disgusted. The next day, when he was back to normal, I told him he had to choose once and for all: drugs, or us. He picked us. He promised that was the last time. But six days later, he said goodbye. He said his freedom was too high a price to pay for us."

Niles was silent for a minute. "You were really strong. It might have been easier to look past it, just to keep your child's father with you."

"I don't know if I was strong. I only did what I had to do. He was no help to us, the way he was. He contributed money to the household, but the stress he caused wasn't worth it. I had my mother to fall back on then. I knew she'd step in and help me through once Devin was gone. She never did like him, although she never said so. I guess she saw through him before I did."

"And did she? Did she come through for you?"

"Of course. I did feel strong when I was with her, because she was so strong. She came through for me that time and every time in my life. To be honest, I don't think I'm the same person anymore since she . . . passed away."

"Oh, I'm sorry." Niles's voice was soft now. "I didn't know. You really are alone in the world."

Claudia felt her grief rising, threatening to overwhelm her.

Tactfully changing the subject, he asked, "You're not from the Midwest, are you? Am I detecting an Eastern accent? New York-ish?"

"Very good!" she said, glad for the distraction. "Northern New Jersey, actually."

"How long have you been here?"

"About three months. I saw an ad for a position as a licensed massage therapist in a chiropractic clinic here, and my intuition told me to go for it, to get out of the rut we were in and come out to the Chicago area. Just to try it for a while, you know, and see if it's good for us. I mean, there was nothing to hold us there."

Niles said, "You could have answered an ad in Hawaii or Santa Fe or someplace like that. Why here?"

"There wasn't an ad in any place like that," laughed Claudia. "And why *not* here? I'd never been here before, and that's what I wanted, mainly. Some place I'd never been before."

"So you're open to new ways of life," said Niles with approval.

Was she? First Maggie and now Niles, telling her what they saw when they looked at her. She didn't know that she was any of the things they saw. She had come here for a new start; that was certain. She and her mom had always moved around. She'd never thought of it as being a sign of novelty-seeking. But Niles seemed to think openness was a good thing, so she had no reason to contradict him.

"That's cool," he continued. "I don't know what winters are like in New Jersey, but you'll find out what a Chicago winter is! In the autumn, it's pretty here. But this winter, you'll be buried under the snow."

Claudia shivered at the image these words made in her mind. *Buried under the snow.* She was, in fact, used to snowy winters, and she hated the cold. But she liked it here, for now. When the winter came, she'd dress herself and Henry warmly.

As they entered the woods and followed a trail, the gravel made a crunching sound beneath their feet. Claudia immediately felt her heart grow peaceful, as it always did in a natural space. The air was filled with layered birdsong. The brown and yellow strewn leaves and verdant groundcover hid scampering little feet, signaling the busyness of the seen and unseen creatures around them. To the left and right, there were fallen branches and stumps of trees that had been struck down, probably by lightning. She thought of the levels of decomposition occurring in this biosphere, most of it invisible, mysterious. She loved the brilliant shade of green on the moss-covered trunks, and the way the great forest trees arched and swayed high above them. Niles walked along confidently, seeming to know where their children would be. They were so far out in the country that no traffic sounds could be heard. Claudia thought that in this place, they could be in a world before cars. They could be in another time. They could be on another planet.

The first class they came to was not Miss Applegate's.

"This is Miss Dalessio's section of fives—the five-year-olds," said Niles.

They paused briefly, and Claudia watched as a teacher seated on a log with six five-year olds showed them how to make dream catchers with found feathers.

Claudia whispered to Niles, "Do they disinfect those feathers somehow? I mean, birds carry diseases."

Niles clapped her on the back affectionately. "Do you worry about *everything*?"

Claudia considered. Yes. The answer to that question would be yes. Since she had become a mother, the number of things she worried about was staggering. She said nothing, and they moved on. For about five minutes, they saw no other human being. At last, they came to a section of sixes.

"But where's Henry?"

"Oh, they're deeper in the woods. But look here."

Claudia saw a teacher supervising her six-year-olds as they lit a fire.

"Now," said the teacher, "bend forward toward the sticks to shield the flame from the wind."

A little girl stood, focusing all her attention on the match in her tiny hands, her long wavy hair making a flowing tent over the flame.

High above them, about twenty-five feet up, another little girl stood on the branch of a tree, shaking its branches and laughing. The teacher glanced at her once, and calmly brought her attention back to the child with the match.

Claudia turned to Niles, who only smiled and led her onward. "Children learn by doing. The question is this: Do you want to keep your child safely insulated in Bubble Wrap—or do you want him to be free?"

"Free, of course. It just seems that with all this freedom, there's bound to be an accident."

"Occasionally. That's how we learn."

Claudia thought about this as she glanced at Niles's profile. She didn't know anyone who took this attitude toward raising children. When she'd seen the other parents pick up their children from Happy Start, they were always giving orders and grabbing their hands to prevent them from running out into the parking lot. But Niles seemed confident and casual in his approach to parenting. His hand brushed hers and he turned to smile at her. It was a dazzling smile. She tried to imagine herself as at ease as he was, and she saw herself and Niles together, romantic partners, working at The Hawthorne School and raising Henry and Taylor together. The movie in her head ran of its own volition. She wished it wouldn't.

Claudia told herself she wasn't looking for a new relationship. She knew she didn't understand men, the way they thought, what mattered to them. Her own father and Henry's father had left. Men always left. When she thought of men, she saw fragments, like shards of glass from something fragile, shattered. Were some men different? Dependable? Invested in their families? The way Niles seemed to be? That was always the hope, the hope that led to disappointment.

Her mother, after heartbreaks, used to say, "We don't need them, do we? We're better off as we are, just the two of us."

From what Claudia could see of her transitory friends' lives, she couldn't contradict her mother.

You couldn't make men stay. You couldn't even stay yourself. Life was constant movement, dizzying. Nothing was forever. And no one was forever.

They came to a clearing, and here was the back of Henry in his blue shirt, walking along the trunk of a fallen tree, both arms extended out to the sides for balance. Claudia felt overjoyed to see him. First, because he was okay, and second, because he looked like he was in his element. He was doing just what he wanted to do, with no threat of failure and no corner for time-out. In the first moment, all she saw was Henry. When her heart and eyes had had their fill of him, she looked for Miss Applegate. Was she watching the children?

Several yards away from Henry, at the edge of a small pond, two children were giving each other a mud shampoo. No one was telling them not to do it. Claudia thought of intervening, or of pointing out the mud problem to Miss Applegate, and scanned the scene for her again.

She was standing on the bank of a gully, holding a rope that had been tied to a tree branch, and she was speaking to three children. Claudia heard one of them, a boy, say, "Can I try?"

Miss Applegate gave him the rope, instructed him to wrap his legs around and hold on, and then swung him across the gully where he let go of the rope and tumbled to the ground.

Niles said, "Check out the kids in the mud puddle." He was smiling, relaxed. Apparently the mud shampoo was not considered something that needed to be stopped. Claudia thought of Henry's favorite movie, *The Wizard of Oz*, when Dorothy says, "I guess we're not in Kansas anymore." If she'd wanted conventional reactions to children's natural behavior, she told herself, she could have kept Henry at Happy Start. The Hawthorne School was a whole different culture, and she would have to adapt to it.

As Claudia and Niles watched, she could not refrain from saying, "That kid swinging back and forth across the ditch like that is making me so nervous. There's water in that gully."

"It's not deep. Just a trickle. That's Anthony Jones. He's done this before. But hey, if he does fall, well, then he'll learn to hang on better the next time. Relax," Niles smiled at her. "Have a little trust."

Claudia wasn't sure it was trust she was lacking. She only knew that Henry could hardly walk across a room without tripping or bumping into something or someone. How could a boy his age handle swinging through the air holding onto a rope without getting injured?

Henry caught sight of her and came running to hug her around her legs.

"Hey!" said Claudia, placing her hands on his head, reassured and full of warmth.

"I found a millipede!" Henry shouted joyfully, looking up to her, his blue eyes wide with excitement and wonder. "They live under the tree bark."

Claudia noticed that Miss Applegate was watching her, unsmiling, and Claudia detached Henry from her leg, giving his little hands a squeeze. "You get back to school. Taylor's dad and I are going to work in the kitchen now." Henry did not need to be told twice, and ran, skidding, toward the mud puddle. Claudia determined not to care. Mud could be washed off, after all. That must be the Hawthorne Way.

Niles, meanwhile, was returning the two thumbs-up sign to one of the little girls at Miss Applegate's side, who was patiently awaiting her turn to try the rope.

"That's Taylor?" asked Claudia. "*You're* not worried about the safety issue. I can see that."

Niles looked at her with amusement. "Safety issue? No, I'm not worried. Evelyn—that's Evelyn Applegate, the teacher—she's been teaching here for over twenty years. She knows what she's doing. Maybe you're just a little anxious," he added more sympathetically. "You're new here, and you're still getting used to things."

Claudia hesitated. What if Henry, after playing in the mud, after Claudia had gone and was working in the kitchen, what if Henry ran to Miss Applegate and asked to swing across the ditch too? What if he fell on the jagged rocks and cut his head open out here? Could she trust this teacher, this total stranger, to know what to do? Out here in the woods, where no one would have a cell phone?

She looked at Henry, who was happy and free, the breeze ruffling his hair. She was in a new reality here. This was a place where children didn't sit at tables and get judged on their paperwork. This was something else altogether, and she wanted it for Henry. And Henry, ankle-deep in the mud puddle and squawking like a bird at his new friends, who were squawking back at him, clearly wanted this for himself.

Claudia walked back toward the school with Niles.

12

T HE KITCHEN WAS cold.

"The first order of business," said Niles, "is the daily smoothie!" He began pulling containers of peeled bananas out of the freezer and handing them to Claudia, who put them on the counter and took the covers off. "Every day we make enough for lunch for everyone in the whole school—students, volunteers, and staff."

"What?" Claudia laughed. "Everyone in the building gets a smoothie every day? How many smoothies is that?"

Niles said, "The total number of smoothies? You don't even want to know! Don't worry, *we* only have to make twenty. Other volunteers have been working through the night to make the rest."

"Volunteers working at night? In the kitchen?"

"Yeah! Sounds weird, huh? You'll learn about the night volunteers. But first—check it out!"

As he spoke, Niles put more ingredients on the counter with the bananas: "You'll love our smoothies, the way *we* make them. They contain superfoods, all kinds of nutrients. The bananas have potassium, B6, vitamin C. Then you have the Medjool dates which give you selenium, iron, potassium, calcium, and magnesium. And cacao powder! The food of the gods, they call it!" Claudia had never seen anyone get so excited about smoothies before. "The cacao also has calcium, iron, zinc, copper, vitamins E, B1, B2, B3,

B5, B9, fiber, protein, antioxidants—oh, and it lowers blood pressure. It does all kinds of good things for you."

"I had no idea," said Claudia. "I would have thought the cacao powder was just to make it taste like chocolate, so the children would like it."

"Yep! It does that, too! And then we have to add filtered water, little green, and a bit of flax oil. The flax oil gives you all your omegas."

"Little green?" asked Claudia, picking up the blue Mason jar and looking at the printed label. "I've never heard of flax oil or little green before."

"You can buy flax oil at any health food store. But little green is our own thing at The Hawthorne School. One day, I'll show you how to dry it and make it into a powder and store it in the jars. It comes from plants we teach the children to grow in the vegetable garden. We put it in juice too. And it can also be a tea. Little green, it's like dates: another superfood, full of good things like antioxidants. Would you mind plugging in the blender?"

After the smoothie mixture was made, Niles and Claudia took a break and each drank a glass of it. Its hue was the most beautiful shade of green she had ever seen. Vivid, deep, and alive. Claudia, who had been hungry since her sewing session in the Pit, was grateful to find that the smoothie was not only refreshing, but also filling.

"So, what kind of lunches do the kids get?" Claudia had dismal memories of cafeteria food from her own school days.

"Oh! Just the best food in town, that's all! Indian dal, tabbouleh, hearty vegetable stews, lots of sweet potatoes—you'll see. Most of the vegetables we grow here, with lots of our own herbs. And it's not just for the kids. All the grown-ups get the advantage of our organic gardens and special recipes too."

They set to work chopping vegetables for salads. As they worked, Niles showed himself to be fascinated with each little detail of her life that she revealed to him. It was a wonderful feeling, after being alone for so long, to have this very attractive man treating her as if she were the most intriguing woman he had ever met. He wanted to know all about her childhood.

What was it like to be an only child? Did she have a lot of friends growing up?

In fact, she had always wanted brothers and sisters, had always envied the big families she knew. At home, it had just been Claudia and her mom. She did remember, at one point, hanging out with a family that was overflowing with children and laughter and games. Their mom was home with them instead of working all the time like Claudia's mom had to do. She used to pretend she belonged to that family, which made her feel guilty.

"And are you still connected to them? Did you get to belong to them, like you wanted?" It was touching that he cared about her life and about the lonely little girl she had once been.

"No. No to both questions. We moved away from that town, and I never saw them again. You see, we moved all the time. So I never got to have a feeling of belonging to any place or group of friends or church—or anything. I always *wanted* to belong, but it's been constant change and moving for me."

"So you don't have old childhood friends who are still in your life?"

"No, unfortunately. I never was good at keeping friends. I always thought it was all my own fault, but now when I think about it, I realize that any kid who moved as much as I did wouldn't be able to keep friends. I was always starting over. I didn't get to have that experience of working things through over years with a few constant friends. And always being new, I started to get shy by the time I was in junior high. It got harder to make new friends. Oh gosh, what a bore I am, going on and on about myself. I'm sorry. Let's talk about you now."

"Oh no. Please, don't be sorry. I'd much rather hear about you. I can see you're a person who really thinks about things. I like that. So then, if you don't mind my asking, what about as an adult? Do you have friends now?"

"Well, I'm neighbors with one of the moms from this school. Do you know Maggie Timmerberg?"

"Of course. Maggie. She's a good friend to have."

"It probably sounds sad, but I don't really have any friends I keep up with from the past. I do strike up superficial relationships wherever I go, but those aren't real friendships, are they? It's still like, why invest in people when I know I'm going to be moving on soon? Even after I grew up, I found that life kept moving me around. I started art school but dropped out. I had a relationship with Henry's father, but that ended. I went to massage school, but that was a short course—one year—and then I started a job. I left that job to come here. It just seems natural for me to go somewhere new, and as soon as I'm getting used to it, something happens, or else I feel like I have to go."

"Sounds like kind of a herky-jerky way to live, if you don't mind my saying so. It sounds like you've been wanting something stable. Am I right?"

"Well, yes. Especially now that I have Henry. He may wind up being an only child like me. But I hope that he can have lifelong friends and a sense of community someplace, like I never had."

"Well, he *can* have that if you stop jumping around like a jackrabbit," laughed Niles.

Claudia really liked him.

"Have you ever heard the expression 'chosen families'? A lot of people are closer to a group of people they've found than they are to the families they were born into. Whether your family is far away, or they've passed away, or you just don't get along with them or whatever, you can, if you're lucky and open, find a new family of your own choosing, a community that becomes a family. Then you spend all your time with them. You know, holidays, spare time, whatever. And it feels right. You have a good feeling when you're with your chosen family. That's what The Hawthorne School has become for Taylor and me."

Taylor and me. No mention of a wife, observed Claudia. He'd opened the door; she could ask.

"What about Taylor's mother?"

Niles looked away and his smile faded. "She disappeared on us. I guess we're like you and Henry that way. Abandoned. But we have a whole extended family in this school. We're okay. We're better than okay: we're great."

"I'm sorry—about your wife, I mean. Has it been a long time?"

"Actually, it's still kind of raw. It's only been six months. See, we started Taylor here when she was three. In the beginning, we both loved it. Then Fiona started talking about moving away and starting over. I didn't want to—Taylor was doing so well here. We argued about it. I told her no way, that wouldn't be fair to Taylor, and that I would do whatever I could to keep her here. I guess those sound like strong words. But I did feel strongly—and so did she. I never expected she would take off on us, though. I thought we'd keep arguing until I could get her to see it my way. But one fine day last April, she left us. Just like that. She didn't bother to leave a note or anything. She just drove away, tires peeling. Taylor watched her go. She was devastated." Niles struggled to compose himself. "So I guess Fiona's 'starting over' like she said, but without us."

"She left her *child*?" Claudia couldn't imagine how a mother could do that. "I'm so sorry." She was a little sorry, but if she were honest with herself, she had to admit she was also pleased that this Fiona was gone and that Niles was sharing this painful part of his life with her.

"Ugh," said Niles, wiping his eyes with the back of his sleeve. There were no tears, and Claudia guessed that his eyes were stinging with the effort of holding them in. His face was contorted with suffering. "Can we talk about something else? Tell me more about you and Henry."

"Sure!" Claudia wanted to give him a chance to pull himself together. He was grieving for Fiona, just as she was grieving for her mother. She understood what he must be feeling.

It was easy to talk to Niles about Henry, and it was a relief. "You know, Henry's been kind of difficult for me; for everyone, I guess. Or maybe it's not fair to say he's difficult. Sometimes I think that he's actually perfectly fine, and the only problem is that I don't know what I'm doing. I might be messing him up somehow. But for whatever reason, he's never behaved well for me—or for any teacher he's ever had."

Niles was paying careful attention, as if he really wanted to understand.

"I mean. I don't want to paint him as a little monster or anything like that. He's a good boy—loving and funny and sweet. He makes jokes; when he's in a good mood, he's affectionate. I think he's super-smart, but then of course, I would, wouldn't I?"

"So then, what's the problem?"

"In one word, 'cooperation.' He just doesn't cooperate with anyone. Tell him to do something, and you can be sure he'll do the opposite. It may not sound like much, but it's wearing and exhausting, and I think it makes his teachers just not like him. I hope they can handle him here. Teachers usually call me in after a few days of school and complain about his misbehavior. He lets the class pet free in the classroom. He hides in the bathroom and colors on the walls in there. He somehow finds the teacher's cell phone and throws it in the garbage. I mean, he can do all of that in the span of ten minutes. He never rests. And he just has to be in control—of himself and of everyone. To tell you the truth, his father is like that. Contrary. Rebellious. Always questioning authority. Arguing just for fun. Henry seems to enjoy frustrating adults. That worries me."

Niles smiled, his eyes looking into Claudia's. "Excuse me, but do you know *anything* about child development? I don't mean to be rude, but someone has to tell you: four-year-olds are just trying to learn how the world works and test out their power. Kids in the typical overprotective environment in most schools and homes today—they don't get to feel enough self-mastery. Kids need that, to grow in a healthy way." Niles paused and added gently, "Claudia, it sounds to me like you're expecting too much from him."

Claudia wanted to feel comforted. "So his teachers have been wrong? Here and in New Jersey too—they always have had so much trouble handling him."

"Maybe so, but that's their own fault. And, yeah, maybe it *is* your fault too, a little bit. I mean, you're doing your best, but it sounds like you don't understand him in some ways. See, I think his so-called 'behavior issues' have to do with his energy level and his need for plenty of exercise and playtime. Those typical, corporate, plastic warehouses for children are like prisons. Naturally, kids go bonkers in those environments. Well, not all kids. The natural paper pushers, the assembly-line fodder—those kids will adapt and conform. But kids with a lot of life in them—no! It's like caging a tiger. It's just not humane, you know? Now, Taylor? She's *thriving* here.

"And hey! I'll tell you what. Another thing that improves kids' behavior, and I know it's been good for Taylor, is the proper nutrition. I mean—" Niles stopped short, as if catching himself just in time before making a rude remark.

"No, it's okay. Go ahead. What about nutrition?"

"Well, I'm not trying to imply that you don't feed your kid right. Don't take offense or anything, okay? But the standard American diet is, you know." Niles gestured with two thumbs down.

"Oh, I *know*. Well, I *do* try."

"Of course you do. But it's hard all on your own, I know it's been hard for me since Fiona left. In our society, single parents may be common these days, but I really think it takes a minimum of two people to raise a child. Or like the saying, 'it takes a village.' I guess that's what we have at The Hawthorne School: a village. Don't think I'm raising Taylor all on my own. Hawthorne has taught me about child development and proper nutrition for children—and adults. Here, everybody is into excellent nutrition, so it's easy to stick with it. No processed foods. You have to think: we're not just feeding our bodies. We're feeding our *brains*. You'll see. The Hawthorne Way will get Henry regulated. Taylor's blooming like a little flower here."

Claudia was feeling calmer now, settled. She wasn't even offended that Niles had agreed she might be making mistakes with Henry. It was actually a relief to have someone helping her think things through. She listened to Niles talk about his own daughter and stopped worrying about Henry. He was in good hands. She had found the right place for him.

"You'll have support here, Claudia. And friends for you and for Henry, too."

She liked that he used her name. She already thought of him as a friend.

"You've made a good decision, enrolling Henry at The Hawthorne School." He put an anchoring hand on her bicep in a sort of partial embrace. "Welcome to the family."

13

"WE HAD A sermonomy!" shouted Henry as Claudia came into his classroom.

The only children waiting for pickup were Henry, Taylor, and Anthony Jones, the boy Claudia had seen swinging across the ditch, holding onto a rope, in the woods. The others had already left. Claudia had wanted to get to the classroom right at three thirty, but Niles had insisted that they had to finish packaging the cooked broccoli and carrots for freezing for future lunches. At three forty-five, Zelma was there with Miss Applegate. Claudia expected a lecture such as she would have gotten at Happy Start about the importance of picking up children on time, but both educators were unbothered.

Zelma only said brightly, "You've gotten through your first volunteer day at The Hawthorne School. How does it feel?"

Claudia said, "It feels great, thanks. Niles has been filling me in on how things are done here. I love it!" She wanted Zelma to know how much she appreciated this opportunity for Henry.

Henry's face and hands were clean, but his clothes were caked in mud.

Miss Applegate, speaking for the first time to Claudia, said, "Tomorrow, if you could bring a spare set of clothes that we can keep here, that would be helpful."

Zelma added, "And his birth certificate, remember."

Henry repeated, "A sermonomy. In the woods, we had it."

"You had a *what*? I don't understand what you're saying, honey. A sermon—"

"A ceremony," corrected Miss Applegate. "Just a little ceremony, bringing Henry into the classroom community."

"Oh!" said Claudia. "I didn't know about it. I would have been there. I'm sorry."

"No worries," said Miss Applegate. "It's not for the parents. It's only for the children. To make them feel a part of the school, you know."

"We wore capes. Mine was gold!" said Henry.

"Capes? Like the ones I was mending?" asked Claudia, looking at Zelma. And then addressing Miss Applegate, Claudia asked, "Were there enough capes?"

"Oh yes, plenty."

Zelma said, "Every classroom has lots of them, in every color. The ones you were working on in the Pit are old ones. We'll probably never use any of those again."

Claudia felt something, like a note off-key, and she asked, "Then why—"

But Zelma had already said goodbye and was leaving the room with Anthony, Niles and Taylor following.

"Goodbye, Claudia. See you—when?" asked Niles.

"My next day here is Wednesday. My days off are Mondays and Wednesdays, and I can be here all day for both of them—if you have enough for me to do."

Zelma, at the door, said, "Oh, there's enough for you to do. More than enough!" With that, they filed out.

Claudia realized that she and Zelma had never discussed specifically the conversion rate between volunteer hours to tuition cost. She had never asked what the actual tuition was, but it had to be astronomical. Of course, she would be expected to give a lot of hours in exchange for what was basically a free ride.

She looked around for Henry's backpack or any papers he was bringing home, and then remembered that her instructions were not to have her child bring a backpack. There were no papers to gather.

Henry looked tired.

"Well," said Claudia, "off we go, Henry. Thank you, Miss Applegate."

"Thank you, Miss Applegate," echoed Henry. "I want to do a sermonomy again tomorrow."

"We'll do other things tomorrow," said the teacher. Firm and factual, like Zelma.

"Miss Applegate?" Claudia began tentatively.

"You can call me Evelyn."

"Thanks. Evelyn, I'm just wondering. About those capes in the Pit. I spent most of the morning mending as many of them as I could. But now I have the impression that they're not needed and will never be used. I'd ask Zelma, but since she just left, well . . ." Claudia trailed off, putting her hands up in an "I-don't-know" gesture. "Like, what was that all about? I mean, don't get me wrong—I'm not complaining. Please don't tell her I said anything. I'm glad to help in any way I can. It's just—"

"Do you have a minute to stay and talk a little? I'll make us some tea." Evelyn's movements were quick and graceful.

Claudia had been asked to stay and talk after school ever since she had started Henry in preschools, when he turned three. Always before, the talks had been about Henry causing problems. But today, she could see, would be different. Henry hadn't caused any problems yet. She wanted to talk to this teacher, develop some rapport with her, before things went south. And she wanted an answer to her question.

While the water was heating, Evelyn gave Henry a glass of green juice, which he drank thirstily.

"The task that doesn't need to be done. When you start here, that's how it is," said Evelyn, as if that explained everything.

Claudia nodded her head yes and then said, "Actually, no, I don't understand. That's how *what* is?"

"Well. Sometimes Zelma will ask you to do things that might not make sense to you. She is the most magnanimous person you will ever meet. She goes to great lengths for the school. She wants to be sure that the people she's being magnanimous to are just as invested as she is. So she'll ask you to do a little something that may seem unnecessary, and then she'll observe your reaction. If you're enthusiastic about helping the school, she knows she's put her trust in the right person. But if you complain or question her, well, then . . ."

She brought the cups to the low table, inviting Claudia to sit down with her.

Evelyn picked up where she'd left off. "Let me give you some advice: don't ask Zelma too many questions." Evelyn poured the tea. Claudia inhaled the pleasant aroma in the steam. "If you do have questions, come to me. Zelma's probably going out of her way for you. She does for every student she takes. If she accepts a family, it's because she believes they already get it, and that they belong here. She only takes the families that are willing to work with us. If you question a lot, she could think she made a mistake. Which she hasn't, of course, in your case. Just the fact that you asked me that question without even knowing how I would react—that shows that you're trusting and open. And that's key."

"Trusting and open?" Claudia glanced at Henry, who was playing quietly on the rug with a prism, tilting the rainbow this way and that. "I feel like I keep hearing how trusting and open I am." Claudia felt a faint sense of discomfort, which she willed away.

"Because those are the qualities that help you to appreciate what we have here, and to adapt to it. We're a different kind of school, Claudia. Parents who are demanding or forceful or closed-minded—you know, the kind of people who march in with strong opinions and think they're going to get on committees and run the school—people like that don't fit in here. We already know what we're about; we have a strong foundation built by Julia Hawthorne."

Claudia looked into Evelyn's hooded, dark eyes.

"I wouldn't think of trying to change The Hawthorne School. I'm grateful that we've found it, just as it is."

Claudia and Evelyn sipped their tea. It tasted like some herb that Claudia could not quite identify. Hearty, not sweet, but surprisingly satisfying. Claudia had lots of herbal teas at home. Some were for detoxing, others for sleep or de-stressing, and still others for building the immune system. She liked this one and made a mental note to ask where she could purchase some.

"Do you like the tea?" asked Evelyn, seeming to read Claudia's thoughts. "It's little green. Our own blend."

"Ah, yes. Niles told me about it."

Henry lay stomach-down on the blue-swirl rug and pretended he was swimming. The women, meditative, watched Henry. He was unselfconscious, not showing off, and not shy either, but focused on crossing his fantasy ocean.

"Zelma told me that Henry's only grandmother passed away recently?"

In answer to Claudia's questioning look, Evelyn added, "She shares with me any information that could be helpful to our work in the classroom."

"Yes, unfortunately, it's just Henry and me here."

"Ah. Do you miss your mother, then?"

"It's still hard for me to talk about." She didn't want to lose her composure in front of Henry's teacher.

"I completely understand that." Evelyn gazed out the window as the wind kicked up, rocking the tree branches. "Come on by after school as often as you like. We can sit and talk like this."

Sitting here, in this quiet room with this kind teacher who was taking time to explain things to her, she felt a growing sense of well-being and a sense that Evelyn Applegate was going to be her friend. Or if not her friend, then at least her collaborator in doing her best for Henry.

"I specifically asked Zelma to put Henry in my class, you know."

"You did? When?"

"As soon as I saw you, while you were taking the tour, I knew that he is just the kind of student I do best with."

Claudia wondered how Evelyn could have made such a judgment so quickly, glancing up as briefly as she did while spooning the corn into the children's bowls. She also thought that if Evelyn knew how difficult Henry could be, she wouldn't have asked for him. She thought she should prepare her, at least a little.

"Actually, Henry is pretty strong-minded."

"I know. I can tell. I like that in a child. He's strong-minded, as you say, and he's also open and ready to learn—when the right methods are used. I feel a bond with him already."

Claudia, rising out of her cloud of well-being, felt the word was out of place. "A *bond*, did you say?"

"Yes. You know, the bond between a student and teacher makes all the difference. See, that's what was missing in his other school. Zelma told me about the issues he's had in the mainstream school."

Evelyn pronounced "mainstream" with a hint of disdain.

"Zelma thought since I was going to have him in my class-room, I should know what his previous school experience had been. Schools with time-out corners and all that judgment and failure and stress." Now she spoke in a voice that seemed to be quoting someone unlikable: "They have to learn to sit still and trace dotted lines. They must learn to hold a pencil and write their letters so they won't fall behind in kindergar-ten. Then, when they get to second grade, they start taking standardized tests. Teachers must teach to the tests. Schools take away art and recess so the children can practice for the ridiculous tests." Evelyn spoke with emotion now, a passion that reminded Claudia of Niles's. "They have *completely* lost any little understanding they ever had of the world of the child. Julia Hawthorne wrote a book—have you read it? *The World of the Child*."

"No, I haven't."

Evelyn got up and went to her desk, and returned with a white book. "Here, take this one. We have lots of copies. Keep it. Read a little each night. This book is our bible, our inspira-tion. Everything we do is based on this book, when you come right down to it."

14

AT HOME, CLAUDIA tried to get as much as she could out of Henry about his school day.

Did Miss Applegate let him swing on the rope in the woods? What happened in the ceremony? Was his teacher nice? Were his clothes warm enough? Where did he get the braided red bracelet that was tied around his little wrist?

His long-sleeved shirt had been covering it until bath time.

All he would say was that all the kids in his class had the red bracelet, that the teacher wore lots of them, that he saw a mama raccoon walking with her babies, and that he liked this school. His eyes grew heavy as he ate his dinner, and for the first time ever, he went to bed without an argument.

Claudia texted Maggie: *Henry's teacher gave me a book by Julia Hawthorne. Have you read it?*

A text came back immediately from Maggie: *Oh, cool. I have that book. Honestly, no. I'm not a big reader. I guess I should read it. It's probably important. Why don't you read it and tell me what's in there lol.*

* * *

Instead of reading the white book, Claudia picked up her phone and did a little research, into Scandinavian forest schools.

TheForestSchoolEducationFoundation.org

Scandinavian forest schools, so-called because they were first developed in Sweden and Denmark, are outdoor educational spaces that emphasize hands-on learning and independence. Forest schools, also called nature schools, capitalize on children's instinctive love of nature. Students of forest schools are encouraged to explore, using all their senses, and they develop a strong sense of self-mastery and superior motor development. The children are permitted to take risks under supervision, and they learn to regulate their own emotions.

Since their inception in the late 1950s, forest schools have gained in popularity as an educational alternative in Germany, the United Kingdom, Canada, and the United States.

Claudia turned from the internet article and closed her eyes. Against her lids, she saw the beautiful campus, Zelma's twinkling eyes, and Henry's rosy cheeks as he ran to her in the woods to hug her. She was pleased. She'd finally made a parenting decision she could be proud of.

CHAPTER

15

HENRY AND CLAUDIA were both irritable in the morning. Claudia tried hard to conceal her bad mood, knowing that it would only serve as fuel on the fire of Henry's orneriness. He intentionally dropped spoonsful of oatmeal on the floor and when Claudia gave him a cloth to clean it up, he threw a roaring temper tantrum that she was sure would wake the neighbors in the next apartment. She was afraid he would have a wretched day at school—and after such a good start too. Today, unfortunately, Evelyn, Zelma, and perhaps the whole school would see the real Henry Vera, and it wouldn't be a pretty sight.

But strangely, as they rode toward the school, and entered through its wrought-iron gates, their moods lifted. Henry stopped whining. Claudia felt a blissful sense of relief. Was it because she was not going to have to deal with Henry today? But he was now talking happily, naming the children in his class: Anthony, Taylor, Mason, Bibi, James, and Valeria.

"They're my friends," said Henry. "And Bibi wants to be my girlfriend and so does Valeria. I'm going to marry Valeria probably."

Claudia smiled at his plans. "And not Taylor?"

"Taylor might marry James."

"You really are busy at school," laughed Claudia.

"And James was crying for his mother, and Miss Applegate gave him a hug."

"Oh, that was nice. I guess kids miss their moms sometimes at school."

"Yeah, especially James. His mom is dead."

Claudia wondered if this were true or just another Henry story. He always had plenty of stories ready about children at school. According to Henry, at Happy Start there was a boy who had to sleep in the bathtub at home with eleven brothers.

Now he fumbled to unlatch his seatbelt.

She took Henry to Zelma's office and gave her Henry's birth certificate and a bag with a change of clothes, in case he should get muddy and need to change during the school day. She was thankful that Henry was bright and attentive with Zelma.

"Hello, Mrs. Huxley," he said. Claudia noticed that he continued to be in awe of the director. He usually ignored adults, as if he didn't want to give them any opening to try to get the upper hand with him. When had he learned to address grown-ups so politely? It must have been in him all along; he just needed to be in the right environment to shine. Because he was shining. He actually glowed. Zelma saw it too. She looked pleased.

"Henry, you look like a real Hawthorne boy!"

Henry puffed out his chest.

Zelma held out her hand to take him to his classroom.

Claudia offered, "I can take him. You must be busy. I have a little time before I start work."

"Thank you, Claudia, but no. Enjoy your day, and we will see you at three thirty. If you need to be late for pickup, that's never any problem. When you come in tomorrow, though, we will work you hard!" She smiled gently, as if to refute the last statement and as if to show she was only exaggerating as a way of friendly teasing.

Driving away, Claudia wondered if she had the arrival time wrong. She hadn't seen other parents at drop-off time. She must be bringing Henry to school late. But wouldn't Zelma have mentioned it?

In the office, in the lull before the first clients arrived, Claudia told the front desk receptionist, Stephanie, and Dr. W about Henry's new school. She was full of enthusiasm and wanted to share it with someone. As she tried to describe The

Hawthorne School, she found herself at a loss to communicate what a state-of-the-art environment it was. She wanted affirmation from them that she had found something incredible for her son.

"It's so health conscious there. All the snacks and lunches are plant based and gluten-free."

Stephanie looked at her with interest.

Dr. W said, "There's no scientific data to support a gluten-free diet for everyone. Only people suffering from gluten intolerance need to be concerned with that."

Claudia was annoyed. "The gluten-free part is not important. That's just a small detail. What's more important is they provide all the food, and it's all organic and locally sourced. Most of it, they grow right on the campus. The children grow it."

Dr. W nodded, half listening. He didn't have young children and was quickly losing interest. Claudia could sense he wanted to go on about his day. But she needed to talk to someone about what she had found. She had felt like a failure as a mother for so long, and she had come in so many mornings with Henry's screams in her ears and no enthusiasm to match their "good mornings." She needed them to acknowledge that she had gotten Henry into a cutting-edge school.

Ignoring Dr. W's cue that he was ready to move on, she described the cold classrooms, imparting Zelma's knowledge: "A cold environment is best for promoting brain growth and stimulating the immune system."

Dr. W made a cynical face. "I've never heard of *that*," he said. She hadn't expected him, a practitioner of acupuncture and chiropractic medicine, to be so closed-minded.

"No, really," protested Claudia, "I can see that it's good for the children. They're outside all morning. Then they come into a cold—well, not cold, *cool*—classroom, and they're quiet. Then they have the teaching. And then they are silent for a little while before they go on to the next activity, so that the students absorb the teaching."

Dr. W and Stephanie raised their eyebrows and exchanged glances, and all of a sudden Claudia hated them.

"The *teaching*?" asked Stephanie, not unkindly. "Is this, like, a religious school or something?"

"No! It's a *nature* school. Like in Scandinavia. It's very progressive. It's based on children's need to be in nature." She felt desperate to make them understand. They hadn't seen it. This school was, in fact, a well-kept secret, and every child should be in a school like this. Why was she so bad at explaining it?

"Oh, *nature*, yes. Nature is good for children—for everyone, in fact. I highly recommend that all my patients make some time to get out in nature. We all seem to be suffering from nature deficiency these days. Very good, Claudia. Well done."

Dr. W shifted his attention from Claudia to his schedule and had a few words with Stephanie about the upcoming day. Stephanie filled him in on an insurance issue she was working on. Claudia stood there, frustrated, before turning away.

Was she irritated with Dr. W, or was the irritation arising from her own thoughts about The Hawthorne School, thoughts that did not match the conviction she wanted, *needed* to have. If she had a doubt now about the school, she was aware that it had not just begun in her conversation with Dr. W.

Doubts. She wouldn't let them in: the unsettling thoughts, the confusion that would have her packing up, making impulsive changes.

Niles had told her she could have stability for Henry at The Hawthorne School.

It was grief, she knew, that made everything tilt sideways, that made her want to run. It's what she and her mom had always done. So what if Dr. W did not share her enthusiasm for nature schools? People were allowed to have different opinions, and The Hawthorne School clearly was not for everyone. And if Dr. W had a wrong impression, it was only based on ignorance anyway.

She felt better. She was on solid ground, with a path forward. In a few short days, she had progressed from exhausted uncertainty to hope.

In the dark massage room, with Zen-like music playing and the air diffuser dispensing the fragrance of eucalyptus to promote relaxation, Claudia worked out the knots in other people's bodies. Some wanted silence, but others, she knew, always wanted to chat. She tried asking them if they'd ever heard of The Hawthorne School, but they brought the conversation back to their bodies. Self-concerned, all enjoying some "me time," they asked her, "Is my neck the stiffest you've ever worked on?" "Are my back muscles tighter than last time?" "Am I your worst case?"

She tried to give them the answers that would soothe them. Perversely, most of them wanted to hear that they were in awful shape, worse shape than anyone she had ever seen, and that the stress in their lives must be just terrible. She cared for each of her clients and wanted them to get better, but they seldom exercised or did anything to help themselves between visits. So many of them were in denial about their worsening condition and refused to see their own responsibility in it. And when they saw her, they wanted her emotional attention as much as her physical attention.

It was demanding work, but Claudia had always loved massage. It was a big part of who she was in the world. She was proud of the specialized knowledge she had continued to gain as she had gone on to study facets of the art in continuing education courses: shiatsu, Thai, and hot stone massage. She was always excited to learn more techniques and improve her skills. It felt good to relieve people's pain. Compared to taking care of Henry, massage felt easy and clear. She always knew what to do to loosen a trigger point. With Henry, she was never quite sure how to deal with him, because nothing she tried succeeded for very long. A technique that seemed effective one day might fail the next. Massage wasn't like that. Her work had been her respite, the sector of her life where she could feel a sense of achievement.

During her half-hour lunch break, Dr. W passed her by with a cursory, "How's it going, Claudia?" as he threw back the last of his kombucha and headed into the examining room to treat a patient. Stephanie was watching a movie on her laptop but glanced up as Claudia approached to take a look at her afternoon's schedule.

"I know, right?" said Stephanie. "It's packed. People really like you, Claudia."

"Oh, thank you. That's nice to hear."

"No, really. People come out of their massage saying they feel so much better, and they book with you again. You're getting to be the favorite massage therapist around here." She added teasingly, "Watch that the other therapists don't get jealous!"

Since Claudia worked different hours from the other therapists and never saw them, she was not worried about their jealousy. She wished that their schedules did overlap. It could be lonely work.

In spite of Stephanie's affirming words that she'd been longing to hear, Claudia still felt "off" and hoped that no one else could see it or sense it. She supposed she missed Henry. She now felt a longing to leave work and go to The Hawthorne School, to be with him. She didn't usually miss him when he was at school; he was the center of her life, but she'd always enjoyed their time apart, to recharge from the exhausting work of raising him.

This was a first, and she could not explain it to herself: the wish to not be at work and instead be with her son at school.

16

THAT EVENING, HENRY was by turns quiet and raging. He'd
been sleepy in the car, too sleepy to tell her about his day.
That was to be expected: he didn't usually get to spend so much
time outside. Even on weekends, she never kept him outside
playing at the park for two and a half hours, and they'd never
had a backyard. The combination of getting used to new classmates and a new teacher, and all that exercise and fresh air,
would make him tired. But then, since he was tired, he should
want to sleep. Instead, he threw himself on the floor, refusing
to brush his teeth, take his bath, put on his pajamas, listen to a
story, or even listen to anything Claudia tried to tell him or ask
him. He'd had tantrums before—lots of them—but this one
was a doozy. It was the longest one he'd had yet. He'd pushed
her away when she'd tried to comfort him and returned to his
world of rage. It went on until he roared himself to sleep.

Claudia picked him up off the floor and carried him to
his bed, feeling depressed. Of course, any mother would feel
depressed, with a child who was so unhappy. She knew she
shouldn't take it personally, but it was hard that he would not
accept her hugs or even pay any attention to her words when he
got like this. She wondered with dread if he'd had a tantrum at
school. How long would they keep him if he acted this way for
them? Henry was attending basically for free as it was, and she
wished he could understand that and behave accordingly.

She collapsed into bed. She knew she should roll out her yoga mat and practice in the living room for forty-five minutes to take time to breathe and to release her own tight muscles. She should stretch and reset herself before sleep. That's what she would do if she were taking care of herself.

As she lay in her own bed, she felt icily alone. Outside her window, the full moon, yellow and mottled, rode high in the sky, eerie and lovely. She wished there were someone loving beside her and that she could say to him, "Look! Isn't that beautiful? Is that what they call the Harvest Moon?"

But she was alone.

She gazed at the night sky until her eyes fell shut.

17

WEDNESDAY MORNING, CLAUDIA and Henry were both eager to drive back in through the tall gates of The Hawthorne School. For her, this would be another volunteer day. Henry, to Claudia's relief, had cooperated in getting ready, even opening his mouth wide to have his teeth brushed and putting on his own shoes. He usually liked to pretend he didn't know how to put on his shoes and tried to make Claudia do it for him, which she often would do so they wouldn't be late. But today, he was the one in a hurry. Claudia hoped her patience and gentleness through the rough evening before had something to do with his improved mood this morning. The books on parenting that she was always reading had instructed her to remain calm and supportive through tantrums, and although it had never helped before, it looked like it was helping now. Maybe she was doing something right with him.

From the beginning, she'd hoped to carpool with Maggie, but this was impossible. The Hawthorne School staggered the arrival and departure times of the various grade levels, so Claudia and Maggie would not have the convenience of sharing the commute.

Again, there was no drop-off line, no hub of parents standing outside or heading for the door. Claudia would have loved to chat with another parent—to feel a sense of comradery with an enlightened adult who understood The Hawthorne School, unlike her coworkers. Claudia and Henry walked hand in hand from the brick-paved parking lot, around the building marked "Unity Hall," to the entrance of the Main Hall, breathing in the sparkle and bright energy of the autumn day. The grayness of the school against the soft blue of the sky and the scent of fall in the air stirred her emotions. She felt excited. The Hawthorne School looked like an Ivy League college, a place that was for specially chosen people. Claudia, considering herself to be ordinary, was amazed and delighted that she had somehow managed to get Henry into this school.

Zelma again met them and, before shepherding Henry to his classroom, said, "No need to wait for me. I'd like you to help Niles in the kitchen again today if you don't mind."

Claudia tried not to reveal her excitement and just stopped herself from saying, "You don't have to ask me twice."

"Check back in with me in the afternoon, say, at two o'clock?"

Niles seemed as glad to be working together again as she was. Now a little familiar with the kitchen tasks, she fell into a rhythm, and the morning passed quickly. They shared stories and laughed. They delivered the trolleys and then ate delicious Thai quinoa bowls for lunch. She began to feel that her relationship with Niles was heading in a good direction.

As Claudia approached Zelma's office at two o'clock, she heard a familiar voice. She stopped in the corridor to listen.

It was a voice from the past, a voice that didn't belong here, didn't belong anywhere near Claudia's new life, and it was coming from the director's office. There had been a time when she had longed to hear this voice again, but she had killed that longing. Any love she had ever had for Henry's father was dead.

What was he doing here?

"Devin."

His cobalt eyes looked up at her as she came in. She couldn't stop her heart from expanding and warming at the sight of him. She had once loved Devin Richards so much. His dark hair was short now, cut close to his scalp. He was wearing old jeans and a red flannel. He stood, and then it was as if they both realized at once that they didn't know if they should hug or not. He gave her a kiss on the cheek.

Zelma looked displeased. "Claudia, I'm glad you're here. It seems that Henry's . . . father? . . . has stopped in to see us." She added primly, "He is taking an interest in our school."

Devin must have said something to irritate her. That was Devin all over. In fine arts school, any day without controversy was a lost day for him. After the initial rush of feeling, Claudia reminded herself that she didn't have any obligation to be polite to him. He had walked out on her and Henry when they needed him most, fleeing the responsibility of fatherhood. He had had no pity.

"What are you doing here?" Claudia asked him. "And how did you find us?" She wanted Zelma to know she had told the truth when she'd said that she was a single mother.

"The internet is an amazing thing."

He was lying. Claudia had no presence on the internet, as far as she knew. She didn't do social media. She was sure her new address couldn't have already shown up on any search engine. So Devin was back, and the first words out of his mouth were a lie. It figured.

His brilliant smile showed that he still hadn't picked up on the fact that he wasn't welcome. Or more likely, Claudia thought, he did know but didn't care.

As Claudia and Devin were talking, Zelma was pouring little green juice. Now she offered the glasses to Claudia, who accepted, and to Devin, who put up a hand like a stop sign. "Ah, no thanks. That looks a little too healthy for me. That is one freaky green color! I'd take a Coke or a Pepsi if you have one, though."

Zelma regarded him coldly. "I apologize. We don't have things like that here."

"No problem," said Devin graciously. "I'm not thirsty anyway."

"Claudia," said Zelma, "I've been telling Devin a little about The Hawthorne School. He's very curious."

"Art and nature." Devin nodded approvingly.

Claudia felt aggravated. What right did he have to come back into their lives now and approve or disapprove of anything? She put down her glass of little green. She'd only drunk half of it.

"Yes," said Zelma, "art and nature. To awaken the spirit of the child."

"Whoa!" said Devin. He narrowed his eyes cynically and scoffed. "'To awaken the spirit of the child'? What makes you think my son's spirit is asleep in the first place?" He wanted to pick a fight with Zelma.

"Devin, let's go have a talk by ourselves," Claudia snapped. She turned to Zelma, wanting to control the damage. "I haven't seen Devin or heard from him since Henry was an infant. I had no idea he would show up here."

"Are you apologizing for me, Claudia? Hey. I'm just asking questions, that's all. I'm not offending anyone. You're not offended, are you, Zelda?"

"Zelma," said Claudia and Zelma together.

Devin smiled, and Claudia knew he had made that gaffe on purpose, to show his disregard for the director. He was no more mature than Henry when he called Miss Patty "Miss Potty." He knew very well what her damn name was. He just never got tired of "speaking truth to power."

She used to think that was attractive.

Now she only wanted to get rid of him.

18

As they walked out of the Main Hall, Devin proposed that they go for a ride. They went down the walk past Unity Hall and to the parking lot behind it. Devin talked. Talking was what he loved to do.

Finally, he thought to ask her something about her own life. "How's your mom?"

"She passed away three months ago."

"Oh no. Claudia . . ." Devin was quiet for a minute. "I can't believe it. She was an incredible woman. So kind. And so strong."

"Yes. Thank you. She was. And she came through for me after you left. I don't know how we would have made it without her."

"I'm sorry about your mom . . . and I'm sorry for what I did. Claudia, I know I let you and Henry down. Does he know who I am? Do you ever show him my picture? I can't wait to see him."

Claudia felt surprisingly calm, and she felt detached from Devin and all he was saying. Yet she knew she had to rouse herself and make it clear to Devin that he couldn't just pop back into their lives. She remembered now that Devin had always pushed her to stand her ground.

He went on. "I know what you're thinking: What right do I have to see him now? But Claudia, listen. You don't know how much I've changed. I mean, I've grown up a lot in four years. When I left you guys, I was just overwhelmed."

Even in her semi-tranquil state, Claudia had to react to this. "*You* were overwhelmed? *You?*"

"Yeah, I know, Claude. You're right. I'm a jackass. Was. I *was* a jackass. But I'm less of a jackass now, I hope. I'm sorry. Back then, I was only thinking about myself. I was immature then. But I want to make things right now. I want to . . ." He tried to put his arm around her, but she stepped away from him. "We had a good thing between us once, you and me, Claude. I've missed you. And I want to be Henry's father now and make up for not being here before."

Claudia thought of the deep love she had once had for this man. If only he had come back three years ago. Even last year. It took a long time for her love to die. Now, it was too late. The love she had once felt for him was beyond resuscitation.

"You're gonna love my car," he promised. "It's cool!"

He was still a child, excited about a stupid car. She didn't care about cool cars. She cared about her son.

Devin's car was an orange Volkswagen Beetle. What else?

As they rode, he shifted gears and talked on and on.

"I've put in job applications all around here: restaurant server, print shop assistant, whatever."

"What about acting?"

"I've done some stuff. I was even in New York City, on Broadway. What do you think of that? I mean, minor roles—I never got the roles I wanted—but still. It was my dream, just to be in that world at all. But you know what? When I got there, I realized I didn't really care about it. Life's funny, huh? You can work and work toward a goal, and then when you get it—"

"You throw it all away," supplied Claudia.

Devin took a deep breath, as if he'd been prepared for cuts like this.

"Here's the thing: I want to help you raise Henry."

"Until you 'realize' you don't want that anymore and change your mind again?"

"No. This time, I'm sure."

"And what about drugs?"

"I don't do that anymore. I haven't for over a year. Well, almost a year. I see everything more clearly now. I want us to be together, you and me, but I understand if I've already screwed that up. Just let me help with Henry . . . Hey, you're not with another guy, are you?" Devin asked as if he had only now considered the possibility that after four years, Claudia might have moved on.

He turned to look into her face.

Claudia thought of Niles. She was not "with" him, of course, but she might like to be. A relationship with Niles could develop, in time.

"It's really none of your business at this point."

Devin looked as if he wanted to argue but conceded. "You're right. I'm not here to demand anything. I'm not trying to make anything harder for you. Just the opposite. I want to fit into *your* life. If you have someone else, that's cool. I can just be here for Henry. I'm his dad. Hey, that director lady, she took me up to see a classroom—real quick. She wouldn't let me get a good look around. But what the heck kind of a school *is* that, Claude?"

"What do you mean?"

"I mean, I never saw kids like that. I'm no expert on kids or anything. But is this a—I don't know . . . a *weird*-kid school?"

"No! What are you talking about?"

"It creeped me out. Kids sitting still, like in a trance or something."

"They're not in a trance! They're tired from being outdoors all morning."

"Being outdoors all morning doesn't make kids tired. It doesn't make them look like that."

"Look like what?"

"I don't know. But don't you see it? It's like something's wrong with them. They're like . . . tranquilized. Or scared. Or suppressed. Or *something*."

"Oh, 'suppressed.' *Oppressed*, you mean. By authority, right?"

Devin shook his head. "It's just weird," he insisted. "I don't think I like this school for Henry."

"*You* don't like this school for Henry? You don't even *know* Henry. The very first thing you ask about him is if he's seen a picture of *you*. Have *you* seen a picture of *him*? Have you ever even asked to? You abandoned us, remember? You gave up any right you had to any opinion about his education. What makes you think you can show up now and try to interfere with how I'm raising him? *I* have been raising him, Devin. *I* have been figuring everything out, all on my own, with no help from you. *I* have been dealing with his teachers, and *I* have found this school for him. This school understands him and supports me—which is more than you can say for yourself. We don't need you now, Devin."

He looked hurt but rallied quickly. "But I *want* you to need me now. I want to be in your lives. I want you to let me see Henry."

"Oh, you *want*? It's all about what *you* want. Is that what you think?"

"What about Henry? What does *he* want? Don't you think he'd want to meet his father if he knew I was here? Doesn't every kid want to know his father?"

They drove through the beautiful rural area, where the land had some low hills, dotted with farms and tracts of woodland. They drove and argued until the end of the school day. It was just like old times. Claudia had forgotten how passionately disagreeable he could be. And yet, she had once loved his feistiness, had loved how much he cared about everything, his assumption that he had a right to whatever he wanted in life. An assumption she had never shared.

Devin wore Claudia down. Of course a boy had a right to meet his own father. Or sperm donor. She would like to introduce Devin to Henry with just that qualification: "This is your sperm donor." After all, that's all Devin had turned out to be. He certainly wasn't a father in any real sense to Henry. He'd done nothing to earn the title of "father." But naturally, she couldn't say "sperm donor" to a four-year-old. Of course she would let Devin meet Henry. She was aware that once Devin saw his son, he would be likely to be even more stubbornly intent on inserting himself into their lives. Yet she could not justify keeping them apart. She would never want Henry to blame her later in life for not letting him have a relationship with his father. She would let them meet—certainly not for Devin's sake, but only for Henry's.

19

Henry's reaction to meeting his long-lost daddy was underwhelming and obviously dampened Devin's spirits. Claudia was glad.

They met in Evelyn's classroom, and the teacher watched with inquisitive interest.

"Henry, this is your father." Claudia tried to make her voice sound cheery.

"Hey, little buddy," said Devin, kneeling down and ruffling Henry's black hair that was so like his own. "Hey. It's good to see you, champ. Hey. You have a good day at school?"

Henry regarded the strange adult wordlessly, as if he were seeing straight through him.

I hope he does see straight through him, thought Claudia. *I hope he sees that he can never count on this guy.*

"Hey, bro," persisted Devin, "you tired, little dude? You hungry? You want McDonald's?"

"We don't eat stuff like that," put in Claudia.

Devin, for once, looked chastened, accepting correction. "Oh. What do you guys eat, then?"

He doesn't even know us, thought Claudia.

"Maybe a smoothie," suggested Evelyn, going to her refrigerator.

"I was thinking of taking him out somewhere. Taking you both out somewhere," said Devin, addressing Claudia.

But Evelyn was already handing Henry a bright green smoothie.

"Is every drink around here that radioactive green color?"

"Do you know how rude that sounds?" chided Claudia. She smiled apologetically at Henry's teacher.

"Sorry. I didn't mean it that way." From his kneeling position, he looked at Evelyn. He looked her up and down, appraisingly. Then he looked around at the classroom: the little throne made of branches, the wardrobe that stood open, exposing a rack of costumes. Claudia realized for the first time that there were no children's books of any kind. She was seeing the classroom through Devin's eyes, and she didn't like seeing it that way. She looked back at Evelyn. The teacher was following her gaze and studying her face.

There was a tap at the door, and Niles strode in, confident, friendly and smiling.

"Hey," he said, "I heard Henry's father was visiting, and I just wanted to stop by to welcome him into the Hawthorne family."

Devin rose and shook hands with Niles.

Claudia was relieved to see him. *Niles* understood The Hawthorne School. He'd explained things so well to her. He could explain them better to Devin, so Devin would stop trying to find flaws.

"*'Family'?*" asked Devin.

"Yeah, we think of it as a family. Hey, let me take you on the grand tour and give you some of our history. We want you to get the full view of what we offer your son here."

Devin was pleased, Claudia could tell, that he was being included in this way and that Niles had referred to Henry as "your son."

"I'd really like to do that sometime," said Devin, "but I'm just now getting to see Henry after a long time—"

Yeah, thought Claudia, *a long time: Henry's whole life.*

"Oh, hey, I promise not to hold you up too long. Twenty, thirty minutes max."

Claudia joined in. "And Henry will need a little downtime at the end of his school day." She was improvising. "We'll be ready in thirty minutes to go out and eat somewhere."

Devin and Niles walked off in the direction of the chapel and cloister walk, and Claudia took Henry downstairs and outside. She hoped to answer any questions Henry might have about the unexpected visitor, but he seemed to have forgotten him already. Gathering energy, he ran past the playground and cried, "I want to go into the hedge maze!"

She followed him through the graveled walkways lined with evergreen shrubs, past sitting areas with benches. She gave him space to run ahead, letting him come to the dead ends and find the winding paths to the center, where a statue of a woman stood, holding a book in her hand.

"That's Julia Hawthorne," Henry informed her matter-of-factly. "When I come here with my class, we have to find her. She's always waiting for us here."

There, just before the metal figure, Claudia sat down on a bench while Henry squatted on the ground, studying an ant hill near the pedestal of the great educator. He didn't try to destroy the ants, as another child might have done, but only observed.

As Henry watched the ants, Claudia had an unsettling feeling of being watched herself, a prickle on the skin, but she knew she must be imagining it.

"Ants live under the ground," Henry told her.

"In tunnels?"

"Yes. Secret tunnels. We're gonna live in tunnels too, like the ants."

"Really? You'd like to live in a tunnel? We could make an ant farm, you know. In a jar. So you could see the tunnels."

Henry, with the four-year-old's skipping attention span, said, "That man said he was my father."

"Yes, Henry. He is your father."

"No, he can't be my father, because I never saw him before."

Claudia could see how this line of reasoning was logical to Henry.

"Anyway. I already saw a picture of my father, and it's not that guy."

"When? Who showed you a picture?" Claudia had never shown him a photograph of his father.

"Miss Applegate has a picture of him on the wall."

She smiled at the thought of Henry assuming that Gabriel Hawthorne was his father. Henry's imagination was as active as her own.

"Henry, you *do* like this school, don't you?"

There was a footstep on the path, and around the hedge came Zelma.

20

"I SO SELDOM GET to come out here and enjoy the hedge maze and the statue."

Sighing, Zelma sat down next to Claudia.

"We always want to meet both parents of our students. Full parental endorsement is essential. When Henry's father came in this morning, I'd hoped that he'd join us, support Henry's education at The Hawthorne School. But I could see from the beginning of our interaction that . . . well."

"I'm sorry," was all Claudia could think of to say.

"This is exactly the kind of thing we want to avoid: mixed messages. It sabotages the students' development. You know, Claudia, not to put too fine a point on it, but we have made a great deal of effort for you and Henry. If it's not too personal a question, may I ask? What do you think his intentions are? Henry's father? Is he going to become involved now?"

"He wants to." Claudia was aware of Henry listening to every word, and knew she should be careful in front of him. Still, she needed to talk about the emotions stirred up in her by Devin's visit. "It's really aggravating. He's been gone all this time, and now he shows up and wants to have a say. He had his chance. That's the way I see it."

"Stand up to him, dear heart," suggested Zelma with motherly warmth. "Don't let him walk all over you. You are agreeable to a fault. Just make sure you are agreeable with the right people. Was he abusive to you?"

"Oh no, never anything like that. He's immature, that's all, and he got overwhelmed when Henry was born, so he just left us. Classic story. But now he says he's changed and wants to play an active role. But I feel like we've finally settled into a rhythm, Henry and I, and found our places. And"—Claudia hesitated here—"he doesn't much like The Hawthorne School so far. He's done nothing but criticize it all afternoon. I hope Niles can help him see it the way it really is, but once Devin gets an idea in his head, he's like a bulldog. He doesn't let go. Facts don't persuade him. He loves to argue and to make people see things *his* way."

"How frustrating," said Zelma. She was deep in thought. "You know, Claudia, it is our policy that both parents must be entirely on board with the Hawthorne Way. If he isn't, well, I don't like to say this, but the fact is, if he is now assuming his role as Henry's father, and he doesn't come around, we'll have to let you and Henry go. As much as it would pain us to do that. It's harmful to have one parent undermining a child's education. I've seen it before, and in my experience, it never ends well. It confuses the child, you see. Niles will try to help Devin see what we are offering Henry, but if Niles fails—well, I hope you understand."

Claudia's spirits sank. Devin was back. And he was going to upend their lives with his stubborn will.

21

THEY WERE AT the Mexican restaurant in town, where sequined sombreros hung on the peach-colored walls and reggaeton music pulsed from speakers in the corners.

Claudia ordered in Spanish, and as the server turned away, Devin said, "That's cool. I wish *I* could speak another language. Maybe you could teach me Spanish."

Claudia didn't remind Devin that he'd tried learning Spanish from her once before. His interest had lasted all of five minutes, and he'd given up when he realized it would require long-term effort. She knew he didn't want to learn Spanish now. What he wanted was to hint that he intended to be around for a while.

"So tell me," said Claudia, determined to expose Devin's lie, "*how* did you find me again? Where am I on the internet?"

"You're not. That's what took me so long to find you. You're the only person under ninety who doesn't have some kind of social media account. What's up with that?"

"I don't like wasting my time. And I value my privacy," she added pointedly. "So how did you find me then?"

"Like I said, the internet. There's a website, Zorba.com I think it is, where you can post a message for someone you're looking for. Then that person, or someone who knows them, can give information. About three months ago, I posted 'Looking for Claudia Vera, mother of Henry.' Then, just last week,

I got an answer: 'Henry goes to The Hawthorne School in Willow Downs, Illinois. Contact Claudia there.'"

Claudia lapsed into silence. Who could have posted that response?

Devin said, "Hey, Henry. Do you like chips? Do you like guacamole?"

He pushed the bowls toward Henry. Henry regarded him somberly.

"Who replied to your post?" pursued Claudia. "Did they have a name?"

"Yeah, I don't know who; they didn't give their identity. Just a screen name: 'Maggiemay.' Was that *you* by any chance? Wanting me to find you?"

The nerve of Devin, to think she would be playing coy games like that. Of course, it had to be Maggie Timmerberg. But why would Maggie do such a thing without asking first? How dare she butt in?

"You don't like hot sauce, do you, Henry?" asked Devin, holding up the red bottle. Claudia absentmindedly swatted the bottle away from Henry. Devin continued, "What do you like, my little man?"

Henry answered without hesitation, "I like my mom."

Devin laughed. "Sure. I like your mom too. What else do you like? Do you like superheroes? Dinosaurs? What are you into?"

Claudia sighed in irritation. Devin ignored her.

"I'd like to buy you a present, dude. But I need to know what you like. Do you want to go to a toy store after dinner?"

"Don't try to buy him. It's so obvious. Stop it."

"That's not what I'm doing. I'm trying to make a relationship here, Claude. I'm trying to show that I care about my son and what he likes." He turned to Henry. "You think about it, little buddy. You let me know what you want some other day."

"Devin. Look, I know you didn't mean to cause trouble, but you *are* causing trouble. Zelma—the director—told me today that if you oppose Henry's enrollment in the school, he won't be able to stay. I don't understand why they'd give you that much say-so. You just turned up out of the blue. I'm not sure what rights you actually have under the law. But their policy is that both parents have to be on board. I'm asking you. Please. If you want to make up for the harm you've already done us, don't screw this up. Tell them, tomorrow, that you're happy to have Henry at the school. I know you want to fight me. And fight them. For no good reason. Just because you love to fight. But just do that one little thing, for me, Devin. For Henry. I'm asking: *please*."

"Wow, Claude. Is that really how you see me? Like, I just want to fight for no reason? Wow."

"Devin. This isn't about how I see you. It's not about you at all, and it's not about me. It's about Henry. His education."

"Okay, since you're the one who's brought up education, let's talk about it. Isn't a school supposed to have an alphabet on the wall or something? Or maybe some books? I'm no expert, but all I saw was costumes and chalk drawings. Is it a hippie school? Or what?"

Claudia scoffed. "*Hippie* school. You're a hippie yourself. You just don't get it. Look. You need to see that I know more about preschool programs than you do. This is a *progressive* school. It offers the best education around. Henry's lucky to even get in. Other kids are on the waiting list."

"Okay. I don't know as much as you do, Claude. You're smart and I'm an idiot. But I still have my opinions. And I'm just not so sure about this so-called *education*. That Niles—nice guy, by the way. I mean, he does have a creepy way of staring, you know? His eyes are kind of—"

"Jeez, Devin, stop with the personal remarks. You're so judgmental! What's wrong with the education—according to you, since you're so well-informed on the topic?"

"Oh, nothing, except there is none. Niles says they don't learn to read until they're 'ready.' I asked him, 'What if they're never ready?' He goes, 'Reading is overrated.' Then he smiles, that goofy-friendly smile of his, like I'm going to agree with that."

"He's just kidding. They learn to read when they're organically ready. For now, their teacher recites fairy tales to them during lunch, and in time they'll learn to recite them just from listening. It's called the oral tradition, in case you've never heard of it. Right now she's telling them 'The Snow Queen.'"

Devin's eyes lit up with amusement. "'The Snow Queen'? That's about Zelda, right? That lady is *cold*."

"You know what her name is, Devin. *Zelma*. And she's only cold to you because you're rude to her."

"I just call it the way I see it. People don't like that. I couldn't care less what people think. That's how I am." Devin grinned and reached across to ruffle Henry's hair, and Henry ducked. "So the kids just run around outside, and then the teacher recites a fairy tale. That's the curriculum?"

"No. They learn to make music and to use their hands. And they learn to play the flute, speak Spanish, and garden, and build things out of wood. They learn tons of things that I would think you would be all over. And you *would* be, if you just didn't like to fight so much. Stop being so oppositional."

"What do *you* think, little buddy?" Devin addressed Henry, who was focused on his burrito, which Claudia had cut up into small pieces for him. "Do you like that weird school? Or do you want to go to a real school?"

Henry looked at Claudia, confused.

Claudia burst out, "No, Devin! Stop it! You don't get to ruin everything I've found for Henry. What are *you* offering us? *Nothing!* Are you ready to make a commitment to him? Or is it all just talk, like last time? Because his school has already given us more support than you ever have."

The server came bustling over, alarmed by Claudia's raised voice

Claudia answered, *"Perdón. Todo está bien. No hay ningún problema. Perdónenos la molestia. La cuenta, por favor."*

As the server prepared the bill at the cash register, Devin said in a low tone, "I'm not leaving you this time, Claude. I'm never leaving again. I'm going to be right by your side from now on. I'm going to be a father to Henry. I'm not here to cause trouble. I really do care about you. You don't have to care about me. I'm not going to push for that. You can be with someone else if you want—"

"Oh, that's so broadminded of you. Thank you so very *much*."

"But Henry is my son. Nothing can ever change that. For his sake, we have to work together now."

"You're trying to interfere with all my efforts. Is that your idea of working together? Do you even have any idea how hard it's been all this time, doing everything by myself? And now, when I've finally got something really good, *you* show up and try to smash it to pieces! I'm not going to let you do it. Do you understand me?"

Devin looked stricken. She had finally penetrated his obtuseness, his thick defenses, and she felt a sense of satisfaction. She pushed on. "If you're really back and you want to support us, then support us. Support us, Devin, or get out of the way. And *I* make all the decisions. Not you."

22

CLAUDIA, HENRY IN tow, rapped on Maggie's door. Maggie's brightness at the sight of Claudia dimmed immediately.

"What's happened?" Maggie stepped aside and waved Claudia and Henry in. Violet grabbed Henry's hand, and the two of them ran off to play.

"You should know."

"What's that supposed to mean?"

"Devin?"

Maggie bit her lip and avoided Claudia's stare.

"Maggie, how could you? What were you *thinking*? You had no right to meddle in my life like that. You went out of your way to find Devin and tell him where I was."

"So it didn't go well?"

"No, of course not, but that's completely beside the point. The point is, why did you do it?"

"I just—I wanted—I *hoped* . . . I thought I could build a bridge. You said you loved him once. And you're all alone with Henry."

"How would *you* like it if I contacted Violet's father and tried to 'build a bridge'?"

Maggie considered.

"Never mind. This is a completely different situation. I *told* you what Devin was like."

"Yes, but he could have changed. People do, you know. And The Hawthorne School likes to have—"

"Both parents on board. I know. Zelma informed me of that policy as I'm sure she did you. But that's not going to happen, as I could have told you if you'd just asked. And now, Devin might ruin everything."

Maggie put her hand over her eyes. "Oh, Claudia, I'm so stupid! Please don't be mad at me. I was only trying to help. I thought you might even fall in love again if you just saw each other after all this time. But you're absolutely right. And now you'll hate me and never be my friend again."

Claudia, forgetting her own indignation for a moment, hugged Maggie. She didn't like seeing her so distressed. After all, Maggie hadn't done it out of meanness, but only out of simplicity. She was like a child.

That night, Claudia's headache was more punishing than it had ever been. Her thoughts—when she could think at all— revolved around Devin. She had been harsh with him. What if he really did want to make amends now? It might be true that he had grown up in the past four years. *She* had. What had he said to make her so angry? He had only pointed out some unusual things about the school. She'd had some of those same thoughts herself until she came to understand better. It was natural to question something so different, so untraditional. Devin was stubborn and considered himself an expert on everything, but he *was* Henry's father. It was good that Henry had an opportunity to have his dad back in his life.

Reluctantly, before the big blowup at the restaurant, she had given him all her contact information, explaining that she wouldn't be able to text during the days she was at The Hawthorne School because they didn't allow cell phones. He had ridiculed that policy, of course, but she was glad that he now could get in touch with her and knew where she lived.

He wanted to try again.

Why shouldn't she give him another chance?

Because, she argued with herself, *I've learned—through hard experience—not to trust him. That's why.*

Last time, he had promised to stay by her side and help her raise the baby, and then he had left them with the lame excuse, "I guess I'm just not a family man."

And now he had the nerve to say that he'd abandoned them because he'd been "overwhelmed." She thought bitterly of how overwhelmed *she'd* been, dropping out of fine arts school and depending on her mom, who had switched to working nights so she could care for the baby while Claudia went to massage school. There, Claudia had requested an empty office where she could pump milk for Henry between classes. At night, she was up with him, walking, nursing, and many nights crying right along with him. And when her mother got sick and couldn't take care of Henry, she'd hired an older woman in their apartment building to babysit while she subdivided her life into caring for her mother, studying, and caring for Henry. She lived in survival mode, where she had remained until The Hawthorne School began to lift some of the burden. Of all the times Devin could have chosen to come back into their lives, why now?

And yet, he *had* come back. He had apologized and said he had changed. She couldn't trust him right away, of course. It would take a lot of time to rebuild shattered trust. But she wouldn't shut him out.

23

TRUE TO HIS word—maybe for the first time ever—Devin met Claudia and Henry in front of The Hawthorne School. He was going to see Henry off to school and then ask Zelma for a volunteer role.

"*There's* my guy!" he exclaimed with the widest smile Claudia had ever seen on him.

Henry wrapped his arms around Claudia's leg.

"Hey, my man! High five!"

Henry buried his face against Claudia's thigh.

"Take it down a notch," murmured Claudia. "Give him a little time."

"What's the matter, little dude? I'm your dad. Don't you know that? We're gonna have good times together, man. We'll go camping and play ball and stuff." Devin reached out his hand toward Henry. Henry screamed and ran around to cling to Claudia's legs from the back.

"Stop pushing him. You're too much right now."

"I'm not too much right now, Henry, am I? No, we're gonna be best buds."

Devin would have kept pressing on in his thick-headed way, but Claudia picked Henry up and opened the door to the Main Hall, and Devin followed.

As they walked toward Zelma's office, Devin said, "Hey, Claude. Guess what? I already got a job. Got the call last night!

Starting tomorrow, I'm a server at Dolce's Italian Ristorante. How do you like that? It's a nice place. You ever been? I mean, I'll do better eventually, but just so you know: I do have a job here now."

Claudia resisted the urge to ask him if he wanted a medal.

"Ah," Zelma said as she appeared at her office door. "I couldn't help overhearing." Henry ran to her and took her hand. He looked up into her face, waiting for her to acknowledge him. "So, Devin, you have a job in town. Well, that's wonderful. And you're willing to do some volunteer work here too? That's grand. Henry, good morning. Isn't that grand?"

"Good morning," said Henry.

Claudia noticed how he stood so straight and proud next to Zelma. He trusted her. Devin had to be noticing it too.

"Yes. My hours will be afternoons and evenings. Dolce's isn't open in the morning. So any morning you like—"

"How about *this* morning?"

"Perfect! But first, I was hoping to observe Henry's classroom, you know, see what's going on in there, what you guys are teaching my son. I gotta say, I don't really get what it is you're doing here. How about if I hang out in Henry's classroom for an hour or so, and maybe volunteer after that?"

Claudia pressed Devin's arm, and he looked down at her hand. She let go. "Devin, you can't just observe a classroom like that, without the teacher having any notice."

Devin paused, looking into Claudia's eyes. It was that touch. She knew he was feeling it still, because she was. He was wondering if there was any chance.

Zelma nodded. She was looking back and forth between the two of them, her sharp little eyes not missing anything. "That's right, Claudia. Well. Good. I'll have Niles come down in just a little while and take you out to the woods, Devin, and—teach you how to gather wild ginseng."

Devin laughed explosively. "Gather . . .? I mean, okay. Sounds good," said Devin. He tried to catch Claudia's eye.

Zelma smiled good-naturedly: "Don't go off the trails in the forest. It's easy to get lost." She beamed down at Henry. "Come along, Henry. I'll take you up to your classroom."

* * *

After school, as Claudia led Henry out to her car, she heard running footsteps behind them.

Devin ran up and threw a casual arm around her shoulder. She shrugged him off, trying not to betray the attraction she was already beginning to feel for him again. He didn't deserve it.

"Claudia!" he said, not acknowledging the rebuff. "Wait till I tell you about *my* day at school. I hung out with Niles the whole day, and you're not going to believe what I saw!"

"Okay," sighed Claudia. They had arrived at her car, and she fished in her purse for her keys. "What did you see?"

Devin pointed vaguely in the direction of the vegetable garden and the greenhouse. "Oh man. Do you even know what they're growing out there?"

"Do tell," said Claudia, trying to sound bored.

"Herbs!"

"Wow. Amazing."

"No! You don't get it. Not just any herbs."

"Devin. I already know."

"You *do*?"

"Yes. The herbs for little green. The mixture for adding nutrition to the smoothies, juice, and teas. It's a superfood combination."

Devin snorted. "Superfood! Is that what they call it?"

"What are you implying?"

"Not implying, my dear little innocent one. *Informing.* You don't know what those herbs are."

Claudia didn't want to admit that she didn't.

Devin, in his element, shared his knowledge. "Common mugwort is one. It's a ditch weed. Looks like ragweed. We sold it in dried leaf form at Health for You. *Artemisia vulgaris* is the Latin name." He was showing off.

"So?"

"So, it's a mild intoxicant!" he said triumphantly. "It's used for calming the nerves."

"Okay. Fine. Devin, they combine small amounts of it with a ton of other ingredients: bananas, dates, filtered water, romaine lettuce, and more things I can't even remember right now. If they add a pinch of—whatever you said—mugwort—I'm not going to worry about it."

"But if it's used in excess, it can damage the liver."

Now he was being ridiculous.

"All right," she said in her best condescending tone. "Well, no one around here seems to have a damaged liver. Zelma drinks the teas—at her age—and look how healthy *she* is." Claudia refused to let Devin see the anxiety that was beginning to creep up on her.

"But wait. Mugwort isn't all. Some of the herbs I can't identify yet. I'll search them later. But one of them I don't need to look up: they're also growing *salvia*! I was like, dude, no way!"

At Claudia's blank stare, Devin expounded. He was so happy to be an authority on something.

"*Salvia divinorum*—'the sage of the diviners.' It has opioid-like compounds. Shamans in Mexico use it for its hallucinogenic effects. They use it to go into visionary trances. Do you get it? What did I tell you?"

Devin looked so gleefully proud of himself. "It looks like mint, and Niles tried to tell me it was mint, but you can't kid a kidder. I know *salvia* when I see it. I've used it myself. I had a terrifying trip on it once. Never again."

It was pathetic that Devin was trying to use his experience as a druggie to make himself important.

"If it looks like mint," she said slowly, as if speaking to a child, "what makes you think it *isn't* mint?"

She glanced at Henry, who had climbed into his car seat and was nodding off to sleep there.

"Because I crushed the leaves and smelled them. Trust me."

Claudia thought that if there was one person she knew she couldn't trust, it was Devin.

"Listen, Claudia. *Salvia* gives you dream-like experiences. Take enough, and you can't tell the difference anymore between reality and hallucinations. It's nothing little kids should be given. We have to pull Henry out of this so-called school—today." Now he was no longer exulting. Now he was serious. His eyes were almost pleading.

"Look, you've got the wrong idea," Claudia protested. "You just pinched some leaves and smelled them, and now you have a whole crazy conspiracy theory about the school, all because you're looking for something to be wrong here."

"No! I know what I'm talking about!"

There it was: his favorite phrase.

She needed to get away from him.

"Tell you what. I'll consider everything you said. I really will, okay? And we'll talk about it tomorrow."

"You're not taking me seriously, Claudia."

"Sure I am."

"I get it." He looked off toward the woods, frowning bitterly. "You've been trying to tell me you don't need me now. I guess you don't. You know it all."

"Devin, I am *not* going to stand here and argue with you."

Claudia drove off, leaving Devin standing in the parking lot, his hands stuffed in his pockets. In her rearview mirror, he looked like a sad teenager. From behind the building, Niles appeared, striding toward Devin. Good. Let Devin argue with Niles. Maybe Niles would set him straight.

CHAPTER

24

TRUE TO CLAUDIA'S expectations—and certainly not for the first time—Devin didn't meet them at school the following morning. Claudia should have known better than to entertain any optimism concerning Devin, cautious or otherwise. He was apparently already bored with the whole thing. He'd been right the first time when he'd said he wasn't a family man.

She tried calling him once, but his phone was off. She didn't bother trying the Italian restaurant where he claimed to have a job. So, true to form, he'd left town as quickly as he'd arrived. Claudia imagined him driving away in his orange bug, ready to break another woman's heart. She pitied and was angry at herself all at the same time.

When Zelma asked about Devin, Claudia brushed it off, and Zelma didn't seem surprised. She could see exactly who he was too.

Henry and Claudia settled back into their routine: calm at school, small tantrums at home. On the verge of a tantrum, he sometimes burst into uncontrollable laughter. Claudia tried not to tell him, "You're just like your father," but she thought it.

One night Henry interrupted their bedtime story. "I know what I want. That man? That guy who said he was my father? He said he wants to buy me a present."

Claudia put the book down.

"Why do you look so sad, Mom?"

"Well, it's just that . . . I don't know if you'll see that man again soon. I mean, it looks like he went away again."

"That's okay. We can get whatever we need anyway, right? We don't need him for anything."

"And what do you want?"

"A puppy."

"Puppies are fun. Maybe someday. When you're bigger."

Predictably, that delay to his wish sent Henry into a melt-down. Claudia wearily waited it out.

As the days went on and there was no word from Devin, Claudia's headaches continued mercilessly, and she felt sick to her stomach. It was all Devin's fault: his showing up and disappearing had brought so much stress into her life.

Fortunately, Henry wasn't fazed. He hadn't had enough time with Devin to get to know him, and certainly not enough to consider him his father. Claudia felt foolish for thinking—even for a moment—that Devin could have changed.

Since her mother's death, she'd needed someone she could count on to help her raise Henry. That someone was not and would never be Devin.

The only stable support in her life was The Hawthorne School.

25

"WHO WAS IT who said, 'When someone shows you who they are, believe them'? I feel stupid for believing him again, even for a minute."

Maggie jumped to Claudia's defense. "Don't say that! You're super smart."

The air was chilled, the sky silver, and black birds flew overhead. They had the park to themselves. Henry, in his bright red sweater, was lying stomach down on a swing while Violet twirled him.

"Don't be so hard on yourself, Claudia. Of *course* you believe people! You're an honest person yourself. So naturally you think everyone else is." Her eyes were pools of commiseration. "Do you still love Devin?"

Claudia was absentmindedly breaking a twig into small pieces. "Maggie, you're a hopeless romantic. Stop with the 'love' already." She threw the broken twig to the ground. "I do feel . . . something. I wish I didn't. Maybe it's not love, though. I guess I feel *bonded* to him. Can you feel bonded to someone you don't love?"

Maggie shrugged, looking to Claudia to answer her own question.

"I mean, I've lost faith in him, but somehow there's still a connection there."

"Because he's Henry's father?"

"Yes—and also because of what we used to have. Or what I thought we had. We were so happy together . . . for a short time. With me, he could be very . . . *tender*, I guess is the word." Claudia roused herself from memories that she did not want to replay in her mind. "Well. It's over now. For good."

Maggie tilted her head, considering. "It sounds nice. I can see why you miss that time in your life with him."

"I won't miss his arguing and criticizing everything, that's for sure. I mean, he never criticized *me*, but the world at large—he had a problem with every little thing."

Henry and Violet chased each other around trees, screaming.

"So much negativity," said Maggie tentatively, as if not wanting to offend. "I mean, so different from you. You're so positive."

"Am I?"

Maggie laughed, flabbergasted. "Well, yeah! Look at your can-do attitude about mothering. You just decide, and then you go for it."

Claudia enjoyed that vision of herself. It was pleasant to think that Maggie saw something in her that she did not see in herself. Blushing with pleasure now, she wanted to move the focus off herself. "What about Violet's father?"

"He's married. Or he was when Violet was conceived. Don't judge me, okay?"

"No, of course not!"

"Well, a lot of people would. But I honestly didn't know he was married. I was just stupid. But I'm not sorry. She's the light of my life, that one."

"So, he's not married anymore?"

"No idea. He's nowhere around. Told you I was stupid."

Maggie now looked so troubled that Claudia regretted prying.

Mercifully, the kids ran up to them, grabbing their hands. "Moms have to play freeze tag. Catch us!"

26

THE NEXT MONDAY, Zelma met her as if she had been wait-ing for her, as if she had nothing else to do. Claudia felt a pang of guilt.

"I'm sorry. I feel like I must have gotten the start time wrong. Are we arriving late?"

"No, Claudia, you're right on time." Zelma smiled at Claudia and looked into her eyes with warmth.

"But where are the other students Henry's age and their parents?"

"The students are going into the classroom through another entrance. You haven't noticed? We do have a dormitory here. Many of the students live on campus. That's why you don't see many parents. Well, you've met Niles, of course. I'm afraid you won't see him today; I've asked him to go off on some errands for me. But you may see Valeria's parents, Yolanda and Oscar. They work here on the grounds as employees. You won't be able to speak to them, though. They speak only Spanish."

Claudia thought to mention that she did, in fact, speak Spanish, but her attention was on the news that she wouldn't see Niles today. She had been looking forward to talking to him again. She had noticed another man, always in the distance, on the grounds. That must be Oscar, then. She hadn't seen Yolanda yet. Of course, it must take a full-time staff to take care of this property. As for the dormitory, Claudia had observed that the school was enormous, and it only made sense that there would be a dormitory. So then, people far away actually sent their children here. Even such young ones as the four-year-olds? She couldn't imagine sending Henry away, but she tried not to judge. She happened to be lucky to have this school practically in her own neighborhood.

"Oh," said Claudia, "before I forget, may I have Henry's birth certificate back?"

The expression on Zelma's face clouded. "You just gave it to me, Claudia. I will need to make a copy of it, and then I can give it back."

"Oh, sorry," said Claudia reflexively. She didn't know why she was apologizing, but it seemed she had annoyed Zelma.

"Of course, we don't have a copier *here*." Zelma stated this as if it should go without saying. "I will need to have it taken into town. There's no rush, is there?"

"Oh, no rush. But I have a printer at home. I can make a copy and bring that to you tomorrow."

"There's no need to complicate things. Since you're not in a hurry, let's just leave things as they are, shall we?" It was not really a question, but a statement.

Claudia didn't want to be a difficult parent. She let the matter drop.

Zelma continued, "I've made you a cup of tea in my office. Have a seat there, and I'll take Henry up."

"Actually," Claudia said, "I would like to take Henry up to his classroom myself—if that's okay with you. I just wanted to have a quick word with Evelyn."

Zelma stood a bit taller. She raised her eyebrows and fixed Claudia with a bright stare. The warm light in Zelma's eyes flickered and faded. Zelma echoed, "A word with *Evelyn*?" Claudia felt herself shrivel. "While she's welcoming the students and getting ready for her *day*?"

"Oh," said Claudia. "Well, no, not if that would be inconvenient."

"It would. It would be *very* inconvenient. Very bad timing. We must *respect* the teachers, and their attention must be on the students—not on the parents."

Claudia felt embarrassed that she had only been thinking of her own need to find out how Henry had been behaving, and not at all considering the teacher's point of view. "I'm sorry," she said again, noticing that she was saying "sorry" a lot. "When would be a convenient time?"

Instead of looking appeased, Zelma looked even more annoyed than before. She answered, "I'll just bring Henry up while you have your tea. We don't want him to miss the morning routine while we stand here chatting, do we? Then I'll come back and I can answer all your questions." Now she smiled sweetly; the kind grandmotherly Zelma returned, and she took Henry's willing hand and led him down the hall.

Claudia, a mass of conflicting emotions, went into Zelma's office and drank her tea.

She had stood blathering on like an idiot, causing Henry to perhaps miss something important in his day—probably the settling-in, welcome-to-school morning routine. She wanted his day to go smoothly so he could be successful, and now she had caused him to be late. She had irritated Zelma with questions, which Evelyn had explicitly warned her not to do. But Evelyn had said that if she had questions, she, Evelyn, was the person to ask. How could she ask Evelyn questions if Zelma would not let her get to Evelyn? And why did Zelma have to take such an attitude about everything anyway? Why on earth didn't they at least have a copy machine in this place? The tea was warm and soothing, and Claudia thought of Devin's wide-eyed assertions about little green. Trances and shamans, he had said. He was ridiculous. Maybe it *was* true that the tea worked to calm her nerves in a subtle way. But to say that little green caused hallucinogenic trips was laughable. She certainly wasn't tripping. In fact, she was getting her jumble of feelings in order: worry, confusion, and aggravation. Not to mention how cold she felt. She felt so cold, although she was wearing a warm jacket. She was glad she'd put long underwear on Henry beneath his flannel shirt and jeans, and hoped that would be enough.

Ten minutes, twenty minutes passed. She wanted to take her phone out of her purse and scroll, but obeying the school rules, she had left her phone in her car. She didn't have a book in her purse either. As she felt the subtle, calming effect of the tea settle over her, she looked around for something to read while waiting, and saw the white book *The World of the Child* by Julia Hawthorne, on a shelf. She didn't know if it would be rude to read one of Zelma's books, but since it was the one about the philosophy of this school, she thought Zelma wouldn't mind. After all, she had been given her own copy. It wasn't as if she could go out in the hall and search for Zelma or ask anyone else what her volunteer work was today. Zelma had told her to wait.

She took the book down off the shelf, finished the last of her tea, and began to read.

> *And of the children, the most special ones are the Indigo children. These are the ones with extraordinary qualities and abilities that must be nurtured.*
>
> *These children commune with the spirit guides that you call their "imaginary friends," but whom the children know to be as real as they are themselves.*
>
> *And as for you, as you grew, you entered onto the road of delusion you are on now. You falsely learned to apply your own will in the world, and from that error comes all your pain. If you could be as a child, you could live forever. Therefore, resist all thought that is your own and open your mind to receive teachings that are wise.*

As the minutes ticked by, Claudia read, but her brain failed to make contact with the words. Her mind was going to sleep, and she tried to rouse it, but it was all blank expanse. She did not comprehend anything in the book. She understood the words, but the sentences they formed were gibberish to her. She remembered that Evelyn had said that everything they did at The Hawthorne School was based on this book. Did others understand it? Had Niles read this book? The inscrutable words had a hypnotic effect on Claudia. She continued reading, although her eyes grew heavy.

> *Childhood, my dear ones, is the ideal state of being. Spirit-knowing falls away from us the longer we are on this plane.*

Therefore, model yourself after the child. It is the children who are our future.

Consider literacy. Because you can read, you perceive these words. And yet, what is their worth compared to total immersion in timeless beingness? For a child's benefit, reading must be postponed for as long as possible. Indeed, the anthropologist will tell you that the happiest people on earth are those who cannot read at all. You, who are reading this: admit that your education has, in fact, subtracted from what you were before. Every piece of your so-called education has taken away from the child you were.

If you would understand this, commune with the spirit guides.

Live a life of purity, celibacy.

And banish all wrong thoughts from your mind.

She sat up straighter and forced herself to keep reading. There was nothing else to do. Two hours had passed, and still Zelma had not returned. She supposed she should take some action, go out to the kitchen and see if there was work to do there, or even go on up to Henry's classroom, but a heavy inertia kept her rooted to her chair. She flipped around the book a bit.

You are in a living universe. You do not experience it as a child does. Do you not perceive that the very rocks are alive? That the moon and the sun are alive? You knew these things once. Humankind knew these things, but when you entered on the path of delusion, you abandoned truth. This is the Science of Spirit, to recognize the aliveness of every part of the universe, and to love the Spirit-self of everything. Meditate on the moon. Make this your nightly practice. Do this until you perceive and commune with the Spirit of the Living Moon.

She didn't like these words of nonsense, and she especially didn't like the word "spirit." She rose up out of her sleepy incomprehension. She had not known this was a religious school.

Why had no one told her? She felt stupid for not realizing. But she had seen no evidence of it. And the juxtaposition of those words that did not belong together in her mind: "the Science of Spirit." For all her love of the arts, she was a practical person. This book and the phrases that pierced her drowsiness were too whimsical for her tastes. It seemed to her that the book—what she had read of it—could not be meant to be taken literally. Zelma, Evelyn, and Niles all impressed her as people who were serious-minded. Their focus was on fostering the most whole-some environment for children. The beauty, the aesthetics of the school had won her heart from the beginning, along with Zelma's kind words about her and her son. The book did not appear to have any connection to the actual school. And the actual school that Henry was attending was all that mattered. She would ask someone—Niles—to explain the book's rel-evance to her. Niles liked talking about the school, and Claudia liked listening to Niles.

She set the book down and decided to try to find someone who could tell her where Zelma was. She got up and went to the door and came face to face with a short Hispanic woman in overalls who was coming in.

The woman—Claudia decided she must be Yolanda, Valeria's mother—smiled at her and nodded. She was carry-ing two green smoothies like the ones Claudia had made with Niles. She mutely handed one to Claudia and kept the other for herself.

Claudia said, *"¡Buenos días!"*

The woman, unsurprised, answered, *"Buenos días."*

Claudia realized that Yolanda assumed that she didn't speak Spanish beyond that greeting. She introduced herself then in Spanish to Yolanda, who lit up with pleasure and friendliness.

"Where did you learn Spanish?"

"My mother was from Costa Rica. Spanish was her first language. When I was little, she wanted me to have the benefit of being bilingual."

As they chatted, Yolanda told Claudia that she and her hus-band were from Michoacán, Mexico, and added proudly that their little girl, Valeria, was a student in the school.

Claudia asked if Yolanda knew where Zelma was. *"Ella me dejó aquí hace dos horas y media y me dijo que me quedara, pero la verdad es que creo que ella se olvidó de mí."* Claudia explained that she had been waiting here, as instructed by Zelma, for two and a half hours.

Yolanda replied that Zelma was busy and had asked Yolanda to come with the smoothies, and then to bring Claudia out to the garden to do a little volunteer work there.

Then Yolanda sat down comfortably at the table, saying with a sigh, "It feels good to take a little break from work!" She smiled at Claudia. "I love these smoothies. They are so healthy, so full of nutrients. They give us the energy to keep working. One of them is really a full meal in itself. I love the green tea too. That is such a treat; I think I love it even more than the *té de manzanilla* we used to drink at our ranch."

Claudia sank back into her chair. It felt good to be speaking in Spanish again, like she had with her mother. It felt like home. However, she was starving and really wanted to grab her purse and car keys and get some lunch somewhere. She had supposed that in her volunteer day, she would be getting lunch in the school's kitchen again, and hadn't brought anything. It was against the rules to bring any food to the school, and she was trying to follow those rules. Now she was at a disadvantage, though, depending on the school to feed her.

The smoothie was irresistible and satisfied her hunger. Yolanda was right; it was a full meal in itself. Claudia had questions for Yolanda.

"How do you like this school for Valeria?"

"We love it! Oh yes! It's beautiful here!"

"Do you know about this book?"

"Oh, the white book? There are a lot of those white books here, you know."

"Have you ever read it?"

Yolanda smiled apologetically. "I am not much of a reader. And I don't read or speak English, you know."

"Right." Claudia smiled and continued questioning. "The book says some strange things that I don't really understand. Did you know it says things like the moon is alive?"

Yolanda tilted her head to one side. "The moon is alive? I don't understand that. But then, I didn't go very far in school." She shrugged. "Only to third grade. But if the moon is alive, what about those men who landed on the moon and walked around up there?"

"Exactly."

Yolanda smiled. "It's a funny idea, isn't it? I guess there are all kinds of ideas like that in books."

"Yolanda, tell me, what has Valeria been learning here?"

"What has she been learning here? Oh! Valeria is getting an education like we never had. The teachers are so good. They tell the children stories and teach them games, and later when they are ready, they will teach them reading and writing and everything they need to go forward in life and be successful. It's very expensive, you know. Very, *very* expensive. Oscar—that's my husband—and I, we work off the tuition. We both work here full-time, about fifty hours a week each, and in exchange we live here." She gestured widely with her arm and her eyes lit up. "It's like living in a mansion. And we eat here—there's always plenty. It's like a dream."

Claudia realized that The Hawthorne School was getting a lot more in "volunteer" hours from Yolanda and Oscar than it was getting from her. And that Yolanda seemed to feel it was not only a fair deal, but that the Garcias were getting the better of the bargain. Zelma's words came back to her: "We'll take everything you have to give," and "We'll work you hard."

But as she drained her glass and her hunger abated, Claudia felt less tense, less urgent about all of it. Her perspective shifted. Yolanda was peaceful and grateful, and Claudia found her mind floating to meet Yolanda's. This *was* a beautiful place, and really, did it matter so much what it said in an old white book? What really mattered was that Henry was enjoying school for the first time, and the school was not complaining about him. Yet.

She said to herself, in fairness, that she hadn't read the whole book. She hadn't retained much of what she *had* read, because she hadn't understood it. There could be later parts that put into perspective the pages that seemed peculiar to her.

And she'd been half asleep as she read it. Anyway, if there was any need for concern, she would deal with it as it came up. She could, after all, just keep Henry here for preschool and then switch him to the public school for kindergarten if The Hawthorne School turned out to be too religious or in any way not right for her boy. So what, if the founder had a few out-of-the-ordinary ideas? At four years of age, Henry couldn't be very influenced by those ideas. Probably most children his age thought the moon was alive. He would learn scientific facts later anyway. This was the time for fantasy and play.

Claudia smiled again at Yolanda. Maybe she, too, could be a friend, like Maggie and Niles.

Claudia followed Yolanda outside. The winding paths bordered by flowers and trees, the beautiful architecture, and the autumn fragrances in the air all combined to intoxicate a person who was susceptible to beauty, as Claudia was.

Apparently, Yolanda and Oscar were both susceptible, too, because they stood and looked around themselves, inhaling and exhaling, before setting to work. From an open window, strains of flute music floated on the air above them. It was lovely and haunting, played as it was by unseen musicians and combining with the autumn breeze.

Oscar, wearing overalls like Yolanda, was friendly and quiet, leaving his wife to give the instructions. They pruned and trimmed and picked up fallen branches and sticks, and as they worked, they talked about Mexico and Costa Rica, and their children and their hopes for them.

They then moved on to work on the hedge maze.

Oscar set to work trimming the sides of the hedges, and Claudia and Yolanda followed suit.

"I'd like to ask you both a little favor," said Claudia, setting down her hedge trimmers as her arms grew tired.

"Certainly," said Yolanda.

"I would like you to just not tell Zelma that I speak Spanish."

Oscar looked concerned, and Yolanda knitted her brows. "A secret? You want us to keep a secret from the director?"

"No, not a secret. A *surprise*! She has no idea, you see. I'm pretty sure I never mentioned that my mother was from Costa

Rica or that she always spoke Spanish with me. I'd like to save it as a surprise."

Yolanda and Oscar didn't fully commit. Claudia could see they didn't want to do anything to jeopardize their positions here.

She didn't know why this idea had come to her so forcefully, but some inner prompting had pierced her cloud of well-being and told her from this point on to keep back from Zelma whatever information she could. It was something in the way Zelma had changed before her eyes this morning, shifting from warm to cold, to warm again. There was an element of control in it. It was probably nothing, but Claudia couldn't forget Zelma's hard stare when Claudia asserted herself. At the time, Claudia had backed down weakly, and she despised herself for it. But still, she would be more cautious now.

She would keep Henry enrolled, she would volunteer, and she would feel grateful and peaceful. And at the same time, she would stop being so "open and trusting." Just in case. Out of an abundance of caution, perhaps.

27

AT A QUARTER past three, Zelma appeared beside them in the center of the hedge maze. Her arrival was sudden. She came through the gravel walkway, and she was wreathed in smiles. Claudia couldn't be sure if Zelma had been listening first, out of sight. She wondered why she would even have such a thought. It was just that this sweet-appearing little woman had become an enigma to Claudia. At times she was motherly and almost even loving; she seemed to understand everything about Claudia's struggle as an insecure single mother, and to sympathize deeply, offering the most down-to-earth help. And then at other times, she turned cold, as when Claudia had asked to see Evelyn before class. She subjected Claudia to odd "tests" such as asking her to mend the discarded costumes. Claudia supposed that leaving her waiting the entire morning in her office was another test. It must have been: to see if Claudia would leave the campus or, against orders, walk up to Evelyn's classroom. And if it were a test, had Claudia passed or failed? She felt, with some confusion, that she had failed in her own eyes while passing in Zelma's estimation. She saw now that a normal reaction would have been to proactively search for Zelma or else go home. Instead, she had done as she was told. She was a rule follower, and she knew it. She had a fear of being rude. Her tendency was to cave under pressure. Devin had always challenged her to stand up and push back. Because of him, she had learned to assert herself—at least, with *him*. But why did she allow this little woman to be so rude and imperious with her? She wouldn't—not anymore.

"*Here* you are!" exclaimed Zelma, her eyes, bright with joy, trained on Claudia. And then, turning to the Garcias: "*Buenas tardes, Oscar. Buenas tardes, Yolanda. ¿Qué día tan precioso. ¿Verdad que sí?*"

The Garcias assented that the day was indeed beautiful, and Claudia gave a secret, conspiratorial smile to them and then looked to Zelma for translation. The Garcias returned to their work.

"I'm just saying that it's a gorgeous day. I see you all managed to communicate despite the language barrier. Yolanda is especially good at communicating with signs and gestures. I knew you would understand each other. You really are a marvel, Claudia, throwing yourself into every little enterprise here and cooperating with everyone. I can't tell you how much I appreciate it." She reached out her hand and gave Claudia's arm an affectionate squeeze. Despite her intention to take a different stance with Zelma, that touch undid her resolve.

Zelma continued: "You fit in so well. I love the way you just go ahead and make yourself at home here. It's a pity, but as I told you this morning, I had to be away from the office all day."

"Oh," said Claudia, "but you didn't. I mean, I guess you *thought* you told me that, but actually you didn't. You said you would be right back after bringing Henry to his class, so I waited for you in your office, like you said. In fact, I waited there for two and a half hours, wondering where you were."

Zelma looked at Claudia strangely.

"You don't remember what I told you?" asked Zelma in a perplexed tone.

"No, I *do* remember. You said to wait for you, and you would come back and answer all my questions."

The look of concern on Zelma's face made Claudia wonder if Zelma was doubting herself now. Was the director slipping mentally? She wondered, not for the first time, how old Zelma really was. Claudia felt guilty for making such a big deal of this issue.

But Zelma said, "I could almost think you're playing games with me now, Claudia. But of course, you wouldn't do that. It's only a misunderstanding, I'm sure. Dear me . . . well, you've had a lot to process in the past couple of days, so it's no wonder— but I do feel bad that you thought you had to wait for me when I had already told you—well, it doesn't matter now." Zelma smiled again and hooked her arm through Claudia's. "Let's go together to pick up Henry."

As they walked along arm in arm, Claudia could feel the embracing energy coming from the director. One small part of her wanted to pull her arm away, but she ignored that. It was a good feeling to be embraced.

"Claudia, I want you to settle in with us and feel at home here. You are a part of our family now. You know, and I have no doubt you *do* know Henry Vera is a very special boy."

"Thank you," said Claudia gratefully. "I'm glad you feel that way." Apparently he still hadn't disgraced himself at school. It was still early days.

"I know that you worry that you're not doing a good job as a mother."

Claudia realized with a shock that Niles must have revealed her confidences to Zelma. She hadn't told him they were confidences, but shouldn't he have known? What business did he have to go to the director of the school and talk about what she had told him in a private conversation? Why would he do such a thing? She had thought that Niles was becoming her friend.

Scanning her face, Zelma said, "Yes, Niles told me all about your little talk. In our family, we share everything, dear heart. And it's all right. Perhaps you *are* the reason Henry's behavior has been problematic. But you didn't *know*—how could you possibly know?"

"Know what?"

"How could you know that Henry—after all, your first and only child—is remarkable. No. I mean it. When I say he is 'special,' I don't mean he's special just like every other child. I mean something else. He is *extraordinary*."

"Extraordinary?" asked Claudia. She hoped that Zelma was not setting her up. The punchline might turn out to be "extraordinarily difficult." She said, "I don't know exactly what you mean. In what way—"

"Henry," said Zelma, "has the mark of greatness on him. I can see it."

"The mark of greatness?"

"You mentioned that his teacher in that *other* school said she had never taught a boy like him in all her years?"

"Yes," admitted Claudia, coloring at the humiliating memory.

"I'm sure she was right. A child like Henry doesn't come along every year. Perhaps only once in an educator's career will there be such a child. The problem there was, *she* didn't have the wisdom to see his greatness. She ignorantly mistook it for a problem. Imagine! The same thing happened to Albert Einstein and many other great people. A child like yours has to be educated in a very particular way—something that teacher wouldn't know anything about, of course. You mark my words. Henry is a future *leader*. He will make history. But he must receive the proper training so that he can step into his greatness when the time comes."

As much as Claudia wanted to believe that Henry was as amazing as Zelma said, she couldn't help but suspect that Zelma was only flattering her to make up for leaving her waiting in her office all morning. All people wanted to believe they were special, and all parents wanted to be told their children were extraordinary. Zelma probably said things like this to all the parents. She must find most people only too willing to believe such honeyed words.

Zelma gave her a sidelong glance and added, "And you, Claudia, you are extraordinary, too. You have periods of confusion, I know, because you are in mourning. Oh yes, Evelyn told me about your little tête-à-tête. Nothing happens here that I don't know about. That's how I'm able to make sure that everyone is well taken care of."

28

BY THE TIME they reached Evelyn's cold classroom, the only children left were Henry and Anthony. Now Claudia noticed that Anthony, too, had a red string bracelet on his little wrist. That reminded her to check Evelyn's wrist, and she saw several of them there, visible from under the rolled-up sleeve of a chunky, hand-knitted sweater. In another circumstance, she would have presumed these bracelets to be part of the boho look. But not on little boys. And presumably the little girls had them too.

It occurred to Claudia that since Anthony was here, she would get a chance to meet his parents when they came to pick him up, if his family lived nearby. To her disappointment, Zelma held out her hand to him and said, "Here we go, Anthony," and the child rushed to her. "I think Claudia has some questions for you, Evelyn. I'll leave you two to talk."

In the kitchen area, Evelyn had her back turned. Claudia, standing at the children's table, could see that she was making little green tea. Claudia was surprised that she felt impatient for Evelyn to finish and bring it to her. It almost made her feel irritable that Evelyn was taking so long. It stood to reason that she would be thirsty. She hadn't had anything to drink—or to eat, for that matter—since Yolanda gave her the smoothie, and that was before she had worked a couple of hours in the garden. While waiting, she turned her attention to Henry. He was sitting on the floor by the book case, his legs stretched out straight before him, playing with small, colorful felt dolls who wore tall red caps. He was lost in play and didn't seem to need her attention, or in fact even know that she was there. She was glad to see him comfortable in his new classroom.

Evelyn came to the children's table with green juice for Henry and tea for Claudia and herself. Now Henry looked up and came running to join them at the little table. Claudia's questions jumbled in her mind like clothes in a dryer, and she started with Anthony.

"Anthony Jones—where did Zelma take him? Is there another pickup area? Or does he live here? I thought I'd get to meet his parents."

"You *have*," said Evelyn.

"I have—what?"

"Met his parent. Zelma. Anthony and Zelma live here."

Claudia saw Evelyn though the steam of the hot cup that warmed her hands. "Zelma lives here? I didn't know that." But then a more concerning thought came to her: "Zelma's his mother? But Zelma has to be—what? Eighty?"

"She adopted him."

Claudia insisted, "But how? At her age, *how*?"

"I know," said Evelyn. "She's unreal, isn't she? He's lucky to have a mother as wise and experienced as she is."

"But she's too *old* to adopt a child, isn't she?"

"Oh, don't you worry about that. Zelma will live forever."

Claudia was drinking the hot tea now as fast as she could. She felt grateful as it revived her, and calmed her turbulent emotions.

"This tea is doing me good," she said. "Would it be rude of me to ask for another cup?"

Evelyn smiled, and the smile looked wrong on her face. "Of course. I'll start the kettle again."

When Evelyn returned from the kitchen, Claudia asked her, "Can you tell me about the red bracelets?"

Evelyn turned her head left and right in that strange bird-like manner of hers. Her right hand moved reflexively to her left wrist as if to cover the row of bracelets there. "Tell you about them? Sure. What would you like to know?"

"Well, like, is there any special meaning behind them, and why do *you* wear them? You know—just in general, what's the story with the bracelets?"

Evelyn said, "Oh. You know how some schools have a special T-shirt that the students and teachers wear? Or some schools even have a uniform? I guess the psychology behind that is to give the children a sense of belonging, right? Of being part of the team or the community of the school. We don't have special T-shirts or uniforms here. But for each child, we do a little ceremony of welcome, and we mark that with a red string bracelet—one for the child and one for the teacher."

"Interesting. And why red string?"

"Well, it's an easy material to come by, isn't it? It's very 'eco.' You've noticed we don't use plastic here. We ourselves make what we have—as much as possible. So this is an easy item to make. And it's a universal sort of thing, the red string brace-let. Jungian, you could say. Archetypal. You find it in so many cultures: Kabbalah, Buddhist, Hindu, on and on. In some cultures, it might be for joining two soul mates. In others, it's for warding off the evil eye—spiritual protection, in other words. You get the idea."

Claudia wasn't entirely sure that she did. Not completely. But her attention was now diverted by a word Evelyn had just used: "spiritual."

"This morning, I had the chance to read a little of the white book—*The World of the Child.*"

Evelyn nodded, her small black eyes intent, encouraging Claudia to go on.

"I found it—confusing."

Evelyn lifted her cup and drank her tea.

"First of all, there's this phrase, 'the Science of Spirit.' The word 'spirit' comes up a lot. Is this a religious school? Because no one told me that it was. I didn't know." Claudia's words sounded more energized than she now actually felt. Somehow, she didn't care anymore about the book or about the sense of caution that had been struggling against her wish to go to sleep as her eyes had skimmed the words. She turned to Evelyn, ready to accept her assurances.

Evelyn spoke soothingly. "There's nothing to worry about. 'Spirit' is a word like 'imagination' or 'creativity,' do you see? Sometimes it's hard to find the right word. Some things are . . . ineffable, meaning there is not any exact word that fits. Words are words."

Claudia had not realized before how soothing Evelyn's voice was. She lost herself in its floating tones, feeling herself carried along as if by meditation music. She was unaware of the words themselves. It was the flow of sound that surrounded her and filled her ears in the most pleasant way, and she could feel a smile lifting the corners of her lips. She felt supremely well in her mind and heart. Her eyes slipped sideways to see the clouds moving slowly across the sky, and they were exquisitely beautiful, so beautiful that tears of happiness filled her eyes.

CHAPTER

29

THE RIDE HOME was quiet. The countryside all around wore an air of enchantment. Everything—the fields, the trees, the clouds—it was all unnaturally beautiful, like a scene from an imaginary world. Claudia could almost have forgotten that Henry was in his car seat behind her. He was not sleeping, but gazing tranquilly out the window. Normally Claudia would have kept up a cheery back and forth with him about his school day, but she had no desire to pump him for information, and no anxiety about what he might have done. It was clear that Evelyn had no concerns about his behavior, so why should Claudia fret?

He began singing a Spanish children's song, breathily, softly, and Claudia felt content listening to him.

That night at bath time, she felt an impulse to get that red string bracelet off him. There was something about the bracelet that she didn't like, but she couldn't say what it was. Her attempt nearly ruined their peaceful evening. Henry fought her and yelled that he needed his bracelet and he wouldn't let her take it from him. He claimed Miss Applegate had told him he was to never take it off, "ever." She gave up immediately. She could always cut it off him while he slept. If Evelyn had questions about its disappearance, she could make up an excuse. But then, Henry would be outraged in the morning and would start off his day in a bad temper. Things were going so well, why antagonize him over such a triviality?

30

WHO ARE THE Indigo Children?
By Aquarian Sunflower, www.enlightenedwaterbearer.net
Are you an Indigo child?
Are you the parent of an Indigo child?
Indigo children began appearing in large numbers in the 1970s. These children are special. Some, in fact, call them "the Chosen Children." They are identified by the color of their auras, which is a rich, royal blue. These are children who are more comfortable on their own in nature than in a classroom with other children. Unfortunately, they have often been misdiagnosed with ADHD or have been seen as hyperactive or difficult to handle.

Indigo children see through the falseness of mainstream society. They cannot tolerate rigid rules. In fact, they know that rules do not apply to them. They challenge authority. They are uncannily perceptive. They often feel out of place in the world as it is and are highly emotional. In other words, these people are different and therefore often misunderstood.

However, Indigo children have a distinct mission. They are old souls. They are being sent here now in greater numbers in order to shift the destiny of humanity and to open up the world to a new age. They are highly gifted. Many of them see visions. Sometimes their parents say that it is almost eerie how their Indigo children perceive things that are hidden from average people.

If you have always felt special, if you have often felt that you did not fit in, and if you have an inner knowing that you are marked for an exceptional destiny of some kind, you are probably an Indigo child. If so, know that you are here in this lifetime to establish paths for the generations that are to come.

*   *   *

Claudia looked up from her browser and rubbed her eyes. Of all the ridiculous things she had ever read, this had to be the most outrageous. It was as weird as the white book. It was so transparently an attempt by adults to claim special status for their children (or themselves) without any justification. Was *this* what Julia Hawthorne believed? Would she have considered Henry, for example, to be one of these Indigo children? He, after all, fit some of the description. So did a lot of people. That did not qualify them all to be world leaders, carving out a new path for all of humanity with their extraordinary perceptions. Claudia didn't like that *The World of the Child* referenced the term "Indigo children." She tried to reassure herself. The book was only a detail in the whole picture of The Hawthorne School. Henry's happiness and ability to succeed in the Hawthorne environment was really the main thing.

Claudia texted Maggie.

Claudia: *Have you ever heard of Indigo children?*
Maggie: *???*
Maggie: *Is it like a brand of clothing?*
Claudia: *Mentioned in Julia Hawthorne's book*
Maggie: *Oh, like I told you, I never read it. My bad!*
Claudia: *So I looked it up. Indigo children ae supposed to be special people with a mission to lead humanity???*
Maggie: *Huh. OK . . .?*
Claudia: *So you don't know anything about it?*
Maggie: *Gee, IDK. Maybe ask Henry's teacher if you're curious. That's what I would do.*

31

IN THE MORNING, Henry was once again excited to go to school. Instead of Claudia hurrying Henry, it was Henry hurrying Claudia, knocking on the bathroom door and yelling, "Mom! What's taking so long? We'll be late!" Claudia had to smile. What a change this was from his days of misery at the old school.

In the Main Hall, she left him with Zelma. She drove away, thinking about Indigo children and about her conversation of the day before with Evelyn and about the idea of Zelma being the mother of a four-year-old. She wanted to think more about that, to try to reason out why Zelma would want to adopt a child at her age, but her temples began to pound.

When she got to the office, she asked Stephanie for ibuprofen and took two of them with water, but it only muffled the pain in her head. She felt depressed and found herself moving more slowly, unmotivated to greet clients, uninterested in their complaints. She thought only of Henry and wished to be at school with him.

She had to wonder if she was getting burned out on massage. She used to love it and look forward to each appointment of her day. Now, quite suddenly, she felt miserable as she looked around her massage room. She didn't want to be here. She felt drawn, as if magnetized, to The Hawthorne School, as if she could only be at peace there. Little concerns about the white book or about expressions on Zelma's face seemed unimportant to her now. There was something binding her to the school, calling her back. She wanted to walk out of the chiropractic clinic, and if she hadn't needed the paycheck, she would have. There was only one place she wanted to be, and that was at The Hawthorne School.

*　*　*

On Saturday, Henry and Claudia stayed at home. Claudia felt despondent. Henry began to tantrum in the afternoon and went on until he wore himself out. She didn't dare to take him to the park or on any errands, for fear that he would throw himself on the ground in a public place and bellow.

Claudia thought how fortunate it was that Happy Start was not seeing this escalation in Henry's misbehavior. She was sure they would have thrown him out if he acted up like this in their school. And yet, he didn't act this way at The Hawthorne School. It was because they understood him and knew how to work with him. *They know how to work with him better than I do,* she thought gloomily, as she watched him writhe on the floor over some frustration he could not even name.

But he slept soundly and woke up on Sunday in a better mood.

At breakfast, Claudia asked, "Henry, did you sleep well? Did you have a nice dream?"

"Um." Henry picked the raisins out of his oatmeal. One day he demanded raisins and couldn't eat oatmeal without them, and the next day he hated them and cried at the sight of them. This was a no-raisin day, but at least he didn't cry. He tightened his face in concentration. "I dreamed about the forest. We were all there, looking for secret people."

"Oh," said Claudia. "Secret people! What kind of secret people?"

Henry frowned. "I don't remember. I need to have that dream again."

*　*　*

Maggie and Violet popped over. As always, Maggie insisted that they all go out into the sunshine. The children played in the park, chasing each other and shouting for joy.

Claudia needed to get some perspective, some reassurance from Maggie.

"I love The Hawthorne School for Henry. But sometimes I have mixed feelings. Or actually, I guess I go back and forth. Like, I wonder about Zelma, for instance. How did a woman her age manage to adopt a four-year-old? It's . . . I don't know. It's kind of weird."

Maggie nodded and shrugged her jacket up closer to her ears as a cold wind blew between them.

"Yeah. Well, Zelma is so maternal, you know? And super-young for her age, right? But I agree with you. It *is* weird. But then again, people in general are weird everywhere you go, aren't they?"

Claudia laughed. "I guess so. *I* always think so."

Maggie frowned, a troubled cloud filling her eyes. "You don't really think it's *weird-weird,* though, do you? I mean, you don't think there's something *wrong* with the school, or anything like that, right?"

"No, I'm not saying that," said Claudia. "But it's just Zelma herself."

Maggie looked at the ground, a crease forming between her eyebrows. "What do you mean?"

"She gave me a volunteer job at the school that seemed like a waste of time. Evelyn implied it was a sort of test, just to see if I would do it. I don't understand that."

Maggie met Claudia's eyes with concern. "Oh? I have no idea what that's about. But then, I think maybe you've had more interactions with Zelma than I have?"

Claudia was disappointed. She wasn't going to get any questions cleared up by Maggie.

Maggie suggested, "Maybe the stresses of her job are a lot for her. Hey! How old do you think she *is*?"

"No idea. But she's got to be up there, right? In some ways she seems very young, the way she walks; the way she moves. But then, in some ways, you can see she's . . . ancient."

"I think someone said she's in her nineties," said Maggie, "but I don't know."

"Wow. That's incredible."

"Yeah, and maybe it explains some things?"

"It does. I'd love to be in such good shape when I'm as old as Zelma. However old she is."

Maggie looked toward the swings where the children were playing. "I mean, Violet is doing so well at Hawthorne. I'd hate to think . . ."

"And Henry is too. For the first time. And I'm so tired of moving and searching, you know? I'm just tired in general."

"Yeah, don't move, Claudia. Please stay. When you really stop to think about it, we're both really lucky to have The Hawthorne School. And I feel lucky to have a friend like you," she added, almost shyly.

Claudia smiled. "Likewise." But she doubted that Maggie could feel lucky to be her friend. She didn't feel she was putting much into the friendship. Maggie always assured her that she felt so supported by Claudia and she didn't know what she would ever do without her. But Claudia knew that she spent most of their time together talking about herself.

*　*　*

For the rest of the day, after Maggie and Violet had left them, Henry was just as miserable as he had been the day before. Nothing she did or said could make him happy. When not raging, he spoke listlessly about "his friend." Claudia questioned him gently. He was not talking about Violet, he grumbled. It seemed he now had an imaginary friend. Claudia had had one as a child too. Her friend had been "Cassie, the girl with the bright hair," and she remembered that figment of her imagination as vividly as she remembered real people from her childhood. Cassie had made her feel comforted and less alone. She was glad that Henry had an imaginary friend, actually. It probably was good for him, as an only child. She thought it had been good for her.

"My friend came to my sermonomy. He only comes when I'm at school. Why doesn't he come here?"

"He *can* come here, Henry. Of course he can. Just imagine him here."

This threw Henry into a rage. "I *can't* imagine him here! He's my spear guy! I don't imagine him! He *comes*! For *real*!"

"Your spear guy? What's a spear guy?"

The term "spirit guide" floated up in her mind. Where had it come from? The white book. Spear guy . . . spirit guide. Is that what Henry was trying to say?

"Henry, are you saying *spirit guide*?"

Henry lunged at her and tried to strike her, but she held his little wrists. "Calm down! Calm down!" she shouted at him. She felt herself in danger of losing control. She couldn't allow that to happen. If she lost control, where would they be then?

Writhing in her grip, Henry spat at her.

"I *hate* you, Mom. You're bad. You don't know anything! You're a bad girl. I want my teacher. I love Miss Applegate. Not you. Go away!"

He threw himself against the wall in a demonstration of his fury. He wouldn't let her come near, but only wailed in misery. All his raging made her headache worse. She checked herself for fever, wondering if she were really ill, but she didn't have a temperature.

Tomorrow she'd bring him to school, where they understood him, and all would be well. She had never found anything that worked for him except this school. Perhaps the only good thing she had done so far as a mom was to get him into The Hawthorne School.

32

O N WAKING THE next day, Claudia and Henry both felt so ill that she considered calling him in absent. Clients in the office had been talking about the flu that was going around. She might have brought a bug home; they both seemed to be fighting something off. Henry was whiny and lethargic, and she would have whined, too, if there had been anyone to listen or care. But they didn't have temperatures, and she didn't think they had complaints that required doctor visits, so she dragged herself out the door, and Henry, blessedly, came willingly along with her.

Once Zelma had taken Henry upstairs and Claudia had been given a tall, cold glass of juice and her first task, all the fragments in her mind slid back into place. She felt well once again. Actually, she felt better than just "well." Her headache was miraculously gone, her omnipresent anxiety was muted, and her heart was peaceful.

Zelma held true to her promise to keep Claudia busy. Her first task was to sort out a wooden bin of used, mixed crayons by color into smaller bins. Zelma had set her up in a tiny, vacant office just down the hall from her own, where Claudia sat at a table and could look out onto the expansive, green lawns throughout the morning as she worked. Of course, she suspected that this might be another pointless task. Were these crayons really needed, or was Zelma again testing her level of cooperation? Well, very likely the crayons were needed. This was a school for children, after all. And if this *was* only a test, then Claudia was determined to pass it. The weekend had proved to her that Henry did indeed have a problem, a problem another school would not tolerate, and a problem that seemed to be getting not better with time, but worse. If Zelma and The Hawthorne School thought that he had no problem, and that he was in fact extraordinary in some way, then she had better do what she could to keep him there. She worked quickly, her hair tucked behind her ears. She did feel that the work was a little demeaning and could have been done by a second-grader, but she gave it her full attention anyway. The Hawthorne School seemed to have a profound psychological and physical effect on her. When she was here, she felt so good. She realized she had never had a headache within the walls of the school but almost always had them at home and at work now. Somehow, she felt peaceful and healed here.

At ten thirty, Niles appeared at the office door to free her from crayon sorting and take her to the kitchen, where together they loaded up trolleys—one for her and one for him—to deliver lunches to the classrooms.

"I made some tea to warm you up," said Niles as they arrived at the kitchen. "Last time, you complained that it was cold in here."

Claudia was touched by his thoughtfulness and his concern for her comfort.

"Who made the lunches?" she asked, imagining that Niles had been one of the chefs and wishing that she could have been working with him this morning instead of sorting crayons. She drained her cup quickly, because the "hot" tea was cooling off rapidly in the icy kitchen.

"Some other folks. They're out with trolleys now. We'll each take a hall."

"Other folks? Parents? Will I meet them?"

Niles had his back to her as he pulled containers from the refrigerator, and didn't seem to hear.

"I'd like to meet other parents," she repeated as he turned around.

His eyes fixed on hers intensely in a way that startled her while it fascinated her, because she couldn't identify its meaning. Had she annoyed him? She couldn't imagine how. But then he resumed his usual friendliness as he said, "We'll all be too busy right now. But you will be with them before long."

As they walked, Claudia felt absurdly proud of her task and her status as a volunteer parent. She felt good about doing something useful to the running of the school. It made her feel like an insider. Niles directed Claudia to go left while he went right. She was to knock, enter, and bring each classroom's delivery to its kitchen area and place the trays on the counter there. Claudia wheeled the trolley as quickly as she could without causing the trays to jump. She would get to see the older children's classrooms in action and get an idea of what Henry would have in his future if she kept him at The Hawthorne School.

She soon found that knocking was an unnecessary precaution. Classroom after classroom was empty. Of course. It was morning. The children would be outside, exploring the vast acreage, climbing trees and studying bugs. She was disappointed not to see the children at work, but then remembered that running and playing outside *was* a major part of their work. The emptiness of each classroom did invite her to indulge her curiosity and look around longer and with more attention than she would have been able to do if the children and teachers had been there.

Each room had musical instruments: a guitar hanging on a wall, a set of bongo drums in a corner. In every room was that same portrait of Gabriel Hawthorne she had seen in Evelyn's class on the day of her tour. And each room had that strange and enchanting art: chalk drawings on the board and framed paintings on the walls. The paintings depicted a bright fantasy world, and the colors shimmered. They gave a feeling of joyful optimism, and Claudia felt happy just to look at them.

In one room, she found a stack of handmade botany books. It looked like the students were creating their own textbooks, with their own drawings of the plants and flowers that could be found in the region. As she turned the pages, she thought that these were the finest examples of botanical art she had ever seen.

Instead of the Latin names labeling the plants, however, each plant was accompanied by a smiling, delightful little winged creature. A fairy. Julia Hawthorne had written in that white book that "the imagination is the direct route to the soul." These handmade books were lovely, works of art in themselves.

At the last classroom door, Claudia didn't bother to knock and brusquely pushed her trolley into the only occupied classroom. She stopped short, embarrassed. The one time she didn't knock, that *would* be the one time she should have.

She heard recorded music similar to the meditation music she played in her massage room. The children, all about ten years old, were seated in a circle on flat cushions on the floor, with large sheets of black construction paper before them. They were drawing colorful swirls—and some of them were drawing intricate mandalas—making striking-looking colored chalk paintings. Oddly, no one was speaking. The teacher's sandals were stepping around the perimeter of their circle, slowly, as if in rhythm to the slow music. Claudia glanced up at her face and realized that the teacher wasn't looking at the children's work at all; she wasn't even looking at the children. She seemed to be in her own world. She apparently hadn't heard Claudia come in.

Claudia, keeping her head down in deference, pushed the trolley as quietly as she could past the children and soundlessly unloaded their trays onto the kitchen counter. As she returned with her trolley to the door, she stole a glance at the class, but remarkably, no one appeared to notice her at all. It was as if she were invisible. She was grateful to not have disrupted the class or attracted the teacher's ire; on the other hand, there was something disturbing about what she had just witnessed.

When she described the strange scene to Niles, he didn't find it strange at all.

"Sounds like they were focused. What's wrong with that?"

She'd spent too long poking around each room and had missed the other parents, who were working on other things, Niles said. Beginning to feel at home here, Claudia took the initiative to put the kettle on to boil to make tea for them again. She needed a warm-up, and the tea was so satisfying; better than coffee even.

"I've always had a very active imagination, I guess." Claudia conceded.

"Well," said Niles, "that's good."

"Mm," Claudia said, hesitating. "Not in my case. I mean, it's great for making art, sure. Not that I have any time to make any art any more. I used to, before Henry. I painted in all media. I loved making murals and children's book illustrations. Maybe that's why the art here touched my heart so much. It's just what I love: bright colors, happy worlds. But sometimes my imagination . . ." Here, she trailed off. Why would she confide in this man, after he had shown that he would repeat anything she said to Zelma? She should not tell him anything that she would not say directly to Zelma herself.

"But sometimes . . ." prompted Niles.

Claudia just shook her head and smiled down into her teacup.

"Sometimes," persisted Niles, "you imagine things? Maybe you have a little paranoia or something like that?"

"Well, 'paranoia' is a strong word. But I guess we can *all* get carried away with our imaginations sometimes. Right? We can all be suspicious of others' motives. Right? I mean, doesn't everyone have thoughts like that?"

Niles studied her for a few seconds, and she immediately regretted those stupid words that had tumbled out of her mouth. Why did she gab like this to him? What made her want to share her insecurities and odd thoughts with him? She should be putting her best foot forward. For one thing, she really liked him. For another thing, he did have the fault of repeating what she told him.

"So you doubt your own impressions."

Claudia didn't like this image he was forming of her. "That's not true. I know my own mind. For example, my boss thinks this school is kind of strange. But I don't question what I've seen with my own eyes—that this is a healthy environment for Henry."

Niles's gaze pierced deeper and his jaw set.

"Why are you talking to people about The Hawthorne School? I mean, there's no way they could understand it. They haven't been here, have they? So nothing they could say about it could have any value for you. I learned that at the beginning, and hopefully you've learned it now too: don't talk to people out there about our school. They won't get it."

He was speaking to her as if he had a right to give her orders, to tell her who she could talk to and what she could talk about. But she was sure he didn't mean it that way. He was just loyal to the school.

Claudia felt she'd somehow lost merit in Niles's eyes.

He continued: "Who else do you talk to, besides people at work?"

That was a good question. Who else *did* she talk to? The cashier at the grocery store. Clients, but those conversations were all about them. "You know, now that I think about it, you, Maggie, Evelyn, and Zelma are the people I talk to most these days."

"That's good. You want to talk to supportive people, people who understand. All the critics in the peanut gallery—they don't matter. Don't make the mistake of trying to make them understand."

Claudia didn't like the way he assumed authority over her. Maybe Fiona hadn't liked it either. But he was so likable otherwise. He was enthusiastic and knew so much about The Hawthorne School and child development. Devin was talkative too, but he only ever talked about himself. Niles conversed *with* her *about* her, and about things she cared about. It felt like their relationship was deepening. She didn't want to mess it up.

"And getting back to what you were saying before, about imagining things about people. See, I think that's a good trait. I mean, it's good to be imaginative, but it's even better to be aware of the fact that you tend to misunderstand people and situations. You waffle back and forth, don't you? You're indecisive. That's because you already know that you can't trust yourself. That's natural for everybody, isn't it? I mean, how often in life do we get hold of the wrong end of the stick, you know?"

"Wait," Claudia objected. "I never said I tend to misunderstand people. And I didn't say that I don't trust myself." But hadn't she said exactly that? And wasn't it true?

Niles shrugged. "No offense. I think we *should* doubt ourselves sometimes. That's just humility. We should be open to
other interpretations. That openness leads to a peaceful heart.
That's what Julia Hawthorne wrote."

Claudia was glad to get off the topic of her doubts and
misperceptions, and onto the topic of Julia Hawthorne. "Okay,
I'm glad you reminded me, because I wanted to ask you. Have
you read that *book*?" She said it with a tone that she hoped
would encourage him to share her impression that the book was
in some ways offbeat, to say the least.

"A few times, in fact. Now, speaking of being open to other
interpretations, *The World of the Child* will lead you to think in
new ways. You've started reading it?"

Niles was brewing more tea for them now that they had
finished their cups.

"What I was surprised by"—and here Claudia noticed that
she was softening her reaction from 'bothered' to 'surprised';
she really didn't feel *bothered* by the book anymore; she didn't
feel bothered by anything at all—"or I guess I should say what I
didn't understand was some reference to the moon? And something about Indigo children?"

Niles set the steaming cup before Claudia. There was something touching, nurturing even, in the gesture. "Some children
have a special—I don't know—sensitivity. We like to call them
Indigo children. In fact, I've been thinking *you* might be one,
Claudia. Sensitive, aware, open, in touch with nature. That's
you, isn't it?"

Claudia held the cup beneath her face, inhaling the aroma.
"Well, I guess anyone would like to think they're all of those
things." She smiled inwardly, wondering if Niles was trying to
flatter her, and hoping that he was. "And the moon," she said.
"Doesn't it say that the moon is alive?"

"You have a problem with that?"

Claudia laughed softly, thinking he was kidding.

"Even molecular biologists are considering these ideas that
came intuitively to Julia Hawthorne. They're starting to see it
now: water is alive. Rocks, planets, DNA—it's all alive, Claudia.
See, the atoms in your body behave exactly the same way as the

planets in the solar system. There are patterns within patterns. It's all about the gyre."

"The gyre?" she asked. The air around her face felt like a soft wave, and she lifted her hands to touch it. It felt blue. Funny to think: she could feel the blueness of the wave in her fingertips.

In her ears, his last sentence echoed. "It's all about the gyre. Gyre. Gyre." Claudia felt so peaceful listening to Niles, and she smiled, thinking of the poem she'd memorized in childhood, "Jabberwocky." How did the lines go? "'Twas brillig, and the slithy toves did gyre and gimble in the wabe . . ." The wabe. The wave. She was *in* a wave. Or a wabe. From far off, she heard Niles's voice talking, talking.

"Yes, gyre. There are more books you could read, if you want to understand it in depth. Books about quantum mechanics and celestial mechanics."

Claudia closed her eyes and thought of celestial mechanics. She pictured gears shining and spinning in the indigo night sky, gears working in precise perfection and making divine music as they turned, and she knew that all was as it should be.

CHAPTER

33

AFTER SCHOOL, CLAUDIA was so exhausted she couldn't imagine making dinner. She couldn't think what reason she had to be so tired. It wasn't as if she had exerted herself physically. She tried to remember what, in her day at the school, could have drained her of all her energy, but she could only remember chatting with Niles and wondering if there was a possibility of the development of something deep between them. She pulled into the parking lot behind Pam's Diner, and Henry stirred from his listless daydream to crow: "Yay! Pam's! I want pancakes!"

Inside, the familiar diner seemed different, distant, although she couldn't see any physical change. Claudia had brought Henry here several times since they had moved to town. She had immediately been fond of the proprietor, Pam, who now came rushing to their booth and laid a solid hand on both Claudia and Henry.

"Hello, my lovelies! I haven't seen you two in just *forever*. Where have you *been*?"

"My new school!" said Henry excitedly. He liked Pam and rarely acted up in her presence.

Pam stepped back dramatically and put her hands to her cheeks. "Your new *school*? Oh my! Tell me *everything*!" She looked expectantly from Henry to Claudia and back to Henry again, as if she couldn't wait for more information.

"The Hawthorne School!" exclaimed Henry, enjoying Pam's theatrics.

"Hawth—wait! Isn't that the one out on Route 171? Oh, I've heard about that school!"

"It's a giant's castle!" said Henry.

"Oh yes," she went on, "that place that used to be a convent or something like that? Isn't that the most exclusive school around here? Now, I know they don't take just anyone. Goodness, Henry, you got into *that* school? Well, I'm not surprised—a smart boy like you. It's private, isn't it?" Pam asked Claudia.

"Well, yes."

"Expensive," added Pam, her eyes widening, and her thumb brushing her other fingers in a gesture signifying "money."

"Yes, I think so, but they're letting me do some volunteer work, and taking Henry on a sort of scholarship."

"A scholarship! Well, aren't you lucky! Aren't you *blessed*!"

Claudia's heart filled with pleasure and pride.

"It's a Scandinavian nature school. They have the kids outdoors, exploring most of the day."

"Well, now, *I* think that's healthy. That's what kids need. They need to run around and be kids. I bet you just love running around outside, don't you, Henry?"

Henry nodded, his eyes bright.

"And they emphasize healthy eating." Claudia was warming to her topic. "All fresh vegetables they grow right there on the campus."

"Isn't that something? Now, look at him: this is the most chill I've seen Henry so far, so I'd say that school is doing him a world of good. And speaking of healthy eating, what can I get for you lovelies today? Blueberry pancakes for my young man? That's what I thought. And for you, Mamma?"

Claudia scanned the menu, feeling the glow of Pam's admiration.

"I'm craving the veggie burrito."

"Coming right up!"

34

CLAUDIA WAS BACK at work with her recurring malaise. Her overactive imagination suggested that the headaches might signal a brain tumor. But then again, there were days when she had no headache and was full of energy. So maybe the headaches were psychosomatic. She didn't get them when she was on that beautiful campus, talking with Niles. She only got headaches when she was isolated at home with Henry or at work in the chiropractic clinic. She felt distant from Dr. W ever since the day he had been so dismissive of The Hawthorne School. And her work itself had somehow lost its luster. More and more, she felt she had completed her career as a massage therapist and that a new chapter was beginning. She had loved massage from the very start and had always assumed that she would be passionate about it forever, but then, that was so typical of her: to be all excited about something one day and ready to move on to something else the next.

She applied pressure with her elbow to trigger points in Janice Brown's back.

"These massages are so great while they last, but already by the time I get home, my pain returns," complained Janice. It was the same complaint she made every week.

"And have you signed up for that yoga class yet? Or any kind of exercise at all? Pilates or weight training would be good, as I've told you before. You have the ability to see what you need. You have the power to improve your own condition. Pick something you can enjoy. Have you started walking every day? Or even a couple of times a week? *Anything?*" Claudia could hear the irritation in her voice, but she couldn't stop herself. These people expected her to work miracles on them while they refused to see that they were sealing their own fate.

"Oh no," chuckled Janice guiltily. "I'm so bad. It's just that I don't have the time."

"And yet you have the time to come here."

Janice raised her head out of the donut hole and peered through the darkness at Claudia. "Would you rather I didn't?" Claudia's frankness had shocked both of them.

"No, no, of course not. You're my favorite client, Janice."

Janice dropped her face back into the hole and sighed. "I know you're right. I've just got to make the time."

What Claudia would really like to do, she thought as she worked the knots out of Janice's muscles, was to work full-time at The Hawthorne School. Maybe she could get a job of some kind there. Yes! That was it. This new and unexpected idea came to her as an inspiration. She always felt ill, with a pounding headache, at the chiropractic clinic. Yet she felt peaceful and stress-free at the school. And while she did have occasional misgivings about Zelma and The Hawthorne School, now she saw that the best way to confirm or deny her doubts, to really see what was actually going on there, was to spend more time on the campus, to become a true insider. That way, she would certainly see if there was anything in the school's environment that she didn't want for Henry. She could ask Zelma if there was some clerical job or if she could work with the Garcias on the grounds.

To her relief, there was a last-minute client cancellation, giving her a half hour to herself. Dr. W was with a patient, and Stephanie was on the phone.

She went to the kitchenette and made herself a cup of black tea, hoping the caffeine would have some effect on her headache.

As she steeped the tea bag, she wished she could have little green tea. Suddenly, her longing for that herbal mixture was overpowering. It occurred to her to drive to The Hawthorne

School, go into the kitchen, and make herself a cup right there. But of course, her next client was due in a few minutes. Still, the urge was so strong; she decided she would ask Zelma or Niles if she could just take some little green home with her, to have on days off, evenings, and weekends. It might even help Henry to feel as calm as he did at school. They both felt so much better under its beneficial influence.

CHAPTER

35

"You'd like to work here?" Zelma arched an eyebrow.

Claudia flushed. "I know it sounds strange—"

"It doesn't sound a bit strange, dear. Most parents *do* ask to work here. The trouble is, there are only so many jobs. We have to be selective about the parents we take on." Zelma steepled her fingers together, pensive.

"I thought maybe I could offer massage to the staff. Or I could also do something in the artistic line. Painting, designing something? Or maybe you might even have some office work I could do? Or I could work on the grounds with Yolanda and Oscar? It doesn't really matter." And Claudia was surprised as she said these words that it *didn't* really matter. She would gladly give up her career to rake leaves and plant flowers at The Hawthorne School. Suddenly it seemed the most important thing in the world that she be able to be here every day.

"Hmm. I see how eager you are to be a part of our mission. I like that. That's good. Let me see what I can come up with. Mind you, I don't promise anything. But I will look into it—today. In the meantime, I'll take you down to the tunnels."

Claudia felt disappointed. She would do any work at The Hawthorne School, but she would prefer not to work down there.

As if reading her mind, Zelma said, "No, not the Pit, dear. We're going to the storage room. I want you to pick out some clothing for Henry. And for yourself too."

Did Zelma think they looked so poor that they needed handouts? She had been on the receiving end of handouts throughout her childhood and had always hated it. She wondered if it showed in some way that Zelma could see.

"You've noticed—with your observant artist's eye—I'm sure, that all the children are dressed in natural fibers. Cotton. Linen. Fabrics that breathe. The teachers, too, for that matter. And in a certain style and certain hues specific to us. There's a special aesthetic that we adhere to. Everything has to have loveliness and grace, you see. We don't have uniforms. We respect the individual. But our aesthetic, you see—we like to share that. Now that you'll be working with us, I want to make these items available to you. We have a Clothing Room in the tunnels where we keep new garments that are appropriate for our environment. Nothing *jersey*," said Zelma with distaste. "Nothing *stretchy*. No words or logos printed across people's chests, turning them into billboards."

Of course, Claudia had noticed and admired the clothing worn by the students and teachers, and just assumed they shopped at some local boutique she didn't know about yet. But apparently they shopped in the Clothing Room down in the tunnels.

Claudia wondered if she would find the red string bracelets in the Clothing Room too. She set down her teacup and followed Zelma into the depths of the school.

36

CLAUDIA FELT EXHILARATED in the new clothes. It had been a long time since she had paid any attention to what she put on every day. At work, she had been wearing scrubs. At home, she wore yoga clothes. Being a single mom left her little time to fuss about—or even think about—her appearance. As she gazed at herself in the three-fold full-length mirror in the Clothing Room, she was thrilled with this new version of herself. These clothes actually *felt* good to the touch. The colors were soothing. She felt graceful as she turned and saw how the material moved with her.

Zelma was so generous, encouraging her to try on more and add more to her basket, and showed delight at each new addition. "Oh, that suits you marvelously, dear. My, that shade of sky blue is your color! You are beautiful!"

Claudia felt beautiful. Just as she'd expected, her headache had left her soon after she'd entered The Hawthorne School. In the yoga classes she used to take—before Henry was born and she lost all free time—they used to say, "Listen to your body." Claudia was listening to her body now, and it was telling her that she belonged in this place, that she could only feel good here.

Zelma invited Claudia to go up to Henry's classroom so he could change into some new clothes.

Claudia knocked on the classroom door and entered, holding up a new outfit for Henry so that Evelyn could see. Evelyn nodded, and her eyes glittered. She was happy, too, about the new clothes. Everyone was happy.

Even Henry was happy, and he usually didn't care what he wore. He changed right away in the bathroom. He looked so handsome when he came out, and so like all his little classmates who were dressed in the same lovely textures and hues.

Claudia hurried away with his discarded T-shirt and shorts, and felt an impulse to throw them in a trash can in the hallway. She never threw away clothes; someone else could always use them, and she passed them on. But these clothes of Henry's and her own old yoga outfit that was in the basket mingling with all her new things, felt like old energy that she needed to get rid of as quickly and permanently as possible. She shoved the old clothes in the garbage, and when the lid swung shut, she felt relieved to be rid of them.

She and Henry were starting a new life.

37

When Claudia asked again for a job at The Hawthorne School, Zelma said, "That's going to have to wait, Claudia: I have very good news."

She paused for maximum effect.

"G is coming."

Zelma sat down at the table across from Claudia. Seeing that Claudia did not recognize the name, Zelma explained. "Oh, dear. You don't remember what I told you about G? The day of your tour of the school?" She sighed. "Then I'll have to tell you again. G is Gabriel. Gabriel Hawthorne, Julia Hawthorne's son, and the president of The Hawthorne Schools. Since the death of Julia Hawthorne, G has been our leader and our north star. He has been visiting the schools in Europe for the past six months, and he's going on to Asia after he stops here. We don't know how long he'll be here or when he is coming. He's only said it will be 'soon.' He likes to surprise us. But you need to know, he is a very important person: *the* most important person in all the Hawthorne Schools. We want everything to be perfect for him when he arrives. We want him to be pleased with us."

Claudia thought it was amusing to see this little old lady so concerned about "pleasing" her boss. So, Claudia thought, she wasn't the only one with the anxious-to-please problem. Surely, at her age, Zelma didn't need her job and she didn't need to kowtow to anyone. But Zelma was staring her down, as if beaming her message into Claudia's skull.

"Well," joked Claudia, "no pressure or anything!"

Zelma's stare hardened.

"We are all thrilled to see him again, and to have his personal supervision for as long as possible. Of course, we are always under his supervision, whether he is physically here or not. *I* am in constant contact with him when he is abroad. He directs us from wherever he is. He is, after all, the president. But to have him here, seeing our work and all that we do as we follow in the footsteps of his mother, well, it's a tremendous honor."

Claudia remained quiet and drained her cup of tea.

Zelma stood up to boil more water. Claudia thought, now that she was feeling more serene, that she wouldn't bring up the job issue again for a while. She could let some time pass before making such a dramatic change. All was well in her world. She couldn't remember at this time why it had seemed so important to her to leave the profession she had studied for, the job that defined who she was to herself, to work here. She did love being at The Hawthorne School, but she could just pick up more volunteer hours here and keep her job. Wouldn't that make more sense?

Zelma handed Claudia the hot tea.

With that strange prescience of hers, Zelma said, "Now, Claudia, about that job."

Zelma's sternness was gone, and she looked into Claudia's eyes like a loving mother. Claudia looked back, and neither of them broke the gaze.

"I am so *proud* of you, Claudia."

Claudia's eyes misted without warning. "Proud? Of me?"

"Of course." Zelma offered Claudia a tissue and continued looking at her with adoring eyes.

Claudia said, "Sorry. I don't mean to get all emotional or anything. It's just been a little tougher than usual at home lately with Henry. I guess I must be feeling a little vulnerable or something."

Zelma's smile widened. "Tough? With Henry?"

"Yes. He seems to be changing, becoming more distant. We've always been so close. Now, he pushes me away."

"But isn't that what you want? An independent boy? He's growing, that's all." She patted Claudia's hand. "Henry is adjusting to a new school, dear. As he develops confidence in school, he feels free to be more separate from you. Try not to let your possessiveness block his growth. I know you want the best for him. His behavior here is perfect. Just give him time to settle in. You'll see. Everything will fall into place. You would sacrifice anything for his happiness. You've already sacrificed so much. You are a very good mother, Claudia. I see that."

Claudia was not offended by Zelma's suggestion that she was too possessive of her son. On the contrary, she felt disarmed by Zelma's words. She felt her whole body relax, all the nervous tension draining.

"And do you know why I'm proud of you? It's because of what you said, dear heart. That you love our school *so* much. That you would quit your job and come to work here, sixty hours a week, doing janitorial work in exchange for room and board and tuition. And that you would donate your car to be sold to benefit The Hawthorne School. You have this sense of gratitude and this longing to give back to the school. I am deeply touched, Claudia, and profoundly impressed, too, by your faithfulness You have a true and deep commitment to the Hawthorne Way. And it didn't take you long. You arrived so recently, and you 'get it' already. But then, I knew right from the start that you are extraordinary. You understand us at some level now, and you will grow to understand us at deeper and deeper levels as time goes on. Deeper and deeper . . . and on and on. On and on . . . and deeper and deeper. We are one mind. *One . . . mind.* And you are *safe*, safe with us. You have always been ours. And now you want to sleep. You are so tired. You need to sleep. And now you may sleep. *Sleep.*"

CHAPTER

38

CLAUDIA MADE PLANS and took actions as if obeying some silent command.

"Please mail me my last paycheck. Send it in care of The Hawthorne School," she heard herself saying to Stephanie over the phone.

"Claudia, is this a joke? Are you all right?"

"I'm not joking, and I'm fine. I'm just quitting."

"But," blustered Stephanie, "with no notice? What about all the loyal clients you have now? You're all booked up. Am I supposed to call them all and tell them—*what*? Dr. W doesn't know about this, does he?"

"No, I haven't told him. I just decided now. Let him know for me, okay?"

"Do you mean, you're not even going to tell him yourself? Do you expect to get a referral from him for your next job?"

"I don't need one. I'm leaving massage." As she said these words, Claudia realized they were true.

"Well! I can't believe you're being so thoughtless, Claudia. And unprofessional."

As she hung up, Claudia realized in a detached way that Stephanie was experiencing strong emotions, but she didn't share them. She was putting everything in order, and she felt calm.

* * *

Claudia had forgotten exactly when she decided to move herself and Henry into The Hawthorne School. It simply seemed that now it was required that she do so. And why *wouldn't* she gladly move to such a beautiful place? Yolanda had described it as "living in a mansion." There was no healthier environment for her and Henry. The Hawthorne School was where they both felt best.

Maggie was at once admiring and envious. "How'd you do it? How'd you get into their inner circle like that?"

"Inner circle?" asked Claudia.

"Well, whatever you'd call it. You'll be one of the people that live there. It's like *you're* more a part of it somehow. They never invited *me* to move in. But hey, we'll still talk all the time, right? We'll still hang out?" She chuckled. "Don't forget me."

The move was easy. She paid the penalty to get out of her lease, with no regrets. The apartment had been a furnished one; all she had to load into her car were their personal possessions, and these were few. Claudia thought with interest about her new job. She'd never liked cleaning before, but she imagined she would get a ring of keys and would be able to see the inside of all the rooms of The Hawthorne School. She would love that. She was sure that there were many beautiful and intriguing things she had yet to discover. And she would prove herself to be a good worker, and then maybe she would get a job she would like better. It didn't really matter now. The important thing was that she was becoming a real part of the school. Niles had said it was like belonging to a family.

Zelma brought Claudia once again to the tunnels, where there was a Janitor's Closet. That's where Zelma introduced her to Irving.

Irving was an enormous man, at least six foot eight inches. He was slow-moving and slow in speech. He gave the appearance of being elderly, but as she looked more closely, she realized he was perhaps in his early forties; it was his posture and his sloth-like way of moving that made him seem years older. Claudia had only ever seen his retreating back as he ambled down hallways in the school. She had never seen his face before, and now she observed that it was pale and mask-like. He showed no interest in his new supervisee, only acknowledging her minimally when Zelma introduced them and then turning away to fill a pail with water in a stationary sink.

Claudia asked Zelma, "Will I need keys?"

"Keys? Whatever for? Irving has the keys. When you need a door opened, Irving will open it. Irving will give you your duties each day. Report to him at five AM, seven days a week."

"Five AM? But I have to get Henry ready for school every morning. Can I start after he goes to school?"

A crease of annoyance formed between Zelma's eyebrows.

"Now that you and Henry are living here, you don't need to worry about *that* any more. Evelyn will get Henry ready for school."

"*Evelyn?* His teacher will get him ready for school? I don't understand. How could she—?"

"Evelyn lives here. All of our teachers live here, of course. You know that."

Claudia did not know that. She knew—from Evelyn—that Zelma and Anthony lived at the school. But all of the teachers? She couldn't take time to wonder about this because she was still absorbing the unpleasant idea that anyone other than herself would get Henry ready for school.

"She'll come to your room at ten minutes to five, so you can leave for work. It's all convenient and will work out perfectly for everyone." Zelma must have seen some protest forming, because she went on, "I have gone to a great deal of trouble to get you this job, Claudia. Some people had to be dismissed, and others had to have their schedules changed so that *you* could have the job *you* requested. I knew that you weren't just asking to work here on a whim. I *knew* you wouldn't let us down. And that you would be grateful for my efforts. Henry is doing so well here, and of course you want that to continue. You want to do your part for him."

"Yes, but what would be the harm if I just get Henry ready for school? I would really like to just work the hours that he's in school. That's how I thought it would be."

"Claudia." Zelma looked at her with a shocked expression. "You *agreed*. You know you did. You agreed to working sixty hours a week. Now, I ask you, is Henry in school sixty hours a week? You know that he isn't. Your schedule, as you yourself decided, is from five AM to five PM, Monday through Friday. On Saturday and Sunday, you work another five hours each day, from five AM until ten in the morning, so you can have time off with Henry. That's what you *wanted*. That's why I set it up for you this way. That's why so many people were disrupted and inconvenienced." She looked Claudia up and down. "What are you trying to pull now?"

Claudia felt confused, panicked, and somehow guilty. Why couldn't she remember? What *had* she agreed to? When had the conversation occurred? She could only say now, stubbornly, "But *I* want to get him ready for school. And after school, I want to pick him up in his classroom and take him back to our room. And have dinner with him and put him to bed."

"Well, of course you will have dinner with him and put him to bed. That's why you are getting off at five PM." Zelma looked distressed, as if she were dealing with someone who was trying to manipulate her or with someone who was mentally unbalanced.

Claudia felt as distressed as Zelma looked. The best thing she could think of to do was to agree for the time being and think about it all later. She could work today, and then this evening, when she was with Henry in their dorm room, she would think it all through with a clear mind, without Zelma staring at her, trying to make her remember something she could not remember. She detached the small thermos she had clipped to her belt, the one that Zelma had thoughtfully provided for her, so that she could have little green juice throughout her day. Zelma had told her she could go to the kitchen and refill it as often as she liked, an idea which unaccountably filled her with joy and relief. She noticed that Irving had an identical thermos strapped to his belt.

After Zelma had gone, Irving shuffled out of the Janitorial Closet, ducking his head under the doorway. He carried the pail of water, sloshing, in one hand and dragged a mop along behind him in the other. Claudia followed.

39

THE WORK WAS hard, and Claudia thought that Irving was too weary for it. He led her through the chores: mopping floors, dusting high light fixtures, emptying trash cans. He moved slowly, his forehead sweating. Irving punctuated his day with frequent returns to the kitchen to refill his thermos. It seemed he needed a refill almost every half hour. Claudia thought he would do better to drink some water rather than the juice every time to quench his constant thirst. Being younger, she didn't need to refill as often as he did—only twice throughout the day—but she found that she didn't want water either. It was the juice that gave renewed energy while at the same time providing a sense of peace.

Irving was not great company, speaking hardly a word, and gesturing instead of talking, as if to save his breath.

They ate their lunch in the kitchen at one o'clock. The food had all been ready-made for them and was waiting in the refrigerator on a tray. There was twice as much food on Irving's tray as hers, although her servings were more than sufficient. It was just the two of them. Irving was glum company but a good eater, shoveling soup, wraps, and salad into his mouth and chewing, chewing, as Claudia made one attempt and then another to reach him on a human level.

She told him a little about her life and about her son. She hoped he would in turn share something about himself, but he remained silent, which unnerved her. She went on then, telling him about her appreciation of The Hawthorne School and what a great opportunity it was for Henry. When he still said nothing, she felt the need to keep on chattering. She told him about Devin and how he had let them down again. Irving just looked at her sadly and returned to his food. She sensed a loneliness in this huge man, and she wanted to make contact with him. She offered him the cup of chopped pineapple on her tray, even though she liked chopped pineapple. Irving accepted it wordlessly, and somehow she felt that he appreciated the small gesture.

But as for conversation, he was apathetic on every topic and even to her very presence. At last she gave up trying to get him to talk. She wondered what his story was.

"Have you been here a long time, Irving?"

She thought he wasn't going to answer, but at last he nodded. She looked into his eyes, searching to read them. When he still said nothing, she stopped pushing, and they settled into a companionable silence. She was surprised at how good she felt. She found her mood lifting and lifting until she felt really well, perfectly well, and realized how grateful she was for this job and for everything in her life and in the world in general. She smiled at Irving, and was not bothered that he did not smile back.

Almost to herself, she continued her reflections aloud. "We're at a turning point, that's how it feels, Henry and I. After my mother died, we had no one in the world, really. Just each other. And now we have this." She spread her arms to indicate their surroundings. "It's like I've finally found something we can count on, you know?"

Irving made a low noise in his throat and stole a glance at her face.

"Ever since I became a mother, I've felt I would do anything for Henry, anything to help him, to make his life better, to give him what he needs for his future. Do you have children, Irving?"

Irving stopped chewing and looked at Claudia mutely with an expression in his eyes that made her think of a suffering animal in captivity.

Claudia thought how good it was of Zelma to give Irving this occupation. It couldn't be easy for someone like him to get a job.

"If you're tired, Irving, I could do the floors in the dining hall by myself. I don't mind. You could take a break."

To this, Irving answered nothing.

In the dining hall, Claudia took the mop from Irving's hands and set to work. With heavy-lidded eyes, he watched her work for a few minutes. Then he took the other mop and joined in at his own slow pace.

*   *   *

Two and a half hours later, at pickup time, when Claudia wished to be picking up Henry, she was instead scrubbing toilets in the administration building. She worried about him now. Who would take care of him from then until five PM? His teacher? Wasn't that asking an awful lot of her when she had been with children all day? In fact, had any arrangement been made? She couldn't remember if Zelma had told her who would take care of him after school. Zelma had said Evelyn was supposed to take care of him before school, but what about after school? Could she trust that Zelma had worked it out? And then, how would Henry feel when she didn't show up for him after school? She hadn't had any time to prepare him for a new arrangement. Finishing her work in the ladies' toilet, she scrubbed her hands and left Irving in the hall.

"Sorry, Irving. I have to ask Zelma a question."

Irving only grunted in reply. His grunt might have been meant to remind her that Zelma didn't like questions.

Claudia didn't care.

She found Zelma and Anthony in the director's office. Anthony was curled up, drifting off to sleep in an oversized chair. Zelma looked up with displeasure as Claudia, dressed in a cotton shirt and overalls splashed with water marks, came through her door.

Zelma stood.

"Sorry to disturb. I just wanted to make sure—who is watching Henry?"

Zelma looked at Claudia in a way that made her feel she needed to explain herself further.

"I mean. I know we probably talked about it, but I just realized, I can't remember for sure that we did. Did we arrange for someone to watch him until I get off work?"

"Claudia, Claudia, Claudia. What am I going to *do* with you?"

Claudia stood her ground, waiting for her answer.

"I have the impression that your mind has become clouded of late. Have you noticed this too?"

Claudia knew she hadn't been herself lately. She'd been forgetful. She'd made major decisions impulsively. And yes, sometimes she did feel that her thinking was clouded, as if she were in a sort of a fog. But she didn't want to admit this to Zelma. She fought to keep her expression calm, unreadable.

Zelma sighed and shook her head.

"I have already told you. And now you come to me, asking me as if you never listened to me in the first place. Why do you do this, dear? And I also told you that G is coming and that we all have to make preparations. Our minds are full of getting ready for him. You *do* remember that? Or have you forgotten that also?"

Claudia pushed aside her sense of confusion. "I'm sorry. Usually my memory is better than this. But what about Henry?"

"As I told you, dear heart, and I hope this is the last time I need to repeat myself, Evelyn has complete charge of Henry while you are working. Naturally."

Zelma clearly expected Claudia to leave after getting the answer to her question, but now Claudia had a new question.

"You say, 'naturally'?"

"Yes! Yes! Naturally! Who else, but his teacher, would have charge of him?"

Claudia didn't know why the word "naturally" bothered her, but it did. She had more questions. Zelma had reached the end of her patience, although Claudia couldn't think what she had said to aggravate her so much. It was probably the mere fact that she was asking questions at all. Evelyn had told her to bring all her questions to her.

So she would. She would go right upstairs and ask Evelyn, "What does 'complete charge' mean?" It probably meant nothing; it was probably just Zelma's manner of speaking. But she needed to ask. Everything was spinning out of control so fast.

"Sorry again," said Claudia, turning to go.

"Claudia," said Zelma. There was a warning in her tone.

Claudia stopped.

"You need to go straight back to work. Your job is a serious responsibility. Breaks are only at the allotted times. I hope I don't have to tell you that. The Hawthorne School is relying on your work ethic. We want these buildings to *sparkle* whenever G arrives. Which could be at any time."

Getting the image that Zelma wished to convey of a "sparkling" school, Claudia thought of another question. Where was the rest of the janitorial staff? All day, she had worked alone with Irving. She hadn't seen anyone else cleaning anywhere. Certainly, on this huge campus, there had to be many more cleaners.

"Zelma," asked Claudia, feeling that she was on the thinnest of ice now. "Where are all the other cleaners, by the way? I haven't seen any. So I was just, you know, wondering about that . . ." Her voice trailed off.

Zelma sighed. "Sleeping, Claudia. Sleeping. The other cleaners work at night. While you will be sleeping comfortably in your bed, they will be cleaning. Of course, we have shifts. You have the day shift for now."

Zelma turned her back.

For now?

Claudia left the director's office, but she didn't return to work.

She had to see Henry.

40

IT WAS ALREADY past four o'clock when Claudia got upstairs. The halls were silent and deserted. She stood in the doorway of Evelyn's empty classroom. The beauty that had enchanted her on the day of her tour did not affect her now. She saw only that no one was there; Henry was not there, and she did not know where he was.

Where could Evelyn have taken her son?

Zelma had told her that Evelyn—and all the teachers—lived on campus. She would need to find the teachers' dormitory. It couldn't be on the third floor of this building—there were more classrooms up there; nor on the fourth floor—she and Henry occupied a dorm room up there, and apart from them, that floor was deserted. She knew from the map in the Janitor's Closet that each building had a name: Freedom Hall, Comfort Hall, Unity Hall, and this one—the Main Hall. But they were not labeled as to their function. She had seen teachers walking along the cloister walk into Unity Hall. Was that the one that housed them? She had to find someone to ask. She hurried down the corridor, stopping to try each door, but one after another, she found them locked. The doors were solid, with no windows in them, so she could not even peek in. Her heart was beating fast now; she was beginning to panic. She tried to calm herself with logic. What was there to be anxious about? Henry was with his teacher, whom he adored. But Claudia had to see

Henry for herself, to know he was safe and that he understood why she hadn't come for him this afternoon. She came at last to one door that opened. Not expecting it to give way, she pushed into the room with a little too much force. There, she found a teacher who stood at an expanse of diamond-paned windows. She turned from the windows to look at Claudia.

It was Miss Kincaid, the teacher of the sevens who had been leading the knitting circle on the day of the tour.

While Claudia gathered her thoughts to ask her question, Miss Kincaid looked her up and down and then nodded.

"You won't find them," she said.

"What do you mean?"

"I mean that Evelyn has taken Henry into the woods." Her words chilled Claudia's heart. "Why? Why would she do that?"

Miss Kincaid looked amused. "Why take him into the woods? Because it's beautiful in there. It's our home, really. It's our home and our classroom and our life, all in one. Nature, our source."

Claudia turned to go. She wasn't going to waste time talking. She needed to find Henry immediately.

"Honestly—you won't be able to find them, even if you try. The forest is too big; there are lots of trails; they could be anywhere in there. Your best plan is to wait until they come back, at five."

Claudia realized with some surprise that Miss Kincaid must know she was working here now and what her hours were. She had only started today; how tight was the communication between Zelma and the teachers, then?

Claudia rushed to the window to stand beside Miss Kincaid and look down onto the lawn below and the woods that began there and went on for acres. The trees were still full of their colored leaves, providing a thick canopy over the forest. She could see no sign of Henry in his bright red sweater.

Claudia's hand flew involuntarily to her heart, and her eyes filled with tears as she searched for some movement below.

"Oh, now. Oh, now," said Miss Kincaid. Her voice was sympathetic, and she put an arm around Claudia. Claudia, in spite of herself, put an arm around the teacher. In that moment, she had no one else.

"Here. Dry your tears. I will help you if you want to try to find them." She handed Claudia a tissue. "There's no chance we *will* find them, as I've already said. But if you want to try, we can. They're very safe, you know."

"But I have to try. I can't wait."

"Okay. How about if you and I walk into the forest together? You might get lost by yourself, but I'll go with you. If it would make you feel better to be out there looking than in here waiting, well then, let's go." She smiled reassuringly at Claudia.

"Yes, thanks. Let's go." Claudia turned.

"Wait—just one thing. Let's refill your thermos. I'll take one too. We don't want to get dehydrated out there." Miss Kincaid filled Claudia's thermos with little green juice. As she did so, she said, "My first name's Lillian, by the way."

"Thanks, Lillian," said Claudia turning toward the door again.

Once in the echoing hallway, Lillian, walking beside her, said, "I assume you don't want Zelma to see you slipping out of the building. Follow me down this staircase." She gave Claudia a conspiratorial wink. "Zelma's windows look out on the front. She won't see us going out the back."

This was the first time she'd seen anyone rebelling against the system of the school or against Zelma herself. But then, Claudia knew there was always bound to be one person a little more free-thinking than the rest. Maybe Lillian was taking her side. She seemed to want to help.

Claudia had no choice but to trust her.

41

Diffused rays of the late afternoon sun streamed down through breaks in the leaves above, and the woods were all yellow and orange, with startling explosions of red. Claudia and Lillian walked along the paths, Claudia with her head turning from side to side, searching for any sign of Henry.

"I never realized until now how huge this place is, how far the woods go, or how many people must live here. How many people *do* live here?"

"I don't know, to be perfectly honest. All of the teachers. All of the students. And the volunteers, of course."

"*All* of the students?"

"Oh yes. They all wind up moving in. It works better for the school that way."

But not Violet, thought Claudia. Maggie and Violet lived away from the school. Why? And where were all the parents? It was strange that she hadn't seen other parents in the dorm on the fourth floor of the Main Hall where she stayed with Henry. In fact, theirs was the only room that was inhabited. Why?

It was all baffling, but she couldn't care about any of that now. What she needed to do was find her son.

As if reading her thoughts, Lillian repeated, "Henry's perfectly safe with Evelyn, you know."

"I'm sure he is," said Claudia. "But he'll be wondering why I didn't show up for him after school. He depends on me to always be there."

"Ah," said Lillian, "but that's already changing. Haven't you noticed? Evelyn has already bonded with Henry."

Claudia burst out in frustration. "What is this *bond* you people talk about? I never heard of a child bonding so strongly with a teacher." She realized that she had said, "you people." Wasn't she one of these people now?

"According to the Hawthorne Way," said Lillian, "the bond between teacher and student is paramount. We are taught that it's a deeper connection; the teacher has much more influence than the parent. The teacher–student bond surpasses the bond between parent and child."

Claudia was not going to be polite now. "That's ridiculous. Nothing surpasses the bond between Henry and me. Anyway, why would it be so beneficial for a child to bond with a teacher when he's only going to have a different teacher next year?"

"But he won't. Teachers move up through the grades with their students. This year, I'm teaching the sevens. Last year I taught the sixes. The year before that, the fives. And so on. I'll be with the same children until sixth grade, when we'll go—the children and I—to the Hawthorne School in California. That's where the older children go."

"What about their *parents*? Do all their parents move to California?"

"Unfortunately, the majority of our students have been orphaned or abandoned, so that doesn't come into it. You'll understand more as time goes on about how it all works. New parents always have to learn gradually. But yes, it's easy to make it all work when our students are, for the most part, under the guardianship of The Hawthorne School."

"Orphans? You're saying that Henry's classmates, for example—Bibi, James, and Mason—they're all orphans?"

"Yes. Taylor still has her birth father, of course: Niles. And Valeria has her birth parents: Yolanda and Oscar."

"The way you say 'birth parents,' it's as if they've already been adopted by someone else. Even though their parents are right here." Claudia wanted to keep her mind on finding Henry, but she was distracted by these disturbing ideas and odd ways of phrasing things.

"Of course, Taylor and Valeria are adopted."

"That's not true—their parents are alive. They're right here, every day."

Lillian stopped, and Claudia, not knowing where she was, had to stop too.

"When parents enroll their children here, they all sign away guardianship on the first day."

They stood, locking eyes. Claudia stopped breathing. Lillian's eyes looked soft and caring. Claudia remembered all of the documents Zelma had handed her that first day, all the paperwork she had signed without reading, excited and grateful.

"Oh, Claudia." Lillian fingered the long fringe on her gold knit shawl. "Oh, Claudia," she repeated, "you didn't know, did you? You didn't read the papers you signed on the first day? You didn't know that The Hawthorne School is Henry's guardian now. And The Hawthorne School has given him to Evelyn."

42

As she stood looking around herself in the forest, Claudia's heart raced, and her breath was labored. Lillian was talking nonsense, of course. Whatever papers she had signed didn't matter—they couldn't be legal. Adoptions didn't happen that way; she was sure there would have to be a court date. This claim of "signing away rights" was just a manipulation tactic. What kind of people *were* they? She couldn't understand how she had put Henry into this insane environment. How had she not realized that this school was not as it had appeared to her? How could she have been so gullible? More importantly, how could she find Henry?

"Look," said Lillian, "you just got a lot of new information to process. It looks like you're overwhelmed. That's understandable. But"—she looked at her wristwatch—"it's ten minutes to five. Evelyn will be back in her classroom with Henry at five, ready to turn him over to you for the evening. Why don't we head back?"

Claudia didn't want to leave the forest without Henry. But she could see that trying to find him here was hopeless. There were paths exiting the forest on all sides. Evelyn and Henry could be heading out toward the school on any one of them. But could she trust that Evelyn would return Henry to her in the classroom at five?

Lillian, seeing her doubt, said, "Come on. They'll be there. I promise. Or how about this? If they're not in the classroom—and they will be; they have to be because it's the rule—but if they're not, I promise I'll come out here with you again with flashlights, and we'll search."

Claudia stalled a for a bit, taking a long drink from her thermos. She must have been dehydrated, because she was very thirsty and drained the thermos quickly. As she drank, she thought, *No, Lillian; if they're not back at five, I'm calling the police.*

Together they retraced their steps back toward the lawn. Claudia glanced at Lillian, trying to understand if she was truly an ally, trying to help her, or simply "one of them." She knew she shouldn't trust any of them. They all appeared to be friendly at first: Zelma, Evelyn—even Niles. He could have told her about the so-called "adoption" scam, but he'd never mentioned it; and he reported to Zelma whatever she told him. And what about Maggie? As childlike as she was, she couldn't have any idea of the deception they had all fallen into. Claudia had to find a way to tell her. Yolanda and Oscar seemed to be unaware too, exploited by Zelma. But were they? She wanted to trust someone, to not be alone, but then, it had been wanting—needing—support that had pulled her, and little Henry along with her, into this school. If it even *was* a school. She remembered Henry's words: "It's not a school . . . it's only pretending to be a school." He was a tiny child, and yet he apparently sensed from the very beginning that The Hawthorne School was not what it appeared to be. And still, he had loved it from first sight. He had wanted to be here. And she, instead of being the parent and overruling him, had yielded to his wish.

She saw her mistakes now. If only it wasn't too late to pull back. But why should it be? She would just take Henry and leave The Hawthorne School and never return. No one could stop her. Henry would cry and protest, but he would recover.

As they reentered the building, Claudia's heart was already beginning to lift. It was as if she'd had a shift in perception, making everything all right. How often she had these changes in mood, in attitude, now. Even before she saw Henry, it was as if she knew she would see him and as if all her worry was behind her. She felt relief. She was back inside The Hawthorne School, she was feeling good, a sense of well-being washing over her, and Henry would be in her arms within minutes.

Nothing else mattered.

43

A s promised, Henry was in Evelyn's classroom.
Lillian left Claudia at the classroom door and went on down the hall. Claudia rushed to her son, who was seated on the child-sized throne. The throne was made of tree branches and wound around with colored ribbons. On Henry's head was a green crown of vines, freshly cut, and he wore a necklace made of vines and bracelets of vines, contrasting with the red bracelet, wound round his small wrists. In his hand he held a stick that served as his scepter.

Claudia hugged him, but he sat limp in her arms, not returning her hug. He smelled of the outdoors. He was safe and sound, and oddly peaceful.

"Henry, I'm sorry I wasn't able to be here for you after school. Were you scared?"

"My name is not Henry," said Henry. "You have to call me *King* Henry."

"Okay," Claudia said, laughing as she wiped away a tear, "King Henry. Did you go for a walk in the woods?"

Henry looked at Evelyn.

"He may feel a little tired," said Evelyn smoothly.

Claudia brushed away the irritation of this woman telling her how her child felt. Henry was fine.

"Evelyn," said Claudia, standing now to face the teacher. It was time for a confrontation. She tried to gather the anger that she'd felt in the woods before she'd drunk the calming little green juice. There was no angry energy in her now, but the questions remained.

"Lillian told me some things that I didn't know. Are you under the impression that The Hawthorne School has *given* you my son?"

Evelyn shrugged her thin shoulders and signaled a chair at the children's table, but Claudia remained standing.

"Zelma gave Henry to me, to be in my *class*. Of course, you know that."

"No. Lillian talked about some kind of 'teacher–student *bond.*' What is that? A bond that surpasses the bond between parent and child?"

"Oh, *that*. It's all very straightforward, Claudia. Let me explain. 'Bond' may be a misleading word. Let's just use the word 'relationship.' Obviously, a teacher has a relationship with each student. That's clear. That's not to say that it's a better relationship than the one the child has with his parents. It's just different. It's of a different nature."

"What's the nature of it?" demanded Claudia. There was a part of her that wanted to fight against these ideas, fight for Henry. There was a bigger part of her that was going to sleep. What was coming over her? Ten minutes before, she had been ready to take Henry and leave. Now, she wanted Evelyn to explain it all in a way that made sense, even while she felt her mind slowly going numb.

"You're asking about the nature of the relationship between student and teacher? Well, it's about learning, of course, educating, training, and forming. Forming young minds. That's what teachers do. *You* know that."

All plans of taking Henry out of The Hawthorne School, of calling the police, receded into the back of Claudia's mind. That would take energy that she didn't have. She needed to give Evelyn a chance to reassure her. She wanted to be disarmed of all her suspicions. She had been imagining absurd things. Evelyn would give her a reasonable explanation for every concern, and then Claudia could go to sleep. She was so sleepy.

"Lillian told me," said Claudia. Now she did want to sit down. She came toward Evelyn and they both took their seats at the children's table. "Told me . . ." What *had* Lillian told her? The word "adoption" floated to the top of her mind. "Lillian told me that The Hawthorne School adopts all of the children, that the parents sign paperwork on the first day, turning the children over to the school. Is that true? I feel like I need to go back and review what I signed. I didn't really read it at the time. There was a lot of paper—just formalities, I assumed. I only wanted to get through it and get Henry started in school. But tomorrow I'm going to ask Zelma for copies of everything I signed." An image of Henry's birth certificate floated through her mind. Zelma had never returned it to her.

"Ah," said Evelyn. "I see the problem. How alarmed you must have been when you misunderstood Lillian. Let me clear that up for you right now. At our school, we use some lingo that can be confusing to newcomers. Hawthornese, some people call it." She chuckled, an odd, false sound.

Claudia rubbed her eyes and yawned. She tilted her head back and drank the last of the juice in the thermos.

"Did you really think that we could actually adopt all these children?" Evelyn sounded amused.

Claudia watched her mouth moving and willed herself to focus on the words she was saying. Her mind wanted to drift. Of course she must be mixed up. Schools didn't adopt children. What was wrong with Lillian? What was wrong with Claudia for believing her?

"What we mean by 'adoption' is what other schools mean by '*in loco parentis*.' That's a Latin term meaning 'in place of the parents.' It simply refers to the duty of the school officials to protect all of the students whenever the parents cannot be present. Believe me, Claudia, there's no need to ask Zelma about it. It's nothing to worry about. After all she's done for you and Henry, you don't want to basically tell her that you don't trust her, do you? She's the most generous person in the world, but she can be touchy, you know. *In loco parentis* is a very common concept. It only means that the school can act in the parents' place for the benefit of the students. It puts the students under the school's authority—protective authority. That's all."

Then there was a lurching forward in time. Claudia did not remember the conclusion of her talk with Evelyn nor climbing the stairs with Henry to their dorm room. A dinner must have been waiting for them on a tray there, and they must have eaten it, because as she became aware of her surroundings, she saw the dirty plates on the tray, and she did not feel hungry.

Henry was already in his bed, fast asleep.

44

THE NEXT DAY, Claudia's suspicions returned. She wanted to ask Maggie if she had ever heard anything about The Hawthorne School taking custody of all the children. She wanted to warn her. Maggie was so simple and unaware. If only she could speak to Maggie in person. But whenever Claudia saw Maggie dropping off or picking up Violet, she was never alone: Zelma had started meeting her at the door, coming and going. The only way to talk to Maggie would be by the landline phone in Zelma's office. Claudia sensed that Zelma would not let her speak privately on the office phone and that she would be angry if she caught Claudia using it.

It was after school, but not yet time for her to pick up Henry. When she peeked into the director's office and found it empty, she decided to risk it.

Maggie couldn't seem to understand Claudia, no matter how she explained what Lillian had told her.

"What? Taking our *children*?" asked Maggie, maddening in her inability to grasp what Claudia was saying. "Violet's okay. She's right here. Say hi, Violet—say hi to Claudia."

"No, Maggie! I don't have time. I'm calling from Zelma's office. Quick, before she comes back."

"Hi, Claudia," Violet's bright little voice said. "What are you doing?"

"Put your mom back on, Violet."

"Mom's making toast. Can I talk to Henry?"

"Henry's not here, honey. Put your mom back on."

Claudia lost heart. If Zelma came back, she'd have to come up with a valid reason to be here, and she had none. She hung up the phone and hurried away.

45

IN THINKING ABOUT her trek in the woods with Lillian, Claudia had the impression that the teacher was the only person who could help her. According to Evelyn, Claudia had misunderstood all that Lillian had told her about The Hawthorne School. But Lillian had spoken very clearly. *Was* it possible that Lillian was exaggerating, or even teasing her to frighten her? Yet her intuition told her that Lillian was trustworthy while that same intuition caused her to pull back now from Zelma and Evelyn.

In the evenings, Henry and Claudia were together, but they didn't seem to have the same quality time anymore.

The dorm room itself was spartan. It contained a sink, a closet, a table and two chairs, and a built-in dresser. There was a casement window looking down on the forest, and the woodwork was dark. The bathroom was down the hall.

Henry was always so tired by five o'clock, and so was she. She had no gusto to even read him the sacrosanct bedtime story, and he never asked for it either. They had their last glass of little green juice after their baths. Then they would brush their teeth and fall into bed, sleeping heavily until morning.

Henry seemed different, as if there was another child in his place. He didn't oppose her; he didn't demand attention; he didn't chatter. He was cooperative and sleepy, and totally unlike himself. But then, did she want him to be ornery again?

She was so weary herself every night; she didn't know how she would have coped if he were as contrary as he used to be. It was good that he was tired out from his long day.

Each night, their dinner was waiting for them. Claudia was always grateful to see it: plant based, gluten-free, highly nutritious, and always with a sprinkling of little green in the sandwich, on the salad, in the soup, or in the avocado taco.

Likewise, breakfast was always waiting for her on a tray outside her door when she awoke. As tired as she usually was now, she appreciated not having to plan meals. Who put their breakfast there? She never saw the deliverer. Sometimes she heard footsteps, and when she went to the door, she saw a figure retreating down the hall. The person's movements were slow, like an automaton, or like the strange and lifeless Irving. This person never turned with curiosity at the sound of Claudia opening her door. It might have been one of the parent volunteers, one of the volunteers that Lillian had said lived on campus. Were they up during the night like the other cleaners? Cooks who prepared breakfasts and then delivered them to the doors of the other residents? She was too busy to wonder about it much, eating quickly and getting ready for work before Evelyn would appear. Then Evelyn would slip into her dorm room to take care of Henry while Claudia headed down to the tunnels to receive orders in gloomy pantomime from Irving.

*   *   *

On Saturday and Sunday afternoons, Claudia and Henry, dressed in their sky-blue and sage-green apparel, went outside and stayed out all day, exploring the grounds. The leaves were brilliant now, coloring the natural world around The Hawthorne School in painterly hues of crimson and amber. Claudia sometimes imagined that they were walking in a vivid watercolor landscape, two small figures in red knit sweaters, beneath the towering trees. The school itself stood as beautiful as on the first day she saw it.

"Henry," she said, as they stood looking up at the gothic splendor of the school, "do you remember the first day we came here?"

Henry nodded.

"Remember, you thought this was a giant's castle?" Claudia smiled down at him and smoothed his black hair away from his eyes. It had grown out too much since his first-day-of-school haircut. She loved his sweet round baby face and everything about him. She'd have to cut his hair tonight, before sleep overtook them.

"It *is* a giant's castle," Henry insisted with a four-year-old's typical confidence.

"It is?" Claudia made a show of looking all around them. "Where's the giant, then? I haven't seen him."

"The giant's coming," said Henry.

CHAPTER

46

CLAUDIA AND HENRY never explored alone for very long. There were always other groups and pairs of children and teachers outside at the same time, and inevitably they were joined by Evelyn. Never Niles, to Claudia's disappointment. He had been sent away by Zelma on important business.

Henry's eyes always lit up when he saw Evelyn, and his then customary listlessness would leave him as he stretched out his arms and cried, "My teacher!" Evelyn expressed affection for him, too, and would give him a green hard candy and then kneel to give him a hug. It made Claudia feel uncomfortable to watch this.

As she followed Henry around the playground, keeping an eye on him in a way that was more protective than the Hawthorne Way, she reflected on this connection Henry had with Evelyn, and Lillian's unlikely claim.

"Mom!" Are you looking at me? *Look* at me!"

Henry worked his way along the monkey bars, hand after hand, a look of grim determination on his face, and fell to the ground halfway across. He was up instantly and running toward the wooden fort.

As for her determination to leave the school once she had Henry in her arms again, she could not account for it, but something was holding her back from taking action. She, who had run from one place to another all her life, now felt that she had no power to move and nowhere to go. Certainly, she could search in the community for a shelter for a night or two, but after that, what then? She had turned over all her financial resources to the school. She had no job, and Dr. W would be unlikely to take her back—or even to give her a good reference—after she had quit without notice. It occurred to her to search for another job. Maybe even without a reference, she could try to get one—anywhere, in any part of the country. And then she remembered that in addition to having no money for a hotel room or a plane ticket to a new city, she had no access to a computer. She had turned in her cell phone as a condition of living on campus. Of course, there were computers at the public library. But it would be a long walk into town for Henry's little legs, and she didn't want to leave him in Evelyn's care any more than she already had to. She already had the feeling she was losing him because she was so seldom with him. If she went on an errand off campus, she would take him with her, but so far, she had never gone anywhere. There were vehicles on campus, but instinctively she knew that she should not ask for a ride to the library. Zelma wouldn't like it. Depending as she did on Zelma and The Hawthorne School for everything, she could not afford to annoy Zelma, and Zelma was so easy to annoy now.

But she knew she was only making excuses. Having no money, no job, no place to take her child—they seemed like valid reasons to stay, but she was getting tired of deceiving herself. The truth was that it was hard now to think anything through to a conclusion. She was in a sort of mental paralysis. All her doubts and urgent realizations melted away as soon as they arose. Why? She had never been like this before. When had she changed?

"Push me! *Mom!*" Henry called from a swing, and Claudia went automatically to him and pushed. Other children ran around them, yelling, discharging energy.

In the beginning, Zelma had been such a sweet and grandmotherly little woman; Claudia had thought she was "adorable." "Twinkly," even. She'd been so supportive and had said that Claudia was an "extraordinary mother." It was impossible now to reconcile that first impression with the Zelma Claudia now knew: terse, irritable, and critical. She could never get Zelma's approval now, so she tried to keep a low profile and avoid her without seeming to.

From where she stood, pushing Henry on the swing and obeying his command to push him ever higher, Claudia looked at the beautiful stone buildings of The Hawthorne School. She had come to know the physical makeup of the campus. In the front and center stood The Main Hall. That was the building she had entered on the first day. On the first floor were the administration offices, including Zelma's. On the second and third floors were classrooms. On the fourth floor were dorm rooms—all empty except for the one Claudia occupied with Henry. West of The Main Hall, was Freedom Hall. That housed children, Claudia knew. East of The Main Hall, was Unity Hall. That was home to Zelma and the teachers and some of the children such as Anthony and Taylor, and Niles lived there too, as did Yolanda and Oscar. Back behind all of these, and in a direct line behind The Main Hall, was Comfort Hall. Here lived Irving, and all the parent volunteers, most of whom were only active at night on the campus—Claudia had come to think of them as the "hidden people" because she never saw them. Each of these buildings was connected by an underground network of tunnels—convenient, she had heard, in the harsh winters, for getting quickly from one building to another without having to put on boots and coats. Outside, the buildings were connected by flower-bordered walkways. Between The Main Hall and Unity Hall there was a cloister walk on the outside, and teachers could often be seen walking along it in both directions between their dorm rooms and the classrooms. Inside, parallel to the cloister walk, was a chapel with stained glass windows, originally built for Catholic masses. The hedge maze where she had worked with Yolanda and Oscar was behind The Main Hall and before Comfort Hall. Throughout the campus were the playgrounds, the woodworking shed, the fountain, the playhouses, the greenhouse, and the bountiful gardens—both flower and vegetable. Surrounding all of this was forest so that the campus was in its own circular world, insulated by acres of trees.

Claudia wondered why she and Henry were the sole occupants of the fourth floor of The Main Hall. When she'd asked Evelyn, the teacher had said, "Zelma is probably deciding whether you belong in Comfort Hall or Unity Hall. When she decides, you'll move."

Claudia would draw the line at living with the "hidden people." Irving was so comatose, and she wondered if the others, those who were "active at night," were like him. She would talk to Zelma and let her know she wanted to live in Unity Hall with the teachers.

One Saturday afternoon, she and Henry met Yolanda, Oscar, and Valeria on the expansive playground. While Henry and Valeria climbed the wooden ladders and chased each other across bridges, Claudia spoke in hushed Spanish with Yolanda and Oscar. She still wanted to keep her knowledge of Spanish between them.

"A question for you," said Claudia, as they watched their children playing. "I'm just a little curious. You live in Unity Hall? With the teachers? What is that like?"

Yolanda kept her eyes on Valeria, and for a few seconds Claudia thought she wasn't going to answer at all.

"It's good. It's very quiet."

Claudia said, "I was told that I'll be moved to either Unity Hall or Comfort Hall."

Yolanda turned quickly to Claudia, her face tense, and then she composed her expression.

"I hope you will be in Unity Hall—with us." She paused, doubtful. "That would be better, I think."

"Why do you say that?"

"It would be nice to have you as a neighbor," replied Yolanda simply. Claudia sensed there was much more Yolanda could say, but she was holding back.

Claudia had come out prepared with extra little green juice as she noticed she was drinking more and more of it, and she offered an untouched thermos to Yolanda.

Yolanda smiled a beautiful but apologetic smile. "You are very nice to offer. Thank you so much, but I am drinking less of the little green. We both are drinking less. We used to drink two smoothies a day, and cups of tea too. And the juice, we were drinking more and more of the little green juice. We finally started to wonder if—"

Oscar interrupted. "If it was making us fat!" Oscar patted his very small paunch. Oscar looked serious, but then he always did.

Yolanda glanced at him and paused. "Yes, we thought perhaps it was making us fat." She looked troubled and added, "Little green is very good. It is nutritious, from plants. Herbs. It makes you feel calm. I am not saying anything against it, you know. Please don't get me wrong. Please don't tell anyone I said there is anything wrong with drinking lots of it. Little green is very good for you. We still drink it every day. Just . . ." She searched Claudia's face and seemed to be in some debate with herself.

Claudia waited.

"Just . . . moderation in everything, no? Pay attention to how much of it you drink and how much you give to little Henry."

Claudia felt a realization dawning on the edge of her consciousness.

There was something not healthy at all about little green.

Devin had been right.

Yes, she had known it, without knowing it, from the very beginning. Little green was the key to Henry's new peacefulness. He never had tantrums anymore. He was never irritable. When they'd lived in the apartment and he'd withdrawn from it every weekend, he'd been beastly. But now that he had an unlimited supply, he was always tranquil like the other Hawthorne children. And as for little green's effect on her? Little green was the reason for her own doubts always drifting away, like the yellow leaves on the autumn breeze.

She, too, was drinking more and more of it. And when Henry began to look unhappy, she found herself rushing to give him a glass of little green juice because she knew it would restore his equilibrium. At least, that's how she explained it to herself. She thought back to times when she had had a sensation of her consciousness being altered as she drank little green—once with Niles, once with Evelyn, and once with Zelma. Those incidents had faded out in her mind and were hard to remember afterward. They were difficult to retrieve now, and yet she knew they had happened. That alteration in consciousness had never occurred when she drank it alone, however, even though her consumption was rising all the time. Why? Had Niles, Evelyn, and Zelma increased the dosage somehow on those occasions without her knowing?

Now she was sure she was being paranoid. Zelma, Evelyn, Niles . . . they would not drug her. They would not . . . She felt chilled now to think of it. They would not drug *children*. They would not drug *Henry*.

"Mom! Push me! Mom-mom-mom-mom!" Henry shouted.

Claudia stood rooted to the spot.

The Hawthorne School was poisoning her and Henry— and all the children and staff as well.

She had to start now, to break free of little green.

CHAPTER

47

Many times in Claudia's life, after reading an article in a health journal, she had determined to cut sugar or excess salt out of her diet. These exercises usually lasted less than four hours. When the craving returned, she always had the tendency to rationalize a regression to the old habit of eating, thinking of all the very old yet healthy people who consumed lots of sugar and salt; thinking of how the popular advice was always changing anyway; and most of all, thinking of how good sugar and salt tasted.

It was similar now with little green.

By the time they got back to their dorm room to find their dinner waiting for them, sprinkled with the herbal mixture, they were both hungry. Why bother to scrape the flecks of little green off the guacamole, when she knew that it had already been stirred into the mixture itself? She filled two cups with water for her and Henry to drink, but they left them untouched in favor of the much more satisfying little green juice. As soon as she began to drink it, she felt the reward going to the pleasure centers of her brain. And Henry, who had always been a ball of tension and nervous energy, was so calm. It wasn't like being drunk or stoned. She knew the difference. It was just a sense of well-being. Wouldn't everyone want to feel this way?

Still, she had lived without little green all her life before coming here. She should be able to reduce it. This was her thought as she reached for one last cup of little green before bed. She would, perhaps, think about it again tomorrow.

She felt cocooned in comfort. For now, with Henry nodding off to sleep in his bed, and her own bed beckoning to her, life was good.

48

THE NEXT DAY, however, the whole school was in an uproar. G's visit was imminent.

"When is he coming?" Claudia asked Evelyn when she went to her classroom at five PM to pick up Henry.

There'd been no use in asking Irving. Anything he could not answer with grunts or pantomime, he did not answer at all.

"Soon," said Evelyn. "That could mean in two days. That could mean tonight. We'll know when he arrives. We think he's getting closer. He'll come when it's the right time."

Claudia thought that this G sounded like an inconsiderate jerk of a president. He must know that all his subordinates were nervous about his arrival. The least he could do was to give a clear date and time. She knew better than to make this observation to Evelyn. Evelyn, like Zelma, seemed to have a profound sort of reverence for this Gabriel Hawthorne.

"It seems like everyone is really excited," said Claudia mildly.

"You could say that!" She sounded like a teenager who was about to attend a concert of her favorite pop idol. "He's like a saint to us. You'll see when he comes. He's Julia Hawthorne's son."

"Yes, I know. I keep hearing that. What's so—I mean, he must be . . .?" Claudia trailed off.

"Inspiring," supplied Evelyn. She shrugged her sharp shoulders up to her ears with the intensity of her excitement. She put Claudia in mind of a crow, shrugging on a fence post. "G is wise. He just exudes love. You feel love in his presence. He has the most powerful effect when he speaks to us. He knows and understands each and every teacher on the most profound level. You've never met anyone else like him. And you never will again, I can guarantee you. It's an incredible experience just to be in his presence."

"That sounds more like a guru than a president. I hope that doesn't sound rude."

"Oh, you're not being rude, not at all. You can say whatever you want here, you know. No one will be offended. We are all free at The Hawthorne School. G *is* more like a guru than a president. Exactly. We look up to him as our teacher and leader—not just professionally, but personally. He takes the time to speak to each one of us individually—from Zelma to the teachers, to the cleaning staff—each and every one of us, and he gives us advice."

"What? G is going to speak to me? Alone? And give me *advice*?"

"Yes. It's almost overwhelming, but yes, Claudia, he'll speak to you. You have to start getting ready for it mentally. But there's nothing to worry about. He'll see through to your very soul and set you on your path. You'll see."

"What if I don't want to meet with him alone?"

"Oh, you'll want to. Of course, you have to. But don't worry: you will definitely want to. Once you've heard him speak at the Love Teaching, you'll get what this is all about, and you will want to be first in line for your one-on-one."

Claudia stared at Evelyn. *Love Teaching?*

Evelyn said, "Until you've met G, you don't really get it. You can't. To you, right now, it probably sounds like we're in a cult!" She laughed.

"It does sound like that. But no, right?" Claudia laughed too.

"No. Of course not. I know. We're so different from other schools. It's profound here. We go deep within the individual. And it's not just about the children; it's about each person, including the parents, the volunteers—everyone. And it's not just about reading, writing, and arithmetic. It's about our personal development. Other schools don't *love* the people in them. That's what makes us who we are. There is no comparison. Because The Hawthorne School actually loves each one of us. Knows what's best for us, directs us."

"When you say The Hawthorne School loves us, you mean—"

"I mean G. Of course. And after him, Zelma. Because G is the human form representing The Hawthorne School—like Julia Hawthorne was before him. And Zelma, in G's physical absence, represents G."

Claudia, seeing Evelyn's passion, knew better than to show the rebellion she felt now. Claudia should have realized from the beginning. But it was this awful brain fog that she had all the time now.

"Sometimes I have a thought . . ." Claudia ventured.

"Yes?"

"A thought that maybe Henry and I aren't right for The Hawthorne School. Maybe we don't belong after all."

"Ah, that only means you are on the threshold of growth! Growing is always uncomfortable, Claudia, don't you know that? This pain and doubt—and it is pain and doubt, isn't it?— this shows that you are almost there. Let it happen, Claudia. There's no life without growth. Let it happen."

Claudia had already decided to begin to force herself to drink water instead of little green—just once each day. Starting today. She hated the taste of water now, and it was an ordeal for her to drink it. And today, when she'd skipped that one thermos of little green, she'd felt miserable. Her mood had become anxious and her skin had felt raw. She had been powerfully tempted to relieve that discomfort by simply drinking some little green juice or tea. Just a sip or two. But then she remembered how, when she quit smoking as soon as she knew she was pregnant with Henry, she would tell herself, "I can skip this cigarette. I can wait just a little while." She had been strongly motivated to quit then, and she had weaned herself from tobacco—although it had been one of the hardest things she'd done in her life up to that point. Because of that success five years before, she knew she had the willpower to at least cut down on her consumption of little green now.

She would not think of eliminating it entirely because that thought made her panic. She would only begin to keep track of how much of it she used, and continue to cut back. Just a little. Just enough to clear her mind and to be able to think clearly again.

49

I T WAS A crisp Sunday afternoon. Claudia and Henry had just come back from a ramble in the woods, and he had proudly shown her the way to Salamander Pond, as he called it. He had let her peek under the rotting log where the salamander's burrow was, and they had stood at the edge of the pond, watching fish mouths popping up to pucker on the surface between floating autumn leaves.

Later, in their dorm room, they sat quietly occupied. Henry looked up from his puzzle and studied her in a way that was almost sly. It was an odd expression on his too-young face.

"A penny for your thoughts?" said Claudia in a lighthearted way that she hoped covered the chill she felt.

"G is coming," he said, watching her expression. "I bet you didn't know that."

"Actually, I did. Everyone is talking about it and getting ready for it."

"Yes, but you don't know *why* he is coming."

"Why he is coming?" parroted Claudia. "Well, he's the president of The Hawthorne Schools, and he visits each school. That's why."

Henry looked self-important and as if there was a lot he could tell Claudia if he chose to.

"That's not why." Henry nodded his head, confirming in his own mind the secret knowledge he had. "He's coming because of me."

Claudia wanted to laugh at his baby grandiosity. To think that the president of several schools in the United States and abroad would be making a special visit for one four-year-old boy. She couldn't imagine Gabriel Hawthorne taking such interest in one small child.

The thought made her feel sick.

*   *   *

In Claudia's long days working with Irving, she continued telling him about her life, especially the parts that involved Henry. She had no one else to talk to. In the first days, she'd felt she was wasting her time, that he couldn't comprehend her words. But as time went on, an understanding grew between them, or so it appeared to her. She learned to read his stiff face and saw a gleam of interest in his otherwise dull eyes. She saw that when she spoke of her son, he was paying attention, and that encouraged her to go on. She'd once gotten him to assent that he had children in the school too, but after that he would give away no more about himself or his own family.

"You love your children, Irving, just like I love Henry." She was speaking as much to herself as to him. "You would do whatever you could for their benefit."

Irving glanced at her and yawned.

"Irving," she said, "have you ever tried to drink less of little green? That's what I'm doing now. You won't tell anyone, will you?" She smiled at the idea. The mop in the corner was more likely to tell tales than Irving was. In spite of his inability to answer, she felt a sort of solidarity with him, a feeling he was no doubt incapable of understanding or sharing.

"I feel stronger and clearer in my thinking when I take less, and I'm drinking more water." She looked at the murky whites of his eyes and felt concern for him. "You should try it."

Irving made no reply and indeed showed no sign of hearing her.

She patted his rough hand.

He looked at her hand covering his.

Then he grabbed his mop and got back to work.

50

Zelma called Claudia to her office.

"It has come to my attention that you have been taking Henry into the woods without authorization."

Claudia knew Zelma too well by now to think she was kidding, but the remark seemed ridiculous. Wasn't the Hawthorne Way all about immersion in nature?

"Yes, I do take Henry for walks in the woods. It didn't occur to me that I would need 'authorization.'"

"It will occur to you from now on."

Claudia met Zelma's hostile glare with an impulse to rebel.

"You've broken a rule. There are consequences for breaking rules. You give me no alternative but to add on working hours. You will need to work on Sunday afternoons now until further notice."

"But I didn't know it was a rule to stay away from the woods. No one told me. How was I supposed to know?"

Zelma and Claudia were locked in a silent battle now, Zelma trying to do her worst with her angry glare, and Claudia pushing back, trying not to be frightened by the power of it. Claudia had skipped her midmorning little green, forcing herself to drink water instead. She knew that this was why, instead of feeling calm and accepting, she was ready to fight back. She longed for little green; she felt slightly sick, and there was a fire of fury burning at the edges of her mind.

Zelma's dark look gave way to one of confusion and then a sudden dawning perception.

"I'm sorry, Claudia. I'm afraid I've forgotten my manners." She rose and went to make tea. "I should have offered you—"

Claudia interrupted, for the second time that morning. "No tea for me, thank you."

Zelma turned and regarded Claudia up and down, as if seeing her anew.

"No *tea?*" It was if she couldn't believe what she was hearing and as if at the same time she now had confirmed her suspicion. "Juice, then?" She gestured toward her small refrigerator but did not move toward it.

"No, thank you."

"I see," said Zelma. She stood with her hands hanging at her sides, looking at Claudia and then at the floor, as if lost in thought for a moment.

Claudia observed as Zelma softened and sparkled before her eyes, taking on the personality she had shown the day of the tour, that day that seemed so long ago now but was only a matter of weeks. Zelma became the adorable little lady with the twinkly eyes, full of love and understanding.

"Claudia, dear heart. I'm sorry if I came off a bit harsh just now." She tilted her head in apology. "The fact is, we're all in a tizzy about G coming. You do know, it could be at any time. He'll come walking through the door, and we have to be ready. I'm a bit on edge perhaps." She smiled sweetly at Claudia. "I hope you will forgive me. I always want to be supportive of you. We are devoted to you and to Henry. I hope you know that."

Claudia foolishly wanted to believe that this version of Zelma was the true one and that her excuses were valid. But she knew better. She wanted to accept the tea after all, but she told herself, *No. Not now. I can wait. I can have it with lunch. I can wait just a little longer.*

Claudia calculated that Zelma had already guessed that she was trying to break her dependency on little green. What Zelma didn't know was whether Claudia was completely free of it or was in some intermediate stage of weaning off it. That uncertainty on Zelma's part was the only card Claudia had in her hand.

"I've been thinking."

Zelma's head pulled back, like a cobra regarding its prey. "Thinking . . .?"

"Yes. There are some things I need." Claudia raised her chin, gathering confidence.

"Things *you* need?"

Claudia felt heady with her growing sense of power. She almost could have laughed at Zelma's echoing her own words back to her. She had the advantage now. Now was the time to use it.

"I want Henry's birth certificate back."

Zelma nodded, unblinking, waiting for the next demand.

"I want a vehicle to use. Sometimes I need to run an errand in town. I need access to a car."

Zelma was watching her warily.

"I want just a few days off, to rest." *And to think,* thought Claudia. *I need time to think. And to detox. And to drive over to Maggie's apartment and tell her about what's going on here.*

"And the money I gave you," she continued. "I understand that is for Henry's tuition. But I need a little nest egg. I need just a little of it back—to be able to buy things for Henry."

"But Claudia, dear, don't we supply all of your needs here? You know if there is anything, anything at all that you need, you have only to ask. You don't have to trouble yourself with money and errands. We're glad to—"

"Four hundred dollars. Just four hundred. I won't ask for more."

Zelma stood, taking Claudia's measure. Her hands clenched and unclenched, her jaw tightened and untightened. There was a silver flame in her eyes.

What she said next frightened Claudia.

"Of course, dear. Whatever you like. We want you to be happy."

Claudia stood grasping this victory that terrified her. If Zelma agreed to all of Claudia's demands, it meant that Zelma was even more determined to keep Henry and her at The Hawthorne School than she had realized.

"If these little things will brighten your life, dear, then of course. And as for the extra working hours, well, forget I said anything about working Sundays. Let's simply call this a warning, shall we? Do not enter the woods without authorization from this point on. And"—Zelma was studying Claudia's face and finding her way as she spoke—"I see now that you're right, dear. Perhaps we are working you too hard. I think you need a little vacation. Two days off to recharge, how does that sound?"

Claudia gave a nod of acknowledgment.

Maintaining her determined tone, Claudia said, "And I'd like the birth certificate now."

"Of course." Zelma went to her uncluttered desk, muttering, "Now where did I put it?" She was the picture of a perplexed senior citizen.

She picked up and put down an agenda and a notebook and a few papers. She put on a look of befuddlement, pretending to search.

"It's not here!" she declared with the mannerisms of a stage actress.

Claudia came toward her. "I'll help you look." She had the upper hand now and was going to use it.

"Oh, *now* I remember."

Claudia sensed the lie before it came.

"Niles has it. I gave it to him to take to the copy shop. He never did give it back to me. We're all so busy, getting ready for Gabriel, you know. When Niles gets back, I'll get the original and the copy from him. And you can have the car that he's using now. He's coming back with G. It could be any time now."

Zelma looked out the diamond-paned window toward the driveway, as if expecting to see him pulling up there right now.

"The second he gets back, I'll send him out to the bank to get the cash you've asked for. You know, I meant to give you a little pocket money. I'm so glad you brought it up. Four hundred, you said. Now, let me just write all of this down. My memory is just terrible lately."

She giggled, and Claudia looked away, black fear overtaking her again.

"By the way," said Claudia, her mind becoming clearer while the sickness in her body became more intense, "you said it had come to your attention that I had taken Henry into the woods? How did that happen?"

"You were reported."

"Reported?"

"Yes, dear heart. All parents, staff, and students are required to make Reports. You will make Reports yourself. Others will make Reports about you. This helps us to understand what everyone in our care needs." Zelma made it sound so maternal: *"Everyone in our care . . ."*

Claudia thought: Who had seen her taking that path into the woods? Who had reported her?

Zelma, with that odd trick she had of seeming to read Claudia's thoughts, answered her unspoken question.

"Henry, dear heart. Henry reported you."

51

"HE'S GROWING INTO his power," explained Henry's teacher.

Claudia had saved the rest of her questions for Evelyn.

To whom had Henry reported her? Since when did little boys report their mothers? She would have thought it was ludicrous if it hadn't been another sign of Henry becoming more and more alienated from her and identifying instead with The Hawthorne School. Still, Claudia was sure, as she sat in the classroom with Evelyn, watching Henry build a tower with wooden blocks, that he hadn't actually "reported" her. That had to be Zelma's spin on it. Henry must have simply *told*—in all innocence—that he had been taking walks with his mother in the woods. Claudia recalled that Henry had been hesitant to go, protesting, "No one is supposed to go without permission." Claudia had reassured him, "It's okay; you're with me." Henry had begun to insist, "No, we can only go with a teacher," but Claudia had tempted him: "But we might see a deer." Henry had held her hand then and walked along with her, adding, "Or the raccoon family? Or the frogs?"

Evelyn regarded Claudia from under her long black bangs. She gestured with her delicate, birdlike wrist toward the colorful poster on the wall, the same one Zelma had in her office, the one Claudia had seen the day they first came to the school:

The Hawthorne School Ideals

1. Be cooperative.
2. Be loyal.
3. Be just.
4. Be self-controlled.
5. Be humble.
6. Be steady."

"It doesn't say anything there about reporting mothers," said Claudia.

Henry looked up from his tower of blocks at his mother and teacher. He knocked down his tower and began again.

"That," answered Evelyn, "would come under number three: 'Be just.' The children learn that they and everyone else, even parents and teachers, have to follow the rules. That's only fair, isn't it?"

"Do you *ask* the children to rat out their parents?" There was aggression in Claudia's tone.

She had refused the little green tea that Evelyn had offered.

She had put off her midmorning dose as long as she could and had finally given in just before lunch. She'd been grateful for the blessed relief it had brought her, and then disgusted with herself for needing it. But that disgust was muted under the now-customary sense of peace, the sense of all being as it should be. Free of her janitorial duties, she'd taken a break in the hedge maze and had sat before the statue of Julia Hawthorne, listening to the birdsong.

After school, she had come to Evelyn's classroom to get to the bottom of this "reporting" business, and the effects of the calming herb were wearing off. She was yearning for more. She should probably go ahead and have some little green, she thought, because she didn't want to try to wean off too fast and sabotage herself. But she wanted to have a clear mind now as she talked to Evelyn. She didn't want to be lulled any more into accepting the unacceptable.

"Yes," said Evelyn simply. "The children have to report on each other, parents, teachers, and everyone else. No exceptions. Rules are necessary in every civilized society. Candy?"

Evelyn opened a green glass dish that had been sitting in the center of the table. It contained green hard candy—like the candy Claudia had once seen Evelyn offer to Henry. Claudia was transfixed by the beautiful green color of the dish and the candy. More than anything, she wanted to take a piece.

"Is that *little green* candy?"

"Of course. This is the adult variety. The ones I give to the children are milder and sweeter." Evelyn watched Claudia with a knowing expression. Claudia was furious with Evelyn in that moment. She was sure that Zelma had let Evelyn know of her suspicion that Claudia was trying to withdraw from little green, and that she was well aware of the battle going on in Claudia's mind as she looked at the candy. To give in and take one would be to give The Hawthorne School another victory over her. And yet, what did it matter? She wouldn't care anymore once that sweet feeling filled her whole being.

She took the candy quickly, unwrapped it, and popped it into her mouth. It was bitter. She thought of spitting it out; there was still time to go back. At the same time, she knew she wouldn't. She comforted herself with the reminder that she had been successfully cutting down. She didn't know how strong a dose was in this candy, never having taken it before, but it couldn't be much: it was so small. It was already melting away on her tongue.

Evelyn was talking. "Let's look at The Hawthorne School Ideals, Claudia. Rule one: Be cooperative. That means obey your teacher, Zelma, and the Enforcers. Henry is an Enforcer."

Claudia tensed. "Why is *Henry* an Enforcer?" The words sounded foreign and surreal as she said them.

"He got to be an Enforcer by reporting the most. We find that when children are the ones who enforce the rules, they learn to manage power. They don't feel that they are subjected to adult whims. Instead, they are a part of the system that maintains stability in everyone's' lives."

Claudia wanted to focus on what Evelyn was saying, but half her attention was waiting for the peaceful relief that would come when the little green would take effect. She eyed the candy dish, and Evelyn pushed it toward her. She didn't hesitate. She took another candy.

"Rule number two: Be loyal. This means we protect our school's privacy. We don't tell outsiders about certain things we do here. And little green can only be consumed here at school; it cannot be taken off campus. That's part of loyalty too, of course."

Claudia was feeling the effects now and sat back thankfully, letting Evelyn go on. Her questions seemed less and less important as her mind slid into that place of ease.

"Number three: Be just. This means that someone must be blamed and punished for each mistake. If the guilty one cannot be found, then someone else is chosen and punished. We call that person the Stand-in. A good choice of Stand-in is usually the one who has reported the least. The Enforcer chooses the Stand-in.

"Number four: Be self-controlled. Our children do not express bad feelings. Bad feelings are anger, sadness, and jealousy. Bad feelings are punished."

Claudia heard these words as rolling waves of nonsense. She felt her heart beating slowly in her chest and a peaceful light spread through every corner of her mind. Questions rose, half formed, as Evelyn interpreted The Hawthorne School rules, but the half questions sank and disintegrated.

My questions don't matter. Don't matter. Don't matter. Nothing matters.

"Number five: Be humble. This means that everyone, including Stand-ins, *especially* Stand-ins, must accept punishments willingly.

"Number six: Be steady. This means that our children cannot change their minds. The Enforcer is always watching for mind-changing. Zelma can change her mind, and G, of course, can change his mind. But even teachers cannot change their minds. That's being steady."

"How?" began Claudia. She saw behind her eyelids the words she wanted to form, and worked to say them. "How is Henry an 'Enforcer'? You said, because he's reported the most? But then, *how* can he report the most? He can't read those rules. He can't read yet." Claudia's hand reached for another candy, her mind barely aware she was doing it. She longed to eat every piece in the dish and go to sleep.

"None of our fours can read. We discourage premature reading. Henry knows all the rules, though, and what's more, he knows what they really *mean*. He's brighter than all the other children. That's what makes him such a good Enforcer. Henry is full of promise."

Claudia's eyelids were heavy. Another question. She wanted to ask another question. But why was she asking questions? She should get up. Take her child. Steal some little green somehow. Walk out of this school. No one could stop her. She could leave at any time. She didn't need to wait for the birth certificate, for the money. She knew that Zelma had no intention of keeping any of her promises. She would never get the four hundred dollars, and anyway it didn't matter. The main thing was to get out. There was no need to worry about where to go. She could figure it all out later. But she was so heavy in her chair. So very heavy. She couldn't get up. She was in a dream. It was all only a dream. She was surrendering. Surrendering made everything all right. Surrendering made the bad dream a good one. She didn't want to get up now. She struggled through the fog in her brain.

A question.

"How . . . are children . . . punished? How have you taught Henry to . . . punish other children?"

"Oh," said Evelyn, "don't worry about *that*. It's nothing dark or creepy, you know. No *physical* punishment. Goodness no. We only practice shunning. That's the most common punishment for children. It's nonviolent. In the Hawthorne Way, we pride ourselves on nonviolence. We simply agree to stop seeing or responding in any way to the punished child; it's as if they're invisible. As if they are not even there. They no longer exist for us. The Enforcer decides for how long. It brings the lesson home, and while it does upset the punished ones, and in fact it causes them intense distress, it doesn't really *hurt* them. If they show they are upset, well, then, they've just broken another rule, unfortunately."

"The Stand-in?" slurred Claudia, trying to rest her chin in her hand. Somehow her chin kept missing its mark. "Who is the Stand-in?"

"The Stand-in could be anyone at all, anyone that the Enforcer chooses. But Henry always chooses Bibi. Yes, if we can't find out who is to blame for something, Henry chooses Bibi for the Stand-in. She never reports anyone.

"So that's just."

* * *

Claudia rose from a pool of unconsciousness to see Evelyn's face in front of hers.

"Time to wake up! It's five o'clock. Time to take Henry back to your room," said Evelyn. Claudia blinked and looked around herself. She was in Evelyn's rocking chair by the window. Henry was standing by the classroom door with his back to her. She pulled herself to her feet and lurched forward.

CHAPTER

52

OVER DINNER IN their room, Claudia talked with Henry. Her mind was clearing. She avoided the little green juice, putting it aside for later.

"Miss Applegate told me that you're an Enforcer. What's that like?"

Henry was eating with gusto. He was always a good eater now, never picking at his food as he used to do in the apartment. He stuffed his mouth and didn't respond.

Maybe he didn't know how to answer that question. She tried another.

"Tell me about Bibi. Is she your friend?"

Claudia thought of Bibi, the tiny Indian girl with the large, solemn eyes.

Henry made no comment.

He was intentionally not answering her. That was okay; he could still hear her.

"I don't want you to be a bully, Henry. Do you know what a bully is? A bully is someone who picks on another person a lot. Makes them feel bad, hurts their feelings. That's not nice, is it? You wouldn't like it if someone was a bully to you. I don't want you to pick on Bibi. She doesn't even have her parents here, so you shouldn't make her sad. You shouldn't make anyone sad on purpose. Do you understand?"

Henry kicked his legs and looked out the window.

"Another thing that isn't very nice is 'reporting' your mom to your teacher. I know you didn't mean to do it, but from now on, don't say things to get me in trouble." Claudia heard how weak she sounded, as if she were Henry's sibling instead of his mother.

"Henry? *Henry!*"

Henry left the table and stood looking out the window, at the darkening forest.

"Henry, are you shunning me right now? You're shunning me, aren't you? Henry. Talk to me right now."

Henry stood small and solid, with his back to her.

CHAPTER

53

CLAUDIA HAD HOPED that having days "off" would mean that Evelyn would not come for Henry before school or keep him in the afternoon, but Evelyn showed up at the usual time in the morning.

She protested to Evelyn, "Oh, didn't Zelma tell you? I have the day off, so I'll keep Henry today."

"Zelma did tell me. She wants me to continue our same routine. She says that it is important for you to have all of your time to recharge and rest. You've been working so hard, she says."

Henry broke his silence as soon as he saw Evelyn, running to her with bright eyes. "Miss Applegate!"

When Claudia tried to kiss and hug him goodbye, Henry stood as stiff as a little tree.

It was okay. Soon, she'd be free of little green. Zelma would withhold all of the things she'd promised. Claudia would pretend to cooperate, to be still under the spell. She wouldn't let Zelma suspect she was taking Henry and leaving for good.

She set out to find a quiet place to think. As she wandered the building, she tried not to cry. She didn't want anyone to see her weeping. Henry seemed to consider Evelyn to be his mother. Claudia told herself to get a grip. Henry was a small child. He couldn't be held responsible. The adults were supposed to be the responsible ones. She had to be the grown-up, the mother.

It was *her* fault that Henry was here, in this toxic place. "Toxic" was the appropriate word, because The Hawthorne School was intoxicating them with little green. But now she had to recognize her own part. The Hawthorne School hadn't come seeking her. *She* had willingly walked in, holding her baby's hand. She was furious with herself as she realized that the facts had been staring her in the face the whole time. She couldn't account for it now, but she had entrusted him, turned him over, to these people.

Why?

Because the building was beautiful and she liked the art on the walls? Because the director had told her she was a good mother and Henry was somehow extraordinary? How stupid she'd been. She had done the very thing she had always been afraid of doing. She was failing her child. She was the one who had gotten them into this place, and she was the only one who would get them out.

The Main Hall was full of nooks and recesses. Claudia curled up in a window seat on the first floor and gazed out the diamond-paned window at the beautiful fall flower beds. Chrysanthemums, asters, goldenrod, heather, and other flowers whose names she didn't know. There were bursts of color everywhere, standing against the background of the gray building and overlooked by whimsical gargoyles. And through the hazy autumn air, scarlet leaves floated down in slow zigzags on the breeze to rest on the grass.

This beautiful place, she thought. *Such a beautiful place.*

She opened her thermos and drank.

CHAPTER

54

Early the next morning, Claudia checked Zelma's office and found it empty. She hurried to the phone and called Maggie again.

"Hello?" Her friend's voice was relaxed and familiar.

"Maggie! Listen. It's very important."

"Claudia?" The voice on the phone sounded alarmed now. "What's wrong?"

"Just listen. I need you to come and pick us up at five thirty. Will you do that? Henry and I will be waiting on the road just outside the front gate. I'll explain everything later."

"What? You're scaring me. What's the matter?"

"I'll tell you tonight. In the meantime, don't talk to Zelma. Don't talk to anyone from here. Don't trust anyone. Promise me you'll be there. Do you promise?"

"Oh my God, Claudia. You sound awful."

"Maggie!"

"I'll be there. Of course, I'll be there. I'd do anything for you. Five thirty."

*   *   *

At 5:25, Claudia was hurrying Henry along the path toward the front gate when she heard swift steps behind her, and she turned.

It was Zelma, smiling kindly and firmly hooking her elbow through Claudia's in a companionable manner, as if the two had met by prearrangement for a cozy stroll through the grounds.

"Awful news, dear. One of our Hawthorne parents. Maggie Timmerberg? I believe you used to know her?"

"*Used* to?" Claudia slid her arm away from Zelma's.

"Brace yourself. She's had an accident."

Claudia felt these words as a punch to her chest.

"But that's not possible. When? What kind of accident?"

"Less than thirty minutes ago. The hospital called. We're assisting in arrangements for little Violet. Apparently Maggie was driving too fast. As soon as I heard, I came to look for you. I wouldn't want you to hear it from anyone else. You were neighbors, I know." She sighed, making a sound that was almost a genteel sob. "Such a shame." She shook her head sorrowfully and pulled a tissue from the inside of her sleeve to dab daintily at the corner of an eye. "So preventable—like most accidents that happen to people. Poor Maggie. Of course, she was never extraordinary like you are, Claudia. Still, it's a tragedy to lose *any* of our school parents."

*   *   *

Alone with Henry in their little room, Claudia sat in stunned silence while Henry ate his dinner. She had just spoken to Maggie that morning. It was not possible that she could be dead. And yet she was and apparently had died speeding toward The Hawthorne School because of Claudia's phone call. It was her fault.

But was it possible it had been no accident?

Now her imagination was getting out of control. But Maggie had been about to help Claudia and Henry escape. At least, Claudia had planned to ask her to help, and she had no doubt that Maggie would have done it. Could Zelma somehow have had overheard her on the phone? And somehow caused Maggie to crash her car? But that was crazy. Now she was suspecting Zelma of murder. That couldn't possibly be.

She thought of her friend's kindness, the times she had shaken her out of a black mood and forced her to come out into the fresh air and sunshine. She thought of the worshipful compliments she had paid her when Claudia's confidence was so low. She had lost her only friend. And now they were "making arrangements" for her daughter Violet.

She thought of Zelma's coldness as she informed Claudia that her friend had died, and she thought of Zelma's crocodile tears.

Claudia's emotions were more than she could bear. There was no way out. Not tonight. There was only little green.

55

T HE FOLLOWING DAY, Claudia used the after-school time, while Henry would still be with Evelyn, to approach Violet's teacher, Lillian Kincaid. The death of her friend brought even more urgency to Claudia's determination to escape The Hawthorne School. If it was possible that Lillian could become an ally, Claudia needed to know that now.

The classroom smelled of lavender, which misted from an air diffuser on a window ledge. Lillian herself smelled of lavender. It was a calming, sleep-inducing scent.

As they sat down at a small wooden table in the sevens classroom, with steaming cups of tea Lillian had prepared, the teacher pulled her gold knit shawl up to her shoulders and asked, "How are you adjusting now to the Hawthorne Way?"

Was she giving Claudia an opening? But Claudia had to be careful. She didn't want to risk a second "report."

"Actually, I've been having some trouble with that. I thought maybe you could help me to understand things better."

Lillian blinked, her face unreadable.

"A question about The Hawthorne School?" echoed Lillian.

Claudia's fingers itched to reach for the cup of little green tea, but she distracted herself by digging the nails of her right hand into her left wrist. She saw a wavering, an opening, with Lillian. If she could just keep her mind clear, she might be able to figure out a way to get herself and Henry free. Her questions came out in a rush.

"Why is the school trying to take Henry away from me and give him to Evelyn? Evelyn denies it, but I know. Why does the school want everyone hooked on little green? I know it's not a nutritional supplement. It's some kind of trance-inducing drug: I *know* it is. Where does the school get so many orphans from? And Maggie—Violet's mom—do you know anything about what happened to her? What's going on here?"

Lillian hesitated. Her face did not have the closed expression that she always saw in the faces of Zelma and Evelyn. Her eyes were not glassy-bright like Niles's. Claudia was talking to a real human being now—she sensed it.

Lillian eyed the closed classroom door. She lowered her voice, even though there was no one to hear them. She looked at her hands, folded on the table. She opened them, palms up, as if to indicate that she would speak openly. Or was that a gesture to hide the deceit that Claudia was beginning to suspect in everyone here?

"Lillian, please. Help me."

"The best way I can help you," said Lillian after a moment of thought, "is by telling you that for as long as you are *in* The Hawthorne School, you are safer not asking questions *about* The Hawthorne School."

Lillian's expression had become tense.

"Thank you for saying that. That means you want to help me. That means that you're acknowledging that what I've just said is true."

Lillian pulled back ever so slightly. "I don't think I said all that," she whispered. "I don't know any more than you do about Violet's mom."

"Please," said Claudia, "tell me why they've made Henry an Enforcer. Evelyn tries to make it sound normal, but it's not normal. What are they trying to do to him?"

"I could be putting myself in harm's way by even listening to what you're saying right now. You could make a Report on me. You should. It's expected. And it would earn you credibility with them. Or I could make a Report on you, you know."

Claudia could see Lillian debating with herself. She reached out and touched Lillian's hand. "We could help each other, Lillian. We could trust each other. Because you don't like whatever it is that's going on here either." Claudia was struck with the realization as she spoke. "*You* want to get out of here. I see it. Am I right?"

Right then, Lillian seemed to make up her mind.

"Look, Claudia. You're asking me what's going on here." She shot a glance at the door again and went on in a rushed whisper. "I'll tell you. The Hawthorne School breaks people. It takes them in and makes them into something they were never meant to be; it spins them and breaks them. I can't get out of here. You can't get out of here. You might as well know it right now. *No one* gets out."

"But—I could just take Henry and leave right now. He's my son. It's a free country. I can leave *now*," insisted Claudia, a hint of hysteria rising in her voice.

"Then why don't you?"

It was true. At any point Claudia could have run out to the road with her son; she could have flagged down a police car; she could have made a way out. Why hadn't she?

She had deceived herself as much as Zelma had deceived her. She answered now, honestly.

"Because of little green."

"Yes. But even if you took some containers of little green from the kitchen, and even if you decided to live in a shelter for a while, you *still* couldn't leave. They'd stop you. They'd bring you back."

"That's crazy. That's illegal. They couldn't do it. Even if they could, I'd just leave again."

"No, you wouldn't. Because they'd take your boy from you and lock you up in the tunnel, in the Holding Place."

Claudia sat back and stared at Lillian. She wondered if Lillian could be on Zelma's side after all. Could she be threatening her while pretending to be her ally?

Lillian went on, "There's a larger picture here. You don't see it all yet."

"Then please *tell* me. What is it that I don't see?"

CHAPTER

56

"WE'RE ALL DISPOSABLE, Claudia. The only people of value in the Hawthorne Schools are the children. They only want the children. And some children are worth more than others. If any adult threatens the organization in the slightest way, they disappear. That's why there are so many orphans here."

Claudia shut her eyes tight. She thought of Violet, now orphaned. Her stomach cramped. The effect of missing another dose of little green, combined with the effect of Lillian's revelation made her physically ill. She had heard enough. How much more did she need to hear? She needed to get herself and Henry out.

And yet, the way out was sealed.

"There are unmarked graves in that forest. Your life is worth less than nothing to the organization, and so is mine. If they even heard us talking like this, we'd be dead and buried before midnight."

Claudia recalled the words Niles said to her on their first day in the kitchen: "This winter, you'll be buried under the snow." She'd thought he was simply saying that it snowed a lot in the Midwest. How much more had she missed? How much more had she closed her eyes to because she had wanted to trust; she had wanted support and to hear that she was a good mother and to be part of a family.

She had known yesterday, when Zelma told her of her friend's "accident," that it had been no accident. She hadn't wanted to see it all at once. She needed to see it all now.

"They *kill* parents? Is that what happened to Maggie Timmerberg?"

Lillian sighed. "I don't have all the inside information. What I can tell you is this: we don't matter. But Henry is worth his weight in gold. All the children are considered precious, but Henry more than the others. Which means, if you stand in their way, you're a dead woman. They're very excited about him."

Claudia's heart pounded, her eyes fixed on Lillian's. "What do you mean? Why are they excited?"

"It's not what you're thinking. A pedophilia ring? No. You're on the wrong track."

"Then . . . what?"

"You'll hear it said: 'G loves the children most of all.' They're malleable; he can form them the way he wants them. You see, he gets these little minds before they are fully developed. They will never question him. They will never be able to leave him because they will never learn to cope with the outside world or even think for themselves.

"All their needs—and all our needs—are met by The Hawthorne School. At first, they make the teachers and the parents feel that they are specially chosen, deeply loved, and pull them in that way. But all the adults have one inconvenient thing in common: they have all known another way of life. G can never be sure of the allegiance of adults. The children, on the other hand, he can mold from the beginning, so they know only this life. He's got a plan in mind, a plan to create a new order, with himself as god-king. It's all based on his own . . . delusion. It *is* a delusion, I know that now, although I didn't always.

"How can I help you understand?" Lillian looked out the window, to where the sun was sinking behind the trees. "Let me tell you about my own beginning here, before it was the way it is now." She traced the rim of her cup with a forefinger. "I was drawn to The Hawthorne School by its idealism. I liked the focus on nature and imagination. I wanted to be a part of this forward-thinking educational movement. I'd heard of Julia Hawthorne, the great visionary in the field of education. I could see myself following her footsteps, so after high school, I went straight into the Hawthorne Teachers' College. I was full of zeal in those early years.

"Julia herself was here in those days, in charge of everything, and I was in awe of her. All the teachers were, I guess. She was a famous innovator. Gabriel, her son, was her assistant then.

"As I look back now, I see that she was an eccentric, but that was part of the fun of it all. She was so different. There was such a thrill in working with Julia!" Lillian was speaking quickly, in conversational tones now, as if still feeling the excitement of the early days. "Everyone in her orbit was swept up in the creation of this dream. Julia had a charismatic presence. Tall, with penetrating eyes and a soft, hypnotic voice. In her day, there was only this one school. Gabriel grew up helping his mother on this campus. He saw how the parents were, how they turned over their children to Julia so trustingly, how they surrendered to her confidence in her own unusual ideas. He saw how worshipful the children were of their teachers. I think that's when he began to work out his plan.

"Nine years after I started here, Julia died, and Gabriel took up the torch. Right away, things started to change. Gabriel stood on the shoulders of his mother to create a religion—with himself as the deity.

"It began with the Promise. That's what they used to call it. The Promise is the fulfillment of all your desires. They taught that you are entitled to get whatever you want and to get it easily. We only needed to unlock our Magnetic Will. We learned that we, here at The Hawthorne School, are the greatest concentration of Magnetic Will on the planet. All we had to do, to get our deepest desires met, was follow the school's teachings and be loyal.

"And it's real—this concept of attracting what you want with just your will. Charisma, lasting beauty, and perfect health. You've noticed how young Zelma is in her body? How there's a special radiance about Niles?"

"But—"

"People are not what they seem. We all made a deal, and we got what we most wanted. There is a strange power here that I wouldn't believe if I hadn't experienced it myself. I had been suffering with a sort of chronic fatigue syndrome. When Gabriel came on the scene and began his teachings, I was all in. Like everyone. And I saw that I was actually healing. I got perfect health after years of illness; Evelyn got her wish: lots of children. They were given to her by The Hawthorne School, of course. Nothing esoteric about that. But some of the other things—there's something real at work here that I can't explain. And what does everyone want once they get what they think they want most? Eternal life. That's the New Promise.

"Gabriel's grown this school into an international organization. He's the one who introduced little green, to break down the minds of adults and children. To separate us from any sense of reality."

"But what is it all *for*?"

"The goal is to get complete control of the children. Little green, trance inductions they call Distance Reality, these are tools to create patterns and chemical changes in unformed brains, changes that will be lasting. From the age of four, the programming begins. Little green makes the mind vulnerable to suggestion. At high doses, it causes hallucinations and delusions. Distance Reality is nothing more than a trick of the mind. Combined with the herbs, it creates an illusion of leaving this reality and escaping to other times and places. Reality is replaced by a group psychosis. Combine these effects with intentionally imposed illiteracy, and you create a population that grows up never knowing what reality is at all. Shells of human beings, unable to think an independent thought.

"They grow up worshipping G in a more profound way than would be possible with even brainwashed adults. For Gabriel Hawthorne, it's the ultimate power trip.

"When you see G, you'll understand.

"The teachers adore him, and the children grow up worshipping him. The children have never known anything else. G goes from school to school—we could say from temple to temple—and finds unquestioning devotees. Lifelong worship-pers, all around the world. He sees himself as the leader of a kingdom of children.

"There's no power greater than the power of obtaining and controlling masses of small children. Children can't leave you if they never grow up in any real sense.

"Think: Why do we keep the children outside, playing half the day instead of studying indoors? Because it's good for them? That was Julia's original idea. But the intention has changed under G. Why do we discourage reading—until the children are 'ready' to learn? Julia Hawthorne wanted reading to develop organically, and her system did work, in its way.

"But since G has taken over, did you know that the students *never* are considered ready to learn? Our students never learn to read. They can't teach themselves. There are no books, in any grade, in any classroom. There's nothing but the poster on the wall, listing the Hawthorne Ideals. Why are there no comput-ers? I think you understand now. The students never learn to inform themselves, think, or question. They grow up depen-dent on little green and believing that G is God."

The pain in Claudia's belly was searing. Her nausea was rising. She reached for the cold cup of little green and drank it down. Although the truth had been knocking at her mind, try-ing all along to wake her up, only now did she let it in, and as it rushed in, it overwhelmed her.

"You said that they're especially excited about Henry. Why?" She forced herself not to cry. Crying would not help her or Henry. She had to be strong.

"As luck would have it, Henry bears an uncanny physical resemblance to G. Blue eyes, black hair, same skin tone. And not only that, Zelma thinks he's like G in his character, the way she remembers G as a child. Because she was a teacher here when he was a kid. She sees Henry as domineering and inde-pendent, 'just like G,' she says. G's been looking for a long time for a perfect 'son.' Zelma will get a lot of credit for finding him, and Evelyn will have a higher position in the organization for being his mother."

"But she's *not* his mother."

"According to The Hawthorne School, she is his only mother."

"They can't have my son!"

"G needs your son, Claudia, and he will have him. Biological mothers are dispensable. He killed his own."

Claudia drew back. Could she believe Lillian?

"Yes, the revered founder of this school, Gabriel's mother, Julia Hawthorne. She wasn't going to allow him to move forward with his own plans. He poisoned her. He does whatever he needs to do to get what he wants. And now he wants Henry. He doesn't have biological children and never will. You've noticed that none of the teachers have biological children either? Part of the Hawthorne Way is strict celibacy. It's against the rules to have sexual relationships. That would detract from the energy needed for worshipping G. G doesn't allow anyone to pay 'excessive attention' to anyone because all attention should be on him. Little green helps with that: among other things, it suppresses the libido completely.

"You might think that a cult leader would use the followers for his own sexual gratification?"

Claudia shut her eyes tight.

Lillian went on. "That's not G's particular sickness. He seems to adhere to his own doctrine of what he calls 'bodily purity.' He gets his power trip not through sex, but through a visceral mind control. What he's after—and what he gets— is fanatical idolization of himself: his thrill is to break people down and own their minds. And actually, he doesn't need to have the pleasure of breaking each person himself, although I've seen how much he enjoys doing it. No. Now, he lets his assistants do that for him. People like Zelma and Niles. Because the international school is growing so fast, he needs his helpers to do some of the work for him. The ultimate goal is to completely own the minds of thousands of people around the world.

"He teaches that the world as we know it is about to end. When the time comes, G's people will live in the tunnels until it is safe to come up. 'We' will be the only survivors. We will be the only people on earth, and G will be our leader. The only people that will survive the End of Days will be these children.

The children—and the adults who have remained faithful and steadfast to G."

"But—the adults? Once they see the price they have to pay, why do they stay?"

Lillian dropped her voice. "What do we get out of it? Safety. Yes, I know, it seems it's the opposite of safety, doesn't it? But as long as we obey, as long as we accept G's teachings, we are safe. If we leave, we know we will be killed. We've seen it happen to others. If we stay, we are provided for, we belong, and we are safe. He cares for all of our needs. He tells us all the time that no one will ever love us as he does. And that no one will ever know us as he does. Of course, he doesn't really know us at all. He uses spying and Reports to give the appearance of knowing our innermost thoughts."

Claudia recalled what she had been told of the other campuses: "And he has schools in Europe and Asia."

"Yes. Oh yes, the Hawthorne Schools are springing up everywhere around the world. Each one with its system of underground tunnels."

"So G is getting power. The teachers and children are brainwashed and feel that The Hawthorne School is their only safe place. But what about Evelyn, Zelma, and Niles? What's in it for them?"

"The same. In addition, they're getting prestige. Significance. Plus, they really believe in G. For Zelma, the purpose of her life is to be G's assistant. She brings the children to him, tends his flock, and keeps everyone in control for him so that each time he returns, he will be happy. She is—they all are—that brainwashed."

"And what do they want to do to Henry?"

"G has been waiting for a little boy like Henry, and Henry's just the right age too. He'll raise him to be his right-hand man and to step into his dynasty. And as for you, Claudia? It could go one of three ways. Oh, it's all been discussed, you know. There's a plan for you. Zelma has shared it with all the teachers."

Claudia felt as if she were dreaming. She felt as if she herself was not real, Lillian was not real, and none of this could be happening.

"If you surrender, you'll live in Unity Hall with the teachers, continue working here, and see Henry from afar from time to time. He will be made to forget he ever had any mother but Evelyn."

"Henry will never forget me!"

"He can be made to forget," repeated Lillian. "They have ways. Henry will live with Evelyn except when G may take him on tours of the schools."

"I won't surrender."

"Then she'll put you in Comfort Hall with the Night People. The ones who work at night. You haven't seen them, but Irving is one of them. He barely sleeps, so they keep him working both night and day. The Night People live on the highest possible doses of little green. Each one is in a sort of walking coma. There, but not there. You may as well say they're zombies."

Claudia thought of becoming like Irving, and shuddered with the realization that there were more people like him, trudging around the campus at night, sluggishly working, and she could be made to become one of them. Had Irving refused to surrender, then?

"The third possibility is that you could rebel against that fate, as a few people have. If you do that, you will join those who fought back. They are buried in the woods."

57

"So they kill everyone who revolts against their plan?"
Lillian nodded, her eyes grave. "The last one was Fiona—Niles's wife. It was in April, the last time G was here. He ordered it. It was because she took Taylor and was about to drive away with her. She'd secretly weaned herself off little green, and they couldn't get Taylor away from her in any other way but to silence her forever."

Claudia knew that if it weren't for the little green she had just drunk, she would feel some emotional reaction to this news. She felt nothing. She only asked, "Does Niles know?" Of course, she thought, Niles couldn't know. She would have to tell him somehow. Yes, when he got back from traveling with the famous G, she would tell him.

Lillian repeated, "'Does Niles know?' Of course he knows. He's the one who made the Report on her."

Claudia could not take this in. *Niles reported his wife? The Report resulted in her murder? And Niles was still here, working for—promoting—The Hawthorne School?*

"Yes. He set her up. He played his part in it. And because of that demonstration of loyalty, he rose to a higher position. He has a lot of power in the organization now."

"But . . ." said Claudia, her mind closing down and telling her to sleep, that all was well.

Lillian finished her thought: "But he seems so nice? I know. That's how he keeps his value in the organization. By knowing how to seem so nice. It works well on most people, especially on young mothers. But it had stopped working on Fiona."

"Lillian." Claudia yawned and forced her mind to focus on forming words. "Why aren't you like them? Devoted? Brainwashed?"

"I was. I was in a waking dream for years. But G is right about one thing. He says that he can only trust the children, the ones he has had from an early age. Everyone else—even Zelma—we all have to keep proving ourselves to him. Because he knows that we all had our own thoughts, our own minds, before we came to him, and any of us can go back at any time. For me, the break happened when they took Fiona. I saw it, you see. From this window." Lillian pointed to the darkening sky outside. "The day they pulled her from the car, I was standing at the window, and I saw the whole thing. I should have felt nothing but satisfaction after so many years here, immersed in the Hawthorne Way. But my humanity, my sanity—*something*—broke the spell."

Lillian had not drunk any tea.

"Since we've been sitting here, you haven't had any little green. How often do you need it?" Claudia wondered if Lillian was trying to wean herself off it too.

Lillian paused, looking deeply into Claudia's eyes.

"Claudia, if you tell anyone this, it will mean my immediate death. But then, I've already told you enough to make them kill me several times over. My life is in your hands, just as your life is in mine.

"So I'll tell you: I'm off little green completely. I've been off it for months now. Every day my mind gets clearer."

Now Claudia understood that different light that she saw in Lillian's eyes. She was the only person on the campus not under the influence of little green.

"I'm not sure what good it does me. It actually probably puts me in danger. If Zelma ever knew, 'the sword would come down.' That's their expression for killing someone. You can't go off little green. It's a big rule. So I pretend. I put water in my thermos, and pray no one will catch on. Some days I say, why am I bothering? I will be here all my life. I may as well go back to sleep. But something—my survival instinct?—makes me do one more day, and one more day after that, without the herbs. Maybe I'm hoping that as I see clearer, I'll see a way out. Because you're right. I want to get out of here, and I want to get all of the children out too."

There was the sound of footsteps in the doorway. They hadn't been aware of the door opening.

It was Evelyn, peering at them through her black bangs and holding Henry by the hand.

Evelyn's expression was blank.

"It's five o'clock."

CHAPTER

58

As Claudia stepped out into the hall, she reached for Henry, who shrank away from her. The teachers were in commotion. They were all streaming down the corridor toward the chapel door. Whatever Evelyn might have said to her at that moment was lost, along with Claudia's opportunity to find out how much Evelyn had overheard. One of the teachers murmured to Evelyn in passing, "It's now. He's here." Evelyn murmured back to the other teacher a reply that Claudia could not hear.

Evelyn picked up Henry and walked as quickly as she could—nearly running—with the crowd, toward the chapel. Claudia, in her cloud of tranquility, followed the thin, flat figure of Evelyn while she reviewed in her mind all that Lillian had told her. She was not alarmed and not angry: these emotions were not available to her. But neither would she let Henry out of her sight. It was past five o'clock. Henry was supposed to be with her. With the throng, she entered the chapel.

Teachers were hurrying silently into pews, and Evelyn brought Henry to the front and center. Claudia took her place directly behind Evelyn and Henry. Henry turned back once to look at Claudia and then shut his eyes tight and turned his head toward the altar.

The sanctuary was empty of any human presence and yet filled with a sense of expectation as all eyes were trained forward, waiting. Claudia glanced around at the teachers, some of whom she had seen before on campus. None of them looked at her or at each other. They were all in their own world of anticipation.

Niles and Zelma, with Anthony trailing by her side, appeared now at a table holding several large chalices. Each took a vessel and started down the rows. Teachers drank and passed the chalice. When Niles came to Claudia's pew, she studied his face, and he caught her eye and smiled his beautiful smile, but now his glassy eyes looked crazy to her. She made herself smile back. When the chalice came to her, she pretended to drink, but only let the liquid touch her lips. Passing the chalice to the woman next to her, she licked the drops it had left on her mouth. It was, of course, little green, but it tasted different, much stronger. She longed to drink it and regretted not taking a big swallow of it when she'd had the chance, but she knew she would need to keep from sinking into a stupor. She'd have to keep her wits about her if she wanted to survive. All around her were teachers with half-hooded eyes and beatific smiles on their faces. Each woman had a child on her lap and others by her side. All the children looked older than their young years, while the adults wore expressions that were unsettlingly child-like; they were like children whose powerful and loving daddy had come home.

Claudia glanced over her shoulder, trying to avoid detection, scanning for Lillian. She looked behind her and left and right, but she only saw the enraptured and worshipful faces of other teachers. Had no one told Lillian that G had arrived? Wouldn't she get in trouble for not coming? Claudia wanted to go and tell her, but she knew instinctively that she could not get up and leave now.

As she scanned the congregation, still searching for Lillian, she found instead a woman who looked exactly like her friend Maggie. She could not comprehend what she was seeing. Maggie could not possibly be here. Maggie was dead. Zelma had told her so. But there she was, or someone who looked just like her.

Maggie met her gaze and stared through her.

Maggie was alive. Zelma had lied. Claudia turned back quickly to the front. What could it mean that Maggie was alive and here in the chapel? Maggie, who had seemed to have so little involvement with the school, who had claimed to have never read the white book? Claudia remembered her friend's apparent envy when she learned that Claudia was moving into the "inner circle." But was it Maggie who had been in the inner circle all along?

And what was the meaning in that vacant stare?

She could feel Maggie was watching her.

In a flash of insight, she understood. From their very first meeting in the parking lot of their apartment building, Maggie had been grooming her for this. Throughout all their meaningful conversations and shared confidences, Maggie had sprinkled strategic mentions of The Hawthorne School. Without appearing to, she had pushed Claudia along, making it seem like it was Claudia's own idea to transfer Henry from Happy Start. She remembered now how Maggie had looked at Henry a little too long, and Claudia had misunderstood, worrying that Maggie was judging. In fact, she had been evaluating. She had seen what Zelma later saw—and Evelyn too—that Henry could be a valuable acquisition for The Hawthorne School—might even be pleasing to G as the protégé he was waiting for.

Zelma and Niles returned the empty chalices to the table.

Zelma announced in quiet reverence, "G is here."

Claudia felt a thrill move through the chapel. Within herself, she felt chilled, frozen in place.

"He will begin with the Silent Discourse."

Zelma sat down in the front pew next to Evelyn, with Anthony on her other side. Everyone waited.

After about two minutes of utter quiet, a door beyond the altar opened.

It was the door that led on to Unity Hall.

A man entered the chapel and walked with deliberate steps up to the pulpit.

A shiver passed through the congregation as the people strained forward.

The man moved with a strange poise. He had that glamour, that unquantifiable charisma of the natural leader. His image was arresting, and it was hard to look away from him. Claudia had to remind herself that he was a psychopath, a murderer. He didn't look evil. He exuded power, but not malice. He did not look like a monster. He was in his late thirties and dressed in the natural fibers characteristic of The Hawthorne School, but his were pure white, contrasting with his hair, which was black, shoulder-length, and gleaming. From where she sat, in the center of the second row, Claudia could see that his eyes were bright blue. His coloring, as Lillian had told her, was just like Henry's. In fact, she could imagine Henry looking very much like him one day.

G stood regarding the congregation, saying nothing. He only looked at each face in turn, and smiled. He stood, completely at ease. No one coughed; no one sneezed; no one whispered. It was as if they were in a group meditation; all around was the sound of deep, relaxed breathing. As if they were all a single organism, breathing as one.

Claudia waited for G to say something. He had been away for six months, she knew. Surely he would want to speak to his followers, his cult. He stood smiling benevolently, as if he were in silent communication with each and every person there. Claudia was sure he had looked for an extra minute at Henry and then at Evelyn next to him. She felt his eyes come to rest on her too. His eyes moved slowly from one face to another, as if he had all eternity at his disposal. There was no sense of restlessness or impatience anywhere in the chapel. Only a great communal sense of ease.

The Silent Discourse, as Zelma had called it, went on for a very long time. Claudia never knew how long. The longer it continued, the more deeply entranced the teachers became. No one nodded off. The children did not fidget or show any sign of restlessness. They simply sat, like the adults, looking forward with shining eyes.

At last, G spoke.

CHAPTER

59

H IS VOICE, AFTER such a long silence, had a powerful effect. It was loud and deep, and he spoke in a slow, mesmerizing rhythm.

"Welcome. It is *good* to be here. Now, close your eyes. Keep them closed until I tell you to open them."

Claudia lowered her eyes so that they would appear closed if G looked at her.

"And just listen to the sound of my voice. There is so much love here for you. Here, with us, is where you are truly loved. You can *feel* that love, can't you? . . . You may open your eyes now.

"The Love Teaching . . . *yes*." He laughed softly, fixing each face before him in a loving way, like a delighted parent. "And so we begin the Love Teaching. Today's Love Teaching is about . . . *thoughts*." He tapped his temples and made a grimace, and then smiled again, looking left and right, taking in each attentive face. *"Thoughts, thoughts, thoughts."*

He chuckled.

The people in the chapel laughed along with him, but softly, tentatively.

"Thoughts!" he shouted, and many congregants jumped. "Thoughts in the form of words, senseless words, that repeat themselves in the mind, all day. *Monkey chatter.* Mixing around and around, causing stress, causing anxiety, causing trouble.

Words. Word salad!" His face took on an expression of indignation, and he repeated, *"Word salad!"*

Claudia saw heads nodding in agreement.

Then he turned angrily on those nodding heads: *"You!* You *think* word salad! You *speak* word salad! You make *no sense.* You make *nonsense!"*

His eyes moved from face to face with profound disappointment.

Then, he seemed to forgive them all.

"You can't help it. At your current state of development, *you* don't know how to stop the mind. It is the nature of the mind to think, to trouble you all day long. The mind is such a burden. Thinking itself *is* the problem, the error. Thinking leads to madness." G's tone had become depressed, and Claudia could feel the sadness all around her as his listeners sank into despondency. Then he changed his direction, stretching out his arms as if to embrace them all. "But! These children! Do *they* think? Are they mad?" The congregation waited, uncertain, for G to answer his own questions. *"No!* The children do not think. They are sane. The only sane ones. They play. They paint. They imagine. They make music. *They are not burdened like you are.*

"Ah!" The exclamation came out as a bark.

"You! You grown-ups must become children. Release your burden. Release your mind. Eliminate thought. Be as a little child." G took several long moments of silence to let these words resonate, his eyes taking in each person in turn. His eyes settled on Henry, last of all, and remained there.

A cold spike moved down Claudia's spine, but she was rooted to the pew.

The congregation waited.

At last he said, "These children—*my* children, these little children are our future."

Claudia had heard the phrase many times before, but never had it sounded so sinister.

60

"'Give us a child until he is seven, and we will have him for life.' *For life.* These were the words of St. Ignatius Loyola. And it is written, 'He alone, who owns the youth, gains the future.'

"I am building my kingdom. It will be a kingdom of thousands of perfect little children."

G raised his arms in the air.

"Where are we going? Where are we taking the children?"

The congregation shifted, trying to keep up with the constantly changing moods and topics of the speaker.

"*Where?* Ah. We don't get to that place with the *mind.* We don't get there with the *body.* No. There is only one way to get there: and that is with the *spirit.* We are all spirits, temporarily housed in bodies. And where did our spirits come from? Where do they long to go? Ha! Into the cosmos, of course. Our home is in space. We came from the living moon. We are stardust and long to return to our place in the Universe. And *will* we return? *Will* we?"

G looked at his supporters with wide eyes. Then he answered his own question in a loud whisper.

"*Some* of us, yes! *Some* of us will live forever in our galactic home. There is no final point in the universe, and there is no final point in life—in the life of those who will live forever. Look around you. See the souls to your left, to your right, and

in front of you. *You* know who among you will live forever—
and who will not. *You* know who you should have reported, and
yet you did not."

G's eyes blazed, and he let his accusation hang in the air.

At last, taking a kindly tone, he advised, "Watch each other.
Save each other. I tell you, each of you has a chance, a very
small chance. The New Promise is not free! Many of you are
on the threshold. It's up to you." He shrugged, the picture of
indifference. Immediately his passion returned. "But will you
do what you need to do? *Will* you surrender to the ways of the
child? *Will* you?"

G let the silence hold his question. The teachers nodded and
bowed their heads.

"Simply surrender," he advised, and as he said it, he smiled
widely and was met with answering smiles all around. "It's easy.
Let go of your mind. It does you no good here." Now he paced
back and forth before his people.

"The End Times are coming!" He repeated: "The End
Times! And do we worry?"

Heads shook from side to side, *No.* There was soft laughter
among the congregation now, the laughter of family members
who all get the same joke and who want to let others know that
they get it, and want to encourage the others to laugh along.

G smiled, indulgent.

"No. Why not? Because we know what to do. We know
how to protect our children. When the End Times come, you
will take the children down to the tunnels. The tunnels are
protected from radiation. There is enough food in storage in the
tunnels to feed you all for seven years.

"That will be the Trial. That will be when you prove yourselves. And after the Seven-Year Trial, you will come up, and
the earth will be ours.

"But will those seven years of trial be hard? Will you be
imprisoned? Will you be always in the dark?"

Again, heads shook. *No.*

"No. You will be joyful! Because you have learned the way to
Distance Reality. The *key* is Distance Reality. You must distance
yourself from reality if you are going to ascend. The *children*

have learned Distance Reality. The art of throwing your spirit! Of flying to other spiritual planes, other dimensions! What is more beautiful than the freedom of children? And so you will reach those planes—how?"

No one dared answer.

G repeated patiently, "Not through the body, nor the mind. Through the spirit. Through Distance Reality. And wherever I am at that time, I will meet with you, in this galaxy or another. We will travel and meet through the spirit. In the realm of *true* reality, Distance Reality. Because we know that *this*—all that surrounds us—is not real. Reality is that beautiful place that we get to only through spirit.

"Now"—G rubbed his hands together—"would you like to live forever in that beautiful place?"

He beamed, gratified by the expressions he saw in front of him.

"Yes. Yes, you would. You already know that these children are guaranteed to live forever. I guarantee that. And I will live forever, and Zelma Huxley will live forever."

Claudia remembered a casual comment of Evelyn's: *"Don't worry . . . Zelma will live forever."*

"And what about the rest of you? You can all live forever, you know. How? Simply surrender your mind. Let it go. Oh, you say, you have already done that? But you know very well, you have not released your mind *entirely*. You see, we can tell. Those of us who have arrived can always tell. You have held back, just a little. You have to break *down* to have the break *through*. Let go. Just let it go, and you can live forever in Distance Reality.

"It all makes sense now, doesn't it?"

He held out his open palms like a father inviting his small children to run to him. "My love for each and every one of you is endless. Endless."

"My children." G signaled to a group of older children who sat with poised flutes, and they began to play ethereal music.

Henry turned his body in the pew to look at Claudia, and he had that sleepy, in-need-of-comfort look. He stretched his arm out to her, the one that wore the red string bracelet. He was still hers. They had tried and nearly succeeded in taking him from her, but the bond between Claudia and her son was still there. She reached out and held his small hand, smiling love and reassurance at him. Evelyn felt his movement and turned to see their clasped hands. She put her hands on both their wrists and detached them, and made Henry face forward, wrapping her arms around him.

Claudia longed to grab him, to take him away from there. She wondered again where Lillian could be.

CHAPTER

61

Zelma turned to murmur to Claudia, "Come with me, dear heart."

Claudia feared this woman now, and yet she didn't dare try to escape. Not here, in front of all G's supporters. She left the pew and followed Zelma through the door into Unity Hall.

They were in a common room, furnished with vinyl-upholstered chairs and a cold and disused fireplace. "I have some good news for you, dear heart." Zelma was projecting her motherly guise. Claudia hoped Zelma could not read her mind, could not tell that she knew that Zelma was behind the murder of countless parents and would be willing to murder her, too, if she stood in her way.

The door to the sanctuary opened behind Zelma.

Maggie emerged and then stood, expressionless, blocking the door. She looked at Claudia as if she didn't even know who she was. She was the same beautiful woman with the flowing golden hair, but her face was hard.

Another figure appeared in the doorway of the corridor that led out of the common room. That figure was Niles. He, too, seemed to be a stranger, all of his charm gone.

Zelma was speaking to Claudia in confidential tones.

"It's a very great honor for you, dear. G wishes to see you *first!* Of course, all the teachers will be envious of you, but no one questions G's choice. He knows best. He has chosen *you* to be the first to have a one-on-one with him. It's all because of Henry, of course! Don't be nervous. I will prepare you."

There was no way out. If she tried to run away, she would be caught immediately, and she had no doubt she would be killed.

She followed Zelma down the corridor and into to a dorm room. The footsteps of Niles and Maggie followed them.

In the room were a bureau, two chairs, and a bed that was covered with a comforter. On a small table was a glass of little green juice. The blind on the single narrow window was drawn, and all was in shadow.

Claudia sat in one chair and Zelma sat in the other.

Maggie stood behind Zelma's chair while Niles lurked in the open doorway.

"Maggie?" asked Claudia. Claudia looked at Zelma for explanation.

"Oh yes, dear, Maggie is here with us. To support you, you know. Maggie is *such* a support to our families. She's our Recruiter. That's why we have her living off campus. She brings the best candidates into the fold." Zelma turned to Niles, who stood silhouetted in the door frame. "Maggie brought *you*, Niles, and Fiona and Taylor. Of course," she added in an undertone, "Fiona didn't work out. Shame."

Then she perked up as if deciding to move on to a more pleasant topic.

"Drink your juice, dear heart."

She watched Claudia with glinting eyes.

Claudia lowered her gaze briefly, trying to think of another option. She could think of none. She drank the little green juice. This time it was different. It burned her throat.

Within seconds, she felt her arms and legs grow heavy, and then numb. She could no longer move her fingers or toes; she couldn't lift her feet from the floor. She was paralyzed. Her breathing was shallow. She tried to speak, but her mouth wouldn't open.

Zelma studied her, and said, "That's good. You don't need to be afraid, Claudia. I wouldn't hurt you for anything in the world, you know. I do hope you know that."

Zelma went then to the bureau and opened the top drawer. From it, she removed a wad of cotton and a syringe. She rolled up Claudia's sleeve and prodded the inner side of her elbow, searching for a vein. "This will be lovely. You'll see."

62

As Zelma and Maggie left the room, softly closing the door behind them, Claudia found herself floating in what she supposed must be Distance Reality. She had never felt so well in all her life. She had no tension, no fear, only bliss. She was flooded with a heart-expanding sense of almost unendurable beauty all around her and within her. She was in a timeless space that expanded into all eternity.

The door opened again, slowly.

Clouds of white came into the room, puffs of brightness, filling the doorway. They were beautiful, fascinating, and she watched them form, unform, reform. The light that streamed in behind and through the puffs of mist was golden-white. She could have watched the vision forever. And then she saw a figure, a human figure, and she saw that it was G, G in his white robes and his long, shining hair, and his brilliant blue eyes filled with such love and compassion—love and compassion for her, and as he stood in those heavenly clouds, she received the knowledge that he was God. Who else could he be in this place of perfection? She was in the presence of God. And now she knew what rapture was. She, who had never had any interest in religion in her life, was now in the presence of pure love, pure energy, the one and only God of the universe. It was sublime. It was almost too much to bear.

He spoke to her. Only to her.

"My child."

Claudia felt that tears were running down her cheeks, yet she was detached from her body. She understood everything, everything now. Now she saw it all so clearly.

She loved this God with all her heart. She wanted to be with him forever. She would do anything to keep this feeling, this incredible love that filled every cell of her being. She had never been as happy as she was right now. She floated with the happiness, on it and above it, a cloud of love, as God regarded her with endless tenderness and caring.

She was one with God.

His voice was beautiful. His words were the Truth. She received them in her spirit—a spirit she never knew she had.

Her senses were all awash. She could not make out God's words, but received their meaning nonetheless, as if perceiving them through new senses. God, in this strange new language, told her that when she could not see him, she must obey Zelma and Evelyn, that they would speak for him until he could come to her again. He told her that in ten days it would be time for him to take Henry and that this was for Henry's highest good, and for Claudia's highest good, too, for he loved them both. It was time to release Henry into God's care, and she was to be completely at peace.

Claudia drifted in a tranquil haze.

63

WHEN CLAUDIA AWOKE, she kept her eyes closed.

She had had the most incredible dream of her life.

She had dreamed, so vividly, of God. It was so unlike her and so unlike any dream she had ever had.

Had it been a dream?

No, it had been real. God himself had come to her and told her that he loved her. It had been so beautiful. She had felt better than she'd ever felt in her entire life. Now, though, the blissful feeling was draining away. She wished for it to stay.

Then she remembered Maggie's cold stare . . . the Love Teaching . . . the Silent Discourse . . . her conversation with Lillian in the classroom . . .

She sat up in bed and saw that she was still in the dorm room in Unity Hall, the teachers' dorm hall, where . . . What had happened?

Now surreal memories floated up, of being paralyzed in a chair and of Zelma injecting her with a drug and telling her, "This will be lovely."

Her few possessions had been brought to this room. But Henry's possessions—his toys, his clothes—were not here. Henry was not here. What time was it? She reached for the blinds on the narrow window and peeked outside. It was still nighttime. The world was drained of color.

Where was Henry? Her mind was working slowly, trying to veer toward panic, but not able to rise to it.

Henry was with Evelyn the last time she saw him. What had God told her? To listen to Zelma and Evelyn, and that it was almost time for him to take Henry?

But had she seen God? She remembered the syringe. She had been drugged. What she saw and felt, it had to be real. She had experienced it with all her senses, senses she hadn't even known she had.

But it couldn't be real.

She needed to get her son. Was he all right? Physically, he would be safe and sound: Evelyn would see to that. But emotionally? Mentally? What were they doing to him?

A warning voice in her mind told her to recognize that she was confused and to think clearly before taking any action. Her life could depend on it. She might only have one chance to get herself and Henry out of this place. She couldn't get hysterical. She needed to appear to be going along with their program, and wait for her opportunity.

Her mind was clearing now.

The little green that burned her throat, the injection, the light and clouds, G's visit, the spiritual experience she'd had—it was all only a drug-induced trance.

And while one part of her still believed that G was God because she had seen him with her own eyes and communed with him in Distant Reality, she knew better in her rational mind. G was a fraud. The white clouds she'd seen had been produced by her own intoxicated brain.

Or . . . what did those white clouds remind her of? She remembered a theater production, back when she was in school with Devin. There'd been a scene in a play where the stage had been filled with clouds just like that. How had they made those stage clouds?

Dry ice.

Could her spiritual experience have been just theater? Just a cheesy trick?

Yes, that's exactly how they had done it. They'd shone a light in through her door, set the dry ice going, and then G had stepped in, looked into her eyes and said some gibberish. Her drugged mind had done all the rest.

Lillian had told her . . . what had Lillian told her? She must remember everything. It was important.

Lillian had told her that Fiona and other parents who had not cooperated with The Hawthorne School were lying in unmarked graves in the woods, that G believed in his own delusions, that he wanted the children as his worshippers, and that he especially would want Henry as his son. Lillian had warned her that her destiny was to live in Unity Hall—where she had been moved now—with the teachers, and that she would see Henry only from a distance. If she showed any resistance, she would be put on high doses of little green and made to live in Comfort Hall and become one of the night-shift workers, the Night People, as Lillian had called them. And if she still rebelled, she would be killed. The Hawthorne School had disposed of people before.

Claudia would only be one more.

64

LILLIAN WAS HER only friend here. Even Maggie was one of *them*. She had to get up and make sure that Lillian was all right. She stood and began to pace the room in the dim lamplight, trying not to make any noise. Why hadn't Lillian been in the chapel with everyone else?

Just before the meeting in the chapel, Evelyn had appeared at Lillian's classroom door. Could Evelyn have overheard what Lillian was saying? Claudia remembered now: Lillian had been admitting that she had weaned off little green. She had said, "I want to get out of here too." That's when Evelyn had said from the door, "It's five o'clock."

The pieces slid into place now.

Evelyn had heard; of course she had. And when a teacher spoke to Evelyn in the hall, and Evelyn had murmured something back—Evelyn had been reporting Lillian.

Now Claudia knew the price Lillian would pay for those words. Lillian had referred to a Holding Place in the tunnels.

Another thought occurred to Claudia. What if Lillian had taken her chance in the excitement and escaped?

She couldn't assume anything. If there was a chance that Lillian was locked up somewhere on the campus, Claudia needed to try to find her. She could not risk trying to get to Henry now. He would be well guarded, and any effort she would make to get him back would be doomed to fail and would prevent any further attempt. She needed to pretend that she was in the mass delusion and under the control of The Hawthorne School.

There was a fluttering knock on the door.

Zelma walked in.

65

"I'VE BROUGHT YOU a nice hot cup of tea, dear heart."

Zelma was carrying a tray with oatmeal, with little green sprinkled on the top, and a cup of little green tea.

Claudia took the cup with shaking hands. She hoped that Zelma would attribute her shaking to hunger and not to fear.

"So!" Zelma was in good spirits. "You've had your first one-on-one!" She said it in a congratulatory way. Claudia was startled by the word "first." Was Zelma going to inject her again?

"Yes," said Claudia. "I never expected it to be like that." She had to play a role now, and she had to play it well. The quality of her performance would make the difference between life and death. "I can't even describe it. I—I understand now. I feel like I can really see for the first time in my life."

Zelma stared coldly at her for a moment, assessing her sincerity.

"Do you, dear heart? Do you really see? And what is it that you see?" Her voice was soft and gentle while her eyes were hard.

"I see—I *saw* the face of God. That's what I saw. And I *heard* the voice of God, speaking to me."

"God, you say?" Zelma tilted her head to one side, drawing Claudia out. "Tell me. Who is God?"

"God is G."

Zelma sat in silence, watching Claudia drink the tea.

Claudia feared that this tea would paralyze her as the juice last night had done, and her hand shook so much that some of the tea spilled. She thought of dumping it on the tray and pretending it was an accident, but she knew it was no use. Another cup would be brought, and she would be made to drink that. Whatever ordeal Zelma might have planned for her, she would have to get through it. She would have to survive and save Henry. She wished she could ask, *Where is Henry?* But she knew better.

"You are correct. G *is* God. And what did God tell you? Do you remember?"

"Yes, it was very powerful. And I heard God's words. God will take Henry. For Henry's highest good. And when G is not here, it's you and Evelyn who are speaking God's words for me to obey. I think it was something like that."

"It was *exactly* that. That is the truth." Zelma was still watching Claudia closely, like a fox watching a rabbit. "Eat your oatmeal, dear heart. You must be so hungry. Your hands are shaking dreadfully."

Claudia had to win Zelma's confidence. She had to be docile and meek. The tea was calming her; it was only the usual little green that she had come to know and depend upon. Zelma was not going to inject her now.

Zelma seemed to be looking straight into her brain.

"It seems you were speaking with Lillian yesterday afternoon."

Claudia felt her heart pound.

"You won't see her again. She has quit without notice."

Claudia would not allow herself to think of what these words might mean. Not now, not in front of Zelma.

"Then," said Claudia, her mind working through the tranquility of little green, "may I get back to work? I want to do something useful for The Hawthorne School." She was thinking that her job allowed her an excuse to wander the tunnels in search of the Holding Place. If she could discover where it was, she might find Lillian there. Irving would have the master key, although how she would get it from him, she didn't yet know.

Zelma watched Claudia finish the last of the oatmeal. Then, she took the tray and stood. She smiled, satisfied.

"You may work," she granted, "Yolanda and Oscar are doing a big fall cleanup on the grounds today. You remember that you decided you would join them outside rather than do the janitorial work? The Garcias will be glad to have your help."

"Thank you." Claudia dropped her eyes, humbly.

"Claudia. Aren't you even going to ask where Henry is?"

"I didn't know if I should," answered Claudia, making her voice soft and meek.

"Why shouldn't you? Everyone is free here, Claudia. Everyone says and asks whatever they like." Zelma leveled her gaze at Claudia. "Henry is living in Evelyn's suite. She has been promoted to a high position in the school, and now she has a beautiful suite of rooms here in Unity Hall. Henry will be staying with her because G has told us that's best. Whenever G leaves us, he will take Henry with him. That will be wonderful."

Claudia looked blandly at Zelma, betraying nothing that she felt. Inwardly, she pushed away any emotion. It was not safe to feel anything now, with the director straining to detect her every thought. Nothing Zelma had just revealed was surprising; Lillian had prepared her for all of it. The "promotion" was no doubt due to becoming Henry's "mother." Zelma was watching her for any sign of pain or dissent, and Claudia gave her no signal at all. Just as some mothers had been known to find super-human strength to save their children from physical danger, lifting a car or confronting a bear, Claudia now found the strength to control her expression regardless of the feelings that struggled to rise up in her. It was the only thing she could do for the time being to save her son.

66

WITH MOTHERLY CONCERN, Zelma had provided Claudia with rubber boots and insulated work clothes with which to face the November wet and chill. With merry eyes, she'd told Claudia that the children used hot potatoes as hand warmers when playing in the woods, but Claudia would need her hands free to help Yolanda and Oscar with the fall cleanup, so Zelma handed her a pair of thick gardening gloves.

Zelma had watched as Claudia had drained her morning cup of little green. She was sure she had shown herself to be a true believer in the Hawthorne Way. She would take advantage of her trusted status to skip every dose of little green she could while appearing to continue to be under its influence. She recalled now that Yolanda had told her that she and Oscar were cutting down, using little green "in moderation." Had they known this was against the rules? Had they continued cutting down? Lillian had gotten away with being free of little green for months without detection. She'd filled her thermos with water instead. Claudia, too, would break free of its grip.

She had hoped to work with Irving and search the tunnels for the Holding Place, but instead she would make good use of her time with the Garcias. She joined Yolanda and Oscar in the flower garden that separated the playground from the forest.

"¡Buenos días Yolanda y Oscar!" called Claudia as she approached. When they looked up from their work, she saw that their eyes were bright, like Lillian's. It was that same, unclouded look. She knew, in that instant: they were free of little green. How had they not been detected? How had they not been reported?

Immediately, Claudia regretted calling out her greeting. No one must know that she could speak Spanish. But Zelma should be in the Main Hall, far from this garden, and no one was on the playground or anywhere in sight. The children were sure to be in the woods with their teachers. And Lillian's class? Now that Lillian had, according to Zelma, "quit without notice"? Where would a school like this find a substitute teacher?

The Garcias greeted her and invited her to join them in clearing the weeds and fallen leaves from the flower beds, and as the three worked together, Claudia asked, "Do you know that G is here? He spoke in the chapel. I didn't see you there." "Of course, we know," said Yolanda.

"He came in a white Rolls Royce," added Oscar, clearly impressed by the car.

Yolanda said, "Zelma told us not to come to the chapel, since we would not understand what he said."

"Have you had your one-on-one with G? Or are you going to?"

"No one has said anything to us about anything like that," said Yolanda. "I think Zelma has actually forgotten about us in the past couple of days. She hasn't given us many orders, but it doesn't matter. We already know what to do. We've been doing this kind of work for years already."

"Here? At The Hawthorne School?"

"Oh no. Other places. We only started here in May."

"Then you just came here four months before Henry and I did."

Claudia reflected. The Garcias had arrived, then, just after Fiona Holloway had been killed and buried in the woods. Just after G's last visit. So they had never had a one-on-one with him. They didn't know—they couldn't know—what The Hawthorne School really was. She thought she should warn them, as Lillian had warned her. But then, they weren't in danger. As long as they were innocent of all knowledge, they posed no threat to the school. And yet they did suspect something. They apparently had understood that little green was addictive, and she was sure they had stopped taking it.

"Yolanda. Last time we talked, you advised me to be moderate with little green."

Oscar stood and put his hands on his lower back. "My wife likes to chitchat. Don't pay attention to her."

Claudia decided instead not to pay attention to Oscar.

"I'm trying to follow your advice because you're right. Tell me, how did you get off it? Because I want to stop. How did you do it?"

Oscar stared with hostility at Yolanda, and Yolanda said, "Please don't misunderstand me. I never said to get off it completely. It's a rule of the school, you know, to take little green. We don't break the rules here. We follow all the rules, Claudia." Yolanda looked pleadingly at Claudia. She was afraid.

If Lillian was gone, Claudia was going to dare to find allies in the Garcias. They might report her. But she felt sure they wouldn't. She felt Yolanda's authenticity, her concern. She would trust her. She had to chance it.

"It's okay. You can trust me. We can all trust each other. We all know little green is a drug." She paused and waited for them to contradict her, but the Garcias kept their eyes on their work. "And we all know that once you start, you want more and more of it. And that it's addictive. And eventually, if you keep taking higher doses, you become a . . . a destroyed person."

Yolanda shivered and stood, looking toward Comfort Hall. Then she looked over her shoulder, as if scanning for anyone who might be overhearing their conversation, but there was no one.

"Quiet. Someone might come. We shouldn't be seen standing here talking. We have to keep working. Come to the rose bushes now. Do you know how to prune rose bushes? Yes? And then we have to train the branches, and then we'll add mulch to their bases. And then wrap them in cloth. There's a lot of work to do."

Oscar came along to the rose garden, too, warning Yolanda to be quiet, to not be stupid.

"Oscar," murmured Claudia. "We can help each other. Don't be afraid. If we are very careful, we can get away from here. And one of the teachers will help us. There's a teacher who has stopped taking little green, and she wants to leave. So there's a group of us now. You both do want to get away from here, don't you? I'm sure you do. Because you've seen things, haven't you? You wouldn't be so afraid if you hadn't seen things."

Oscar looked troubled. He didn't want to speak, but almost unwillingly, he said, "I've seen things. We both have. I don't like it. We saw children in a—what do you call it?—a trance. We were trimming the branches of the hedge maze, and we saw them there in the center, a group of children with their teacher. It wasn't normal. I asked Valeria about it, if they ever did that in her class, and she knew what it was. They—send their spirits out—that's the way she said it. Into the stars, they send their spirits. Me, I didn't go very far in school, but I know that is not a normal thing to do in school. But what can we do?"

"Why don't you leave?"

Oscar and Yolanda looked at each other and then returned to pruning the rose bushes. Yolanda pointed with her chin toward Comfort Hall and whispered to Claudia, "Have you *seen* them? *Los nocturnos.* The way they walk? Their faces?"

"No. Only Irving."

"Oh yes, Irving is one of them, but the others are much worse. *Much* worse. Horrible!"

"When did you see them?"

"Just before dawn, this morning. I can't get the image out of my head."

"This morning?"

"Yes, it was still dark. Zelma gave only one order yesterday. She wanted firewood for the fireplaces. We never got to it, we have so much work to do—it's just the two of us—and I woke up at about four in the morning, worried that she would be mad at us. I woke Oscar up and said, let's get that firewood now and put it behind the Main Hall so that when she wakes up, she'll see that we did it. Oscar didn't want to, but I insisted, so we came down and started gathering sticks and fallen branches. That's when we heard them.

"We heard their footsteps crunching the leaves, and they came out of the woods in a single file. They had shovels. And the way they walked . . ." Yolanda's face contorted itself into an expression of horror. "They *dragged* themselves. We were standing close by them, close enough to greet them, but it was as if they never saw us. Their faces were like stone, and they stumbled one after the other, like dead people. I thought at first that they were ghosts. They walked from the woods into Comfort Hall." Yolanda gazed into space, as if seeing it again. "And that's when I realized who they were. Zelma told us about them before. She called them *los nocturnos* and just said they are people who work at night. We thought they were regular people. We didn't know they were like *that*. I've never seen people like that."

"How many were there? And they had shovels?"

"Five of them. Shovels, yes." Yolanda stopped. "I've said too much."

"It's okay. I'm on your side."

Yolanda searched Claudia's face.

"I said to Oscar, 'Why would they need shovels in the woods?'"

"Did you go into the woods, try to find out where they were digging?"

"No. The forest is enormous, and there are many paths. It would be useless to try to find where they'd been. And it would be dangerous, we think, if someone knew we were trying to find things out. We have to mind our own business. And we don't need to see."

"What do you mean by that, you 'don't need to see'?"

"We don't need to see where they've been digging. *What* they've been digging. Because," murmured Yolanda, "the truth is, we already know why the Night People take shovels into the woods."

Oscar hauled a bag of mulch from a wheelbarrow and tore it open. He muttered to Yolanda, "Are you going to tell her what Valeria told us?"

Yolanda turned to Claudia, her face grave: "You had a visitor a few weeks ago. We saw you with him."

"He had an orange Volkswagen beetle," added Oscar.

"Yes," said Claudia. A realization was dawning on the edges of her mind, a sense of something that she had known, but had in some way kept hidden from herself, all along. Something that she was still not ready to know.

"That was Devin, Henry's father. Why are you asking me about *him*?"

"Valeria told us that the children have something new to play in when they go deep into the woods." Yolanda looked away, through the trees.

Oscar said, "It is a little orange car."

CLAUDIA'S LEGS GAVE way beneath her, and she crumpled to the ground. The world around her faded out.

They had killed Devin.

Zelma, Niles, and maybe Evelyn too—they had murdered him because he had come questioning and arguing and they knew that he wanted to take Henry out of The Hawthorne School. And for that, they had murdered him and buried him where they had already buried Niles's wife and everyone else who had gotten in their way. Devin's face appeared before her. He hadn't left them again after all. He had come to begin a new life with his son, and he hadn't understood what he had walked into. He really had meant to stay. All Claudia's experiences with him from that time they had first met ran like a roaring train through her mind, culminating with his last promise to her: *"Henry is my son. Nothing can ever change that. For his sake, we have to work together now."* And she saw him as he looked that last time, as she drove away, leaving him in the parking lot, with Niles coming up behind him.

The hysteria that had been threatening to overtake her for so long now ran through her mind and body uncontrolled. She heard her own sobs as if listening to them from a long way off. The crush of emotions was unbearable: the sorrow for Henry's loss of a father who had wanted to be a true father to him; the pity for Devin himself, who had come with good intentions;

the guilt because Claudia had put him in harm's way; and the anger for the injustice of it. She struggled to breathe through it, to straighten her hunched spine, to regain self-control.

She couldn't grieve now. She couldn't let herself feel the feelings. She had to pull herself up out of this pain. To be seen suffering would be to guarantee her own destruction. She wasn't supposed to suspect what had happened to Devin, and she couldn't be seen mourning him.

Her survival instinct told her to open her eyes to everything around her, to face the whole truth at last. She had been deceived, yes, but she had also deceived herself. She had wanted to believe. She had dismissed early misgivings. She had chosen to be unaware.

There could be no more self-delusion. She thought she was seeing clearly now, but how could she be sure? Could she still be blind to something?

Devin was dead. Lillian was possibly dead, perhaps buried early this morning by the Night People. Or else she was in the Holding Place, wherever in the tunnels that might be, and would be placed in her grave soon. And Claudia needed to face the fact: there could well be another grave waiting in the woods.

Her own.

68

THE GARCIAS KNELT next to Claudia, Oscar pretending to pat the mulch into place and Yolanda whispering, *"Tranquila, tranquila, Claudia. Cálmate. Respira y cálmate."* Yolanda placed a hand on Claudia's back. *"Viene la señora."* The lady is coming.

Claudia pulled herself together. Zelma must see her as complacent, cooperative, and under the influence of the herbal sedative. She was coming toward them with a group of seven-year-olds in her wake: Lillian's class. The children were quiet, simply following Zelma with their hands at their sides.

Zelma spoke to Yolanda and Oscar, while casting an occasional smile at Claudia.

"¡Qué día tan bonito, ¿verdad?"

Yolanda replied, *"Sí, señora."*

"Sí, señora. Pues, un poco fresco, pero no tanto," Oscar answered.

"Veo que le está cuidando bien. Oigan. Quiero que me hagan un servicio," Zelma said.

"A sus órdenes, señora."

"Tengo un cambio de plan. Llévenla abajo, ¿me entienden?" Zelma asked.

"Claro que sí, señora."

"Gracias. Ya saben que cuento mucho con ustedes. Y su hija también cuenta mucho con ustedes. Hasta luego."

"Hasta luego, señora," Oscar and Yolanda said in unison.

*   *   *

Then Zelma nodded encouragingly at Claudia and glided on with the children toward the hedge maze.

Zelma hadn't known that Claudia would understand what she had told the Garcias—after making small talk about the cool weather: *"I see that you're keeping an eye on her. Do me a favor. Take her downstairs."*

As Zelma sauntered away with the children, Yolanda clarified, "She wants us to show you the Gardening Storage Room—in the tunnels. We have to take an inventory of the supplies we have left, so we will know what to order for the winter and spring."

They walked across the lawn toward a rear entrance of the Main Hall. All three of them pushed wheelbarrows.

Claudia said, "This is an opportunity. While we're down there, I'll try to find the Holding Place. The teacher I told you about, the one who wants to leave—she might be down there, if she's still alive. I'll search. Will you help me?"

Yolanda looked uncertainly at her. "We can't get in trouble, Claudia."

"Of course not. But Zelma is outside. We could look real quick. Maybe no one is in the tunnels right now. Do you know where the Holding Place is? Have you ever heard of it?" Another thought occurred to Claudia. "What was she saying about your daughter? That she counts on you?"

Claudia's head was beginning to pound, reminding her that she needed another dose of little green. She took a drink from her thermos—which contained only water.

"Zelma wants Valeria to move to a children's dorm room in Unity Hall. Up until now, we've been able to keep Valeria with us. I think she worries that Valeria may be telling us things about the school—like about the trances. She has been trying to convince us for a couple of weeks. Of course, we have been saying no. She has told us that all the children live with teachers, but still we say no. Yesterday, she said she would let Valeria stay with us as long as we remain as cooperative as always."

"Yes, that's what you have to do; that's what I have to do too. Let her think we're cooperative and under the spell."

Once in the Main Hall, they put the wheelbarrows, one at a time, into a lift. Oscar went down the stairs to unload the wheelbarrows as they came down.

Claudia said, "You're right to hold on to your daughter. Keep her. Don't let her go. They've got Henry. They consider Evelyn his mother now, and they plan to 'give' him to G. I've got to get him back and get us both out of here. You and Oscar and Valeria too—you all need to get out of here. We can do it together." When Yolanda didn't answer, Claudia insisted. "We *can* do it—don't you believe we can? We have to be bold, and work together. Yes?" Claudia needed Yolanda's vote of confidence, needed the reassurance that she had allies in her fight.

Yolanda said simply, "We all want to save our children."

They went down the stairs to meet Oscar.

69

ONCE IN THE tunnels, Claudia despaired of ever finding the Holding Place. All the numbered metal doors that lined the walls of the tunnels looked exactly the same. Oscar told her that the walls of the rooms were so solid and thick, they were sure to be soundproof.

"But the doors," insisted Claudia, hanging onto hope. "If she's inside one of these rooms, she would be able to hear pounding on the door. She could pound back!"

Oscar frowned as Claudia began pounding on the doors as she ran along. "Calm down, please; be quiet!"

"It's all right," said Claudia. "No one is down here but us."

At that moment, around a corner just ahead of them, came the gigantic figure of Irving, slouching along with a vacuum cleaner that he pushed forward on its wheels.

Claudia stopped abruptly and greeted Irving, who only blinked and stood still, looking from her to Oscar, to Yolanda.

"We're just going to the Garden Storage Room," stammered Claudia. "To take inventory. You know, to see what's in storage there."

Irving's face, usually so expressionless, looked skeptical now. Was it only her fear of being reported that made her think so? She couldn't imagine Irving getting up enough energy to report anyone. Still, she didn't know if he might be a threat to them. She wanted to keep explaining about their purpose in the tunnel and get the reassurance that he believed her, but he only passed them, taking the vacuum cleaner toward the lift.

They went on, turning corners, Claudia feeling anxiety that Lillian might be kept prisoner behind any one of the doors. She passed each metal door now without knocking. The Garcias were too afraid to let her try. They were in a hurry to start the task Zelma had set for them.

At last, Yolanda admitted in a whisper, "We do know where the Holding Place is." Her voice was shaking. "Not only that. We have a master key. We could open it." She looked over her shoulder, and then back at Claudia. Her eyes were filled with fear.

"Why didn't you tell me before? Will you show me?"

"It's very dangerous. If anyone, even Irving, knew that we'd shown you—we could lose our daughter, do you understand? We could lose our lives. Our daughter needs us."

"I understand. Please." She looked from Yolanda to Oscar. "I will be very quiet. No one will ever know. If Lillian is still in there, we could save her life. We have to try. Please help me find her."

Yolanda and Oscar shared a look, then nodded, and led the way past doors on the left and right until at last they came to one that looked exactly like all the rest except for the number marked in white paint: 506.

"It will be dark in there. There is no light. If your friend is in there, she may be injured. Just so you are prepared for what you might find."

"Thank you. Thank you," whispered Claudia as Yolanda put the master key in the lock and the door swung open.

Claudia knew she needed to go quickly. She was putting the Garcias in danger by asking them to do this. She stepped into the darkness. Behind her, she heard Yolanda's voice.

"¿Claudia?"

"¿Sí?"

"Perdónanos."

"Forgive us."

The door slammed shut.

CHAPTER

70

CLAUDIA'S FIRST THOUGHT was that the Garcias had let the door swing shut by accident. She stumbled to the door in the pitch blackness and yelled.

"¡Yolanda! ¡Oscar! ¡Ábren! ¡Ábrenme por favor!"

And then Yolanda's last words echoed in her mind: *Forgive us.*

They had done this intentionally. Zelma's words to them on the lawn took on a new meaning. *"Take the lady downstairs. I'm counting on you. So is your daughter."*

They would be walking away, down the tunnel now.

And what about Lillian?

"Lillian? Lillian, are you in here? It's me, Claudia."

She groped blindly, with her hands before her and her feet shuffling so as not to trip over whatever might be in the room. All senses but her sight were hyper-alert now. The room smelt of—something familiar. Lavender! Lillian's scent. She heard nothing, nothing except for her own ragged breath and her own feet scuffing along the cement floor. She called out again, "Lillian! Lillian, are you in here?" In the faint echo, she perceived the hollowness of the room. She was desperate to find Lillian here, not only to save Lillian but to have someone on her side, someone to help her get out of this room and away from The Hawthorne School.

Lillian could be lying senseless on the floor.

She could be lying dead on the floor.

Claudia's hands found a cold cement wall, and she traced her way around the perimeter of the room. Then she walked cautiously back and forth. She found that the room was empty—completely and utterly empty. At last, her foot hit something soft but solid. With a sense of dread, she knelt to touch her fingertips to it. It was dry, and it was soft and giving, and yet slightly rough against her fingers. It was fabric—no. Yes? As she moved it through both her hands, she felt straight fibers about four inches long, attached to it. It was something knitted with fringe hanging from it.

It was Lillian's knit shawl.

She held it to her face, to her nose, and breathed in the lavender. Lillian had certainly been here, but when? The knitted shawl could hold that scent for hours, certainly.

If Lillian had been in the Holding Place and now she was gone, there was only one scenario that made any sense. She couldn't have escaped, any more than Claudia could escape now. Therefore, someone had taken her out of here. And the only reason anyone would have taken her out would have been to murder her.

Claudia knew: Lillian must already be dead.

She also knew: she would be next.

CHAPTER

71

WHAT FOLLOWED WAS sheer excruciation.

Claudia was hungry, grieving, and frightened, but what was the most torturous of all was her withdrawal from little green.

What she experienced now was one thousand times worse than the most horrible flu imaginable. By evening, or what she supposed must be evening, she was huddled on the floor, nauseous, shaking, her nose running. She vomited there where she sat, and had nothing with which to clean up the mess; but even if she had, she couldn't have lifted a rag. Her skin was slimy with sweat and vomit and covered in goose bumps. Every joint in her body ached. The pain and shaking were unbearable. She longed only to sleep, to escape the agony, but she could not sleep at all. She lost all sense of time, there in the darkness. She was in a hellish eternity. Would she be left here to starve to death? Would someone come for her and kill her? She didn't care if they did. She wished for death. Nothing mattered anymore but an end to this suffering. She didn't know or care how many hours or days were passing, but could only suffer in her world of pain. She longed not for food, but for little green. She cried and sobbed, and it was not for Devin and not for Henry, but for little green. She had no thought for Maggie and her betrayal, and no concern for Lillian. Depression engulfed her completely, and she remained in its icy embrace for a period of time she could not measure.

Time dragged on.

All was torment.

And then, at long last, she lifted her head from her knees. She felt light, with the lightness of hunger, yes, but also with the lightness of freedom after a long imprisonment. She was still in the Holding Place, but her mind and her body were free. Energy returned. She struggled to her feet.

She removed her vomit-covered jacket. She realized now that she was wearing long underwear beneath her overalls, and although she was cold, she removed the long undershirt and did the best she could to clean her face and hands with it. Then, wearing her shirt, overalls, and boots, she moved away from where she had been sick and felt her way to the door.

Yolanda and Oscar would come back for her. They were the only ones—besides Zelma—who knew she was here. They would feel remorse, and they would come back.

It was her only hope.

72

YOLANDA AND OSCAR did not come back.

Of course they didn't. With their daughter held hostage, they wouldn't. In their place, wouldn't she put Henry before anyone else?

Claudia leaned up against the door, pounding, scratching, calling out until her voice was hoarse, although she didn't have a friend or ally who would open the door for her even if she could be heard. When she grew tired, her pounding became a slow, soft knock, and then she would gather energy and beat at the door violently again.

Finally, there was a new sound. It sent a shock through her system, after days (she didn't know how many) in solitary confinement. The new sound was a key in the door.

It would be Yolanda and Oscar, somehow having found a way to save Valeria and then to come and rescue her. Or it would be Zelma or Niles, come to murder her.

It was neither.

73

THE LIGHT OF the tunnel came flooding into the black room, blinding Claudia. She put a hand to her eyes, and stepped forward before the door could shut again. There was a large form before her, and it took her a few seconds to realize that the form was her savior and that her savior was Irving.

Behind him were two others, a woman and a man she had never seen before. One look was enough to tell her: they were Night People. Had they come to kill her at last? Were they charged by Zelma with that duty? Not only to bury the dead but also to kill whomever Zelma marked for death?

Irving offered her an opened thermos.

Claudia, still adjusting to the sight of Irving and these strange, hollow-looking people, didn't dare accept. She would never go back to little green.

Irving said in his taciturn way, "Water."

Claudia spilled a little on her hand to make sure. It was, blessedly, water. She drank.

He then held out to her some food: a bread roll. Her stomach clenched.

"Slow. Slow," advised Irving.

She took a small bite, swallowed, and then took another.

Claudia had rarely heard Irving's voice. He spoke now, through thick lips.

"Save yourself."

She echoed his words. "Save myself? You're letting me go?"

Irving stepped back clumsily and gestured down the tunnels as if to say she was free to go.

She wanted to ask why he was doing this, wanted some assurance that it wasn't a trick, but she knew he wouldn't speak. In his weary eyes, she thought she saw that gleam of interest, that same light she had seen during their long days together when she'd spoken trustingly to him and expressed interest in him as a fellow human being, and in his family. And was there a dawning clarity in his eyes as well? Had he taken her advice to begin breaking free of the toxic herb? She felt now she could trust him.

"My son. I can't leave without my little boy."

Irving lifted his right hand and shoulder as he turned from Claudia, mutely signaling her and the strange man and woman to follow him.

"What time is it?" asked Claudia, as they walked.

There was a long silence. At last, the woman said, "Two o'clock in the morning."

Her voice echoed through the tunnels.

The four of them walked slowly along until they came to the stairway leading to Unity Hall, the teachers' dormitory. Henry, she knew, would be sleeping there in Evelyn's suite. Did Irving know that too? Of course he did. He knew every inch of this campus and where everyone slept.

They mounted the steep stone stairs past the first floor, then the second, and on up. Claudia was weak from hunger and from her ordeal in the locked room, and was grateful for the slow pace of her companions. For balance, she traced the cold and clammy wall with her fingertips as she climbed.

At the top of the stairs there was a light. Although they could not see its source, they continued to climb.

When they reached the third floor landing, they heard the voice behind the light.

"Dear heart, what are you doing up at this hour?"

74

"CLAUDIA, CLAUDIA. DON'T you know by now? There isn't a thing that happens at The Hawthorne School that I am unaware of. I have eyes and ears *everywhere*, dear."

Claudia's desperation to get to her son had become a buzzing in her ears. Her weakness and hunger were gone, and all that was left was a pure red rage.

Zelma shone her flashlight into the faces of Claudia, Irving, and his companions.

Zelma shook her head, bitterly disappointed. She spoke in low tones; it was the middle of the night, and all of the teachers lay sleeping only yards away. "So many years of loyalty on our part, concessions made, tuition waved—*all* of it—only to end this way. *This* is how you repay years of maintaining you here, educating your children. I regret ever giving you the opportunities you have had." The glare of the flashlight hit the face of each one in turn. "And *you*, Irving? I think it's *your* betrayal that hurts the most. It's a betrayal of trust, Irving, after all of the special faith I have placed in you." Her injured tone changed to one of resolve. "I'll have to deal with you first, won't I? You've been with us long enough to know how this ends. So you already know: some have to be made to suffer for quite a while before their final release. And that is just."

Claudia's weakness and hunger were gone. Her mind was clear, and her body was gathering strength.

Zelma turned to call out for backup from the dormitory rooms. In a moment she would have teachers at her command to overcome Irving.

But before Zelma could raise her voice, Claudia stepped in front of Irving and knocked the flashlight from her hands. The hallway was at once shrouded in darkness.

In an instant, Zelma's hand was on Claudia's shoulder, clutching. Behind Claudia, Irving picked up the flashlight and shone it into Zelma's face, a face of hatred.

Zelma was elderly and Claudia was young, but there was inordinate strength in those grasping fingers. Claudia twisted in their grip and turned to see Zelma's mouth opening to cry out for help. In that moment, Claudia pulled her shoulder free, turned to put both palms against Zelma's chest and pushed her toward the steep stairwell.

Time slowed down. Zelma was falling back, reaching out to Claudia with her clawing hands. Her eyes were at first shocked, then fearful, and then pleading. Claudia, obeying a natural instinct, reached out to save the old woman. As Zelma got a stronghold, grabbing onto Claudia's sleeve, her eyes again became victorious.

Claudia thought of Henry.

She yanked her sleeve free, and Zelma tumbled backward down the steep stone stairs.

Her descent seemed to go on and on, outside of time. At long last she landed, slumped and broken on the floor below.

Claudia took the flashlight from Irving and ran down, to her horror passing streaks of blood, until she got to Zelma. Her left leg was bent at odds with her body; one shoulder was dislocated, and her blue eyes were staring. A pool of liquid was spreading out behind her white hair.

Zelma was dead. *"Zelma will live forever."* The words came echoing back to her. She had half believed them. But they weren't true. Zelma had fallen to her death in an instant. Or had Claudia pushed her? It had all happened so fast. And there were only minutes left for her to get to her son before she was stopped. Claudia left Zelma's body there. She rushed up the steps to find Irving, who had stopped at a door. He moved the keys on his key ring quietly, with more stealth than Claudia would have thought him capable of. He inserted a key in the lock and stepped forward. Claudia followed, and after her came the woman and the man.

The moonlight and lamplight from outside the building shone through falling snow into the suite to reveal a living room and other rooms beyond, with open doors. One was a bathroom. The other two must be bedrooms. The man and woman went to the left, while Claudia and Irving went to the right.

In the moonlit room, on a child's bed, lay Henry. He was deeply asleep. Claudia's heart filled with relief, love, and joy at the sight of him. She moved to his bed, and with one finger to her lips, she gently woke him. As he awoke, she lifted him in her arms, and he looked from her to Irving and back to her again, and then closed his eyes, smiling. Then he opened his eyes wide at Irving. He murmured, "Is it *you*? Are *you* the giant of this castle?"

Irving spoke.

"Yes. I am."

Henry stirred to attention. "I knew it, Mom. Remember? Remember when I told you this is a giant's castle? I was right."

"Yes, Henry," whispered Claudia. She smoothed his hair as he rested his head on her shoulder. "You were right."

"They said G was coming for me. I thought G was the giant. But he's not. G is just a regular man." Henry lifted his head to watch Irving lumbering toward the door.

From the other room, there was a stifled cry, and then silence.

Claudia, her boy in her arms, was ready to leave The Hawthorne School.

CHAPTER

75

C LAUDIA FOUND HERSELF on the state route, in the middle of the night, in the first snowstorm of the season, walking along, holding her son's hand.

The snow was already ankle-deep and still coming down heavily. The flakes coated Henry's eyelashes, and he looked up in wonder, as every small child does, at the first snow. The white gusts swirled around them, propelled by an icy wind. The sky was black, and the world was cold and silent.

This was the snow under which she might have been buried. Devin was buried under this snow.

Zelma, Niles, and Maggie had set the whole thing up. Claudia's mind was becoming clearer by the minute. Zelma had not wanted to risk Devin showing up at some point in the future, claiming his paternal rights. Not when Henry was destined to be G's "son." She saw it all now. Zelma had ordered Maggie to find Devin and bring him to The Hawthorne School, where Zelma would either acquire him as a supporter of the school or dispose of him. And Devin had made Maggie's job so easy by posting online that he was searching for Claudia. Zelma had seen almost instantly that Devin would never cooperate. And once Devin had shown Niles that he knew all about the herbs they were growing and using to subdue everyone at The Hawthorne School, the only possible fate for Devin was immediate execution.

Claudia picked Henry up again although she was weak and he was heavy for her, and she trudged on. He wore a coat she had taken from a hook in Evelyn's suite, but she herself had no coat.

She had no car; she had relinquished that to the school as part of Henry's tuition. She had no phone; The Hawthorne School had taken that contraband from her. She had no money; she had turned over the contents of her bank account to Zelma too. She had no identification. She had no friends. Henry's father was dead.

She had no destination, and she had no plan.

When the police cruiser pulled up on the side of the road, she hurried to it.

76

Willow Downs Police Department Report
Time: 05:16
Officer Name: Jonathan Heinz   ID #3042
Case #010004

On December 2, at 05:16 hours, I was dispatched to Route 171 four miles south of the Willow Downs city limits in reference to a woman walking through a snowstorm along the highway with a child in her arms.

When I stopped my vehicle on the shoulder of the highway, the individual, identifying herself as Claudia Lee Vera, approached and asked for help. She and the child got into the cruiser. She stated her name and that the child was her son, Henry Vera. She had no identification and no proof that the child was hers. However, the child clung to her and said, "Mom, does Miss Applegate know where we are? Mom? I want little green juice." She stated that she was escaping from a cult and that this cult is housed in The Hawthorne School. She further stated that people are being held against their will in the building called Comfort Hall and that there are murder victims buried in the woods on the property. Ms. Vera appeared to be in need of emergency care. I took her and the child to Willow Downs Memorial Hospital emergency room and saw them admitted for examination there. In the meantime, I notified the dispatcher of the claims Ms. Vera had made concerning The Hawthorne School.

77

Chicago Tribune   December 2
SUBURBAN CULT EXPOSED, 37 DEAD

Willow Downs Police and Fire Department were called to The Hawthorne School on Route 171 in unincorporated Willow Downs at 5:47 a.m. on the morning of December 2, where they found 148 children between the ages of 4 and 12 years old, safe and assembled on the lawn while flames leapt from the windows of the four 4-story, gothic-style buildings there.

As firefighters battled the flames, they discovered the bodies of 37 adults who appear to have died of causes unrelated to the fire. Evelyn Applegate, 46, appears to have died of strangulation and was discovered in a bed in Unity Hall.

In the chapel, which was untouched by the fire, emergency technicians were met by a gruesome finding. Dead of an apparent mass suicide caused by a narcotic overdose were Gabriel Hawthorne, 33, president of The Hawthorne Schools International; Niles Holloway, 30, an administrator; and Maggie Timmerberg, 34, a recruiter; as well as 33 teachers.

The director of the school, Zelma Huxley, 92, was found in a stairwell, apparently having died from a fall down the stairs.

The children, who have been interviewed by police, have claimed that the fire was intentionally set by a group they refer to as the "Night People." They have stated that these so-called

"Night People" woke all of the children from their beds, brought them out and assembled them on the lawn, and then proceeded to set fire to all the buildings.

Some children have also claimed that there are murder victims buried in the woods on the property. Police are looking into these claims.

All of the children appear to be orphans. The Department of Child Services is charged with their care.

*   *   *

The Hawthorne School Cult
Allthingscult.com
The Hawthorne School International was a chain of children's schools with campuses in the United States, Europe and Asia.

The school fed into a cult headed by Gabriel Hawthorne, who inherited leadership of the first school in Illinois from his mother, Julia Hawthorne, who was a visionary in the field of education.

In the 1960s, she formed a school that borrowed from the mainstays of popular systems that were outside the mainstream: Montessori, Waldorf, the Scandinavian forest schools, and others. To these, she added ideas of her own to create a unique blend of pedagogy that emphasized hands-on learning, independent outdoor discovery, art and music. As time went on, Julia Hawthorne seems to have developed a concept of herself as a spiritual conduit of some sort, and added her own brand of "spirituality" into the curriculum. Her ideas can be found in her book *The World of the Child*, 1982.

After her death, her only son, Gabriel Hawthorne, took on leadership of The Hawthorne School and expanded to build more campuses in the United States and abroad. The philosophy of the school at this point took a dark turn, as Gabriel Hawthorne created a cult of personality. He used a mixture of narcotic herbs that all staff and students were required to take every day. This helped him to keep his subjects under control and assist in creating mind-bending effects that led them to believe that he was God. He engineered "spiritual experiences" using psychedelics and dry ice to create other-worldly effects.

The cult idealized children and taught that adults needed to become like children—presumably to make them easier for Hawthorne to control.

Gabriel Hawthorne required parents of students to give custody of the children to him. The documents signed by the parents were of dubious legal value; however, soon after signing over their rights to Hawthorne, the parents "disappeared." Some of these parents became night-shift janitors on the campus, where Hawthorne and his administrators kept them in a constantly drugged state. They were referred to as the "Night People." Others were murdered and buried in the woods on the property.

Several murders are attributed to Gabriel Hawthorne and his followers. Six bodies were exhumed in the woods on the campus: one teacher and five parents of students. They were presumably murdered by The Hawthorne School staff, although this has never been proved. The names of the deceased were parents Fiona Holloway, Devin Richards, Jonathan Todd, Kashvi Sharma, and Molly O'Neill, and teacher Lillian Kincaid.

Among the missing are Yolanda and Oscar Garcia and their child, Valeria. Oscar and Yolanda Garcia worked at the school, and their 4-year-old daughter was a student. Their whereabouts remain unknown.

The cult ended in an uprising when several adults who had been kept drugged and held against their will on the campus for years, the so-called Night People, set fire to the buildings after strangling one teacher, Evelyn Applegate. The director, Zelma Huxley, was found dead in a stairwell on the campus. At the time of the uprising, Gabriel Hawthorne and his followers took a fatal dose of narcotics. All 148 children survived the incident, thanks to these same Night People.

In an unexpected turn of events, the above-mentioned Night People turned themselves into the police a day after the fire, claiming full responsibility. Initially, they had hidden themselves in the woods. When they appeared at the Willow Downs Police Department, they stated that they were the parents of some of the children and wished to be reunited. They told police they had been forcibly drugged and kept apart from their children. Addicted to a narcotic herbal mixture called "little green," which they had been forced to take for years, they now required medical detoxification. After completing treatment, the parents were reunited with their children, many of whom had been sent to The Hawthorne School campus in California and had to be brought back by authorities.

CHAPTER

78

O N THE PLANE to Costa Rica, Henry was looking out the
window and kicking his legs. Claudia was filling out her
application for a work permit on the fold-down tray table. She
was sure to find work as a massage therapist, although it might
not pay much. Then again, it also didn't cost much to live in
Costa Rica. She'd find a way to make it work. She'd already
found a way to get her old job back and save a little bit. Now it
was time to take the lessons learned and move on. She'd create
a new reality for them both.

She looked at the sunlight reflecting off Henry's face, giving him a beautiful glow. He was safe and he was well, she
reminded herself with gratitude.

The morning they were admitted to the hospital, the thing
Claudia had dreaded most was Henry's withdrawal from little green. Her own experience had been horrific. As with the
majority of dreaded events, it was not nearly as bad as she had
anticipated, as his weaning occurred under medical supervision
at the hospital, where he was administered carefully titrated
doses of a medication to assist in his withdrawal.

Henry hadn't noticed the loss of his red string bracelet,
which Claudia had cut from his wrist while he slept in the hospital. What bothered Henry most was the loss of his teacher.

Claudia told Henry honestly that Miss Applegate had died
the night of the fire, but of course she kept back the fact that

the cause of her death was murder. At four years of age, Henry's grasp of the concept of death was weak.

"But she'll visit us in Costa Rica?"

Claudia shivered and only pointed to the sunlit clouds so distant beneath them.

"Look, Henry. We're so far away already. Look how far we've come. Look at all the light."

CHAPTER

79

THE HAWTHORNE SCHOOL, gutted, ruined, and empty, still stands rooted to its spot, surrounded by its hills and forest. The vines that clothed it in the fall are brown and leafless now. A crow flies in through an empty fourth-floor window and out through another.

The small pale faces carved into the stone moldings of the buildings blanche, turning their blind eyes up toward the heavens as the dark day ends, and the night rushes in.

If, on the air, there are echoes of long-gone voices, there is no human ear to hear them. If The Hawthorne School is haunted by its past, no living person knows it.

Nature is taking over the school. It is now the domain of bats and birds, and feral cats, creatures sheltering from the snow and ice.

The Hawthorne School stands ruined, but its heart still beats.

It lies sleeping.

It dreams of rising again.

DISCUSSION QUESTIONS FOR *THE HAWTHORNE SCHOOL*, BY SYLVIE PERRY

1. As you read *The Hawthorne School*, when were you surprised? What were some of the twists you did not see coming?
2. How did you feel about Maggie's efforts to bring Claudia back together with her ex?
3. After finishing the book and looking back, what do you think was the cause of Claudia's headaches earlier in the book?
4. When did you have a sense of foreboding?
5. At the end, the whereabouts of Yolanda, Oscar, and Valeria remain unknown. What do you think most likely happened to them?
6. Which character or characters were you most interested in, and why?
7. *The Hawthorne School* can be read either as an entertaining gothic psychological suspense story or as an allegory representing narcissistic abuse. What are some of the aspects that might symbolize a narcissistic relationship?
8. Using your imagination, what do you believe lies in store now for Claudia and Henry?

ACKNOWLEDGMENTS

THIS NOVEL IS the result of collaboration with many kind and clever people.

I would like to thank my beta readers, who read the story before it was fully formed and gave me valuable insights and encouragement: Tom Davy, Rosemary Davy, Claire Smolinski, Rose Ann Vonesh, Jeanette Beauregard, Lisa Marquez, Hilary Ward Schnadt, and Corinne Farrell.

Thank you also to Jenny Chen for believing in this book and for your skillful edits. Thank you to Melissa Rechter for shepherding this book into the world. Many thanks also to the entire Crooked Lane Books team.

And to my agent, Danielle Bukowski, my profound gratitude for your encouragement of my ideas, your spot-on editorial suggestions, and your faith in my efforts.

I am forever thankful.